The Big Boat to Bye-Bye

Also by Ellis Weiner

Drop Dead, My Lovely
Published by New American Library

The Big Boat to Bye-Bye

Ellis Weiner

NAL NEW AMERICAN LIBRARY

NEW AMERICAN LIBRARY
Published by New American Library, a division of
Penguin Group (USA) Inc., 375 Hudson Street, New York, New York 10014, USA
Penguin Group (Canada), 10 Alcorn Avenue, Toronto, Ontario M4V 3B2, Canada
(a division of Pearson Penguin Canada Inc.)
Penguin Books Ltd., 80 Strand, London WC2R 0RL, England
Penguin Ireland, 25 St. Stephen's Green, Dublin 2, Ireland (a division of Penguin Books Ltd.)
Penguin Group (Australia), 250 Camberwell Road, Camberwell, Victoria 3124, Australia
(a division of Pearson Australia Group Pty. Ltd.)
Penguin Books India Pvt. Ltd., 11 Community Centre,
Panchsheel Park, New Delhi - 110 017, India
Penguin Group (NZ), cnr Airborne and Rosedale Roads, Albany, Auckland 1310,
New Zealand (a division of Pearson New Zealand Ltd.)
Penguin Books (South Africa) (Pty.) Ltd., 24 Sturdee Avenue, Rosebank, Johannesburg 2196,
South Africa

Penguin Books Ltd., Registered Offices: 80 Strand, London WC2R 0RL, England

First published by New American Library, a division of Penguin Group (USA) Inc.

First Printing, March 2005
10 9 8 7 6 5 4 3 2 1

NEW AMERICAN LIBRARY and its logo are trademarks of Penguin Group (USA) Inc.

LIBRARY OF CONGRESS CATALOGING-IN-PUBLICATION DATA
Weiner, Ellis.
The big boat to bye-bye / Ellis Weiner.
p. cm.
ISBN 0-451-21396-3 (alk. paper)
1. Television programs for children—Fiction. 2. Private investigators—Fiction. I. Title.
PS3573.E39323B54 2005
813'.54—dc22   2004021835

Printed in the United States of America

To Two Great Gals:

Gillian Weiner,
the swellest daughter a guy could have,
and
Barbara Davilman,
without whom this (and everything) would be
twice as difficult and
half as much fun

ACKNOWLEDGMENTS

The author would like to thank:

Steve Radlauer for good notes

Doug Grad for canny cuts

Mark Saltzman for (disturbingly) thorough advice on un-orthodox ways to use an Emmy

Cathy Rabin, Larry Siegel, and David Yazbek . . . friends in need (Mine. Not theirs.)

And James Ellroy, a portion of whose *American Tabloid* pro-vided the "inspiration" for the exchange between Bounce and Pounce in Chapter One

A self, according to my theory, is not any old mathematical point, but an abstraction defined by the myriads of attributions and interpretations (including self-attributions and self-interpretations) that have composed the biography of the living body whose Center of Narrative Gravity it is. As such, it plays a singularly important role in the ongoing cognitive economy of that living body, because, of all the things in the environment an active body must make mental models of, none is more crucial than the model that agent has of itself.

—Daniel Dennett
Consciousness Explained

LADY CLAIRE: *How do you know you're God?*
JACK: *Simple. When I pray to Him I find I'm talking to myself.*

—Peter Barnes
The Ruling Class

ONE

It was Monday morning and I was deep in thought—maybe too deep; yeah, maybe in over my head. Introspection is good, clean fun until you start asking inconvenient questions, like, "Who do we talk to when we talk to ourselves?" and "How is it possible to think?" Then it all goes bad.

"Hey, Pete. You look weird." My assistant, Stephanie Constantino, sounded concerned, or at least curious. "What's up?"

We were in the front office, the main reception area where she mans the desk and does the important things, like eating peach yogurt and studying lines for her acting class. She looked trim and casual, her primo gams discreetly sheathed in pressed blue jeans, under a pink cotton T-shirt item with shortie sleeves. "You look like you got something on your mind."

Normally when I sing the blues I keep it in the shower and spare the staff. But this wasn't normal. "I'll tell you, doll." I pulled up and parked in the visitor's chair. "Last night I caught a movie on TV where the lead character is this psycho who thinks he's God. And when someone asks, 'How do you know you're God?'

he says, 'Because every time I pray I realize I'm talking to my-self.'" I paused and braced for impact.

It never came. All she said was, "Great line."

"But I suggest to you that that's not crazy."

"Yeah. So?"

"So, the guy who said it isn't really God. But his statement makes sense. So there's your paradox, angel. And I don't like para-doxes, although actually I do like them somewhat." I tried a new angle. "Maybe what I'm asking is, how is it possible to talk to yourself?"

"You should see this book I'm reading. It says you don't even *have* a self."

I bristled. Or maybe I thought of bristling. "Who doesn't?"

"Everyone." With a white plastic spoon she twiddled and probed in the yogurt. "That inner observer you think is your one true self? That, like, essence of your personal being? That maybe goes to heaven when you die?"

"That'll be the day."

She smirked. The high cheekbones, the almond-shaped green eyes, the smooth-planed cheeks and the strong, forthright chin, the wide, thin mouth, the whole presentation amplified by a little but not too much makeup: She was the kind of woman who made smirking look good. "Okay, but that part of you that you think is really the real you? Forget it. There's no such thing."

Shocked? Get in line. But I did what I always do when the youngster and I broached the larger philosophical issues: I ping-ponged back with the Socratic method. "Sez who?"

"This book my friend David gave me. *Consciousness and How It Works.*" She scooped and spooned up more yogurt. "He said it might give me some ideas for acting techniques. It says we have no central self. There's no little *me* in my head that takes it all in and makes sense of everything, and makes decisions and has thoughts and all that."

"Then who's in charge, angel?"

"No one. Nothing. The mind is a bunch of whatchamacallits. Processes." She twirled an unmanicured finger in a circle on the side of her head, her reddish light brown, short-cut hair shimmering. "All going on at once. Like computer programs running at the same time. There's a process that sees. There's a process that connects the image of what you see to the idea of what it is. Then there's a process that connects that idea to other ideas, and the ideas are connected to feelings, and each other—and that's it!"

The phone rang. But there are some things that are more important than a ringing phone. Some things like truth. "Sorry, doll, but assuming I understand you—which is not an assumption I'm prepared to make—where does it all come together? Who's driving the bus?"

"Nobody. The reason you feel like you're in control of all those processes is because there's one process that looks back on all the other processes and thinks, 'I'm the boss of all this.' But it isn't. Because that's all it does! It thinks it's the boss. It's just one among many." She pointed. "Shouldn't I answer that?"

"In a second." I had taken some punishment, body blows to the very ego that existed in the self of the mind of my brain. It was time to punch back. "You're saying I don't have one self, but a hundred? I'm saying I have one self with a hundred ways of appearing. They're like clothes. Or better yet, try roles. That should appeal to you. Like Shakespeare says: All the world's a stage and every man's a player, who fits and starts his fifteen minutes of fame and outrageous fortune, and then shuffles off to Buffalo."

She looked at the phone. We had ignored it and now it was sulking. "Well, either they'll call back or it wasn't important."

She got up and dropped the yogurt cup in the circular file. "Anyway. Sorry. I know it's weird. But it makes sense. There's no permanent, single self."

I dodged that and came in with a combination. "What about when you talk to yourself, sugar? You use that private, inner 'I' then, right?"

"Nope. I mean, you say it, but it doesn't really exist. There's no private 'I.' It's a myth. Or an illusion. It *acts* like one. But it's not what it thinks it is."

I let my thoughts wander—at least, I thought they were my thoughts. After what Stephanie had just said, I wasn't so sure anymore. If I understood her correctly, not only was I not who I thought I was, I wasn't who anybody else thought I was, either. And neither were they—no matter what I thought.

And that made a certain amount of sense. In my line of work I've seen plenty of people who act as though they don't really believe I am who I say I am. You say to me, "Gosh, Pete, that sounds rough." I say: I'm used to it. But who am I kidding? You never get used to it. You never get used to anything.

Now there was this new idea to chew on. It was unsettling. You spend your life thinking your mind is like a car, with you in the driver's seat, getting info from your dashboard instruments like your eyes and ears and similar items. (Okay, I don't drive. I live in New York. But believe me, I've been outside, I've crossed the street, I've looked both ways. I know what a car is.) Now I had this savvy young skirt telling me my mind was actually a department store, with lots of different floors and boutiques and specialty shops, and each with its own staff person, ready and willing to assist me twenty-four hours a day. Whoever "me" was. Meanwhile, I'll tell you who "me" wasn't: I wasn't even the manager of the store. I was just some guy who worked there.

That thought brought another. *Ingalls,* I said to myself, *stop griping. At least you have a job.*

Then the phone rang and Stephanie answered.

"Pete Ingalls, PI . . . Yes, we do. One moment, please." She covered the receiver. "This lady sounds upset. Are you in?"

"Try to keep me out." I went to my office in the rear and picked up. "This is Ingalls."

"Mr. Ingalls? My name is Charlotte Purdy." The voice was lively and expressive. "I got your name from Max Goldman, who's our friend and who knows Tony Smith. Mr. Smith spoke very highly of you." I replied that I had done some work for one of Smith's clients and the lady had been pleased with the result. "Well, the reason I'm calling . . . I guess you could say we're being blackmailed."

"And who's 'we'?"

"My husband and I, and our company. We produce children's television shows, and we have one on PBS right now. . . . Oh, God, look, I can't talk about this on the phone. But it's very urgent. Can you come to our office right away so we can show you what's going on?"

I said I could, and had Stephanie take the horn for the details. After about half a minute of quiet, all-biz murmurings in the outer room, she suddenly let out a delighted yelp and came waltzing into my office. "Oh, my God!" She was thrilled. "Guess who works there! Ellen Larraby! She's Charlotte Purdy's assistant. Do you believe it!? We did *Pippin* together in North Carolina!"

I dodged that one—what drugs she took, and with whom, and where, were strictly none of my affair—and got the specs. I was halfway out the door when I realized that Stephanie was, too. I gave her the look of a man who doesn't know why his secretary is accompanying him. "Kind of early for lunch, isn't it?"

"I'm coming with you." She suddenly squared off, ready for an argument. "Oh, come on, Pete! You know I'm always a big help."

"You're an even bigger help at the front desk."

"Look, I know Ellen. And she's Charlotte's assistant." Her eyelids suddenly drooped. She gave me a sexy smile. She was playing "crafty." "That could be a big bonus. Knowing someone on the inside."

Normally, at being conned by a dame turning on the charm, I would have drawn the line and hollered nix. But something in me had changed. Now I heard some little voice—not mine, but also not not-mine—say: *Buy it, flatfoot. It might pay off later.*

"Sold," I said.

She said, "Hot dog!" kissed my cheek, and we cabbed uptown.

The offices of DD Productions occupied the penthouse floor of a long, old brick building situated as far west as you can get in midtown without actually sinking into the Hudson. The space was a single open loft, divided by charcoal-gray barriers into work carrels and brightly illuminated by an array of skylights. The far wall was all windows and gave a splendid view of the river and New Jersey beyond. The gal at the reception desk up front took my name and announced us into the phone.

A frail in a tank top and jeans, who I assumed was Ellen Larraby, came literally running from the rear of the place. She was in her twenties, with a cute, schoolgirl face and a nimbus of dark, fuzzy curls. In a moment she and Stephanie were squealing and hugging as I vamped off to the side. They both spoke at once and I didn't catch any of it. Then Stephanie introduced me.

"Cool," Ellen said. She eyed my suit, the fedora, the wing tips.

I couldn't tell whether she was impressed or confused. I get lots of both and have no preference. "Nice outfit," she said finally. "Meanwhile, Charlotte's, like, pacing the floor. Come on."

She led us toward the rear, past a lively, with-it array of young people, mostly gals, all in their twenties, in jeans and khakis and T-shirts and pullovers. They looked up from their computers or telephones, under their task lighting, surrounded by their personal items—mugging photos, bug-eyed stuffed animals, wisecracking coffee mugs—and smiled. There were bookshelves everywhere, packed with thin, brightly jacketed kids' books.

Finally we reached Ellen's desk, equidistant between two private offices. She pointed to our left. "Here's Charlotte."

Entering the boss's office was like moving from a kid's den to a master bedroom, where Mommy and Daddy do grown-up things that the youngsters aren't allowed to see. The floor was carpeted; there was a massive, overstuffed sofa near a low glass coffee table, and an actual mahogany desk, with drawers and a blotter under a brass lamp wearing a frilly white shade like a dame's tearoom luncheon hat. A framed poster on a wall had its own cheery spotlight. It showed six puppets, all kids of different racial and ethnic groups, wearing everyday kid clothing, arrayed around a jungle gym, mugging or grinning at the camera, and the logo of *Playground Pals*.

"Mr. Ingalls, I am *so* glad you're here." Charlotte Purdy walked toward us, a slim hand extended. She was a pleasant-looking broad, around forty-five, a little over five feet tall, and of medium weight. She wore a conservative white blouse and dark slacks, tiny gold earrings, and a small gold pin. She had short, dark hair in a helmet of waves, and showed just enough makeup to let the world know she cared. Her merry blue eyes looked happy to see me. "I'm Charlotte Purdy, and we seem to have bought ourselves a peck and a half of trouble."

I shook the hand and introduced Stephanie. Charlotte practically hugged her, saying, "You're the one who worked with Ellen! Don't you love when that happens? When you run into old friends! I just think that's the greatest thing in the world."

The woman radiated warmth and good humor and sensitivity. They say show business is a nest of vipers populated by sharks and cannibals, but you couldn't prove it by this jolly, welcoming skirt.

But then, it made sense. This wasn't the world of adult television, with its big money and big sex and big greed and big egos. This was kids' TV. This was the candyland of pastel flowers and yummy treats, where media was educational and wholesome, where they respected the viewer as a living creature, to be nurtured and developed and improved, instead of as a sucker with a wallet, a consumer on the make to be seduced and fleeced and sold down the river.

Then a smiling gent in a plaid shirt and chinos appeared in the doorway. "Are you our private muscle?" he asked with a grin. "I mean, I love the hat." He was Donnie Dansicker, Charlotte's husband, five-six and with the paunch of a guy who liked his cheesecake. He had an affable, open face, and a slightly fuzzed bald head. In the glittering metropolis of show business, these two were the mom-and-pop proprietors of an ice cream shop.

We all got settled. Charlotte and Donnie took their places in twin armchairs facing the couch and offered us drinks. When we declined, Ellen shot Stephanie a discreet good-luck roll of her eyes and then bounced, shutting the door.

"First, we should tell you about the show," Charlotte said. "Are you familiar with *Playground Pals*?" It was, she said, a daily TV show on PBS for little kids. "Preschool, two to six. It's all about differences. Appreciating differences in skin color, and hair, and racial and ethnic background, and custom—what we wear, what we eat, what holidays we celebrate, the different kinds of families we have, all that good stuff."

She went on: They had wanted to tell stories about kids without the expense and difficulty of using child actors. So they created kid puppets: Jenny was a white girl; Jimmy was a white boy—

My associate interrupted. "Jimmy? Jimmy Farlow? My sister's kids love him!"

Charlotte gave the proud but qualified smile of a mom pleased to hear one child praised but careful to promote the others, too. "Jimmy's gotten kind of popular. But all our characters have their fan clubs." She went on: Latisha was an African-American girl; Ramon was a Hispanic boy; Tamiko was an Asian girl; and Victorio was a Native American boy. There was a talking dog and cat for extra fun.

"Can we move along?" Donnie was getting restless. He grabbed a remote off the coffee table and shot it at a TV across the room. The unit came on with a dainty electronic click, and a VCR silently began to operate. As he fast-forwarded past the standard opening, he said, "Here's an episode from last season."

The setting was a sandbox. Three kids sat in the sand, surrounded by plastic buckets and shovels and toy trucks. Three others sat along the surrounding benches. The puppets were elaborate affairs, with disproportionately big heads, and eyes with eyeballs that moved and lids that blinked. Some had arms that flexed and hands that grasped; others seemed to have arms lashed to their sides. The mouths, of course, flapped open and shut.

Yeah, it sounds about as lifelike as a bad day at the wax museum, but the puppeteers were adults, not kids, and they could act as well as manipulate the dolls. Once they started talking, the kids came to life and you bought the whole presentation.

"I think Christmas is one of my most favorite holidays in the whole year!" Jimmy Farlow said.

"We don't celebrate Christmas," Jenny said. "We're Jewish. We celebrate Hanukkah."

"Hanukkah? What's that, Jenny?" Tamiko said.

"Et fucking cetera," Donnie Dansicker murmured, and clicked the tape off. "We just wanted you to see what the characters are like. They're like kids."

"Well, mainly." Charlotte twinkled, as though pitching the project. "Nominally they're nine-year-old kids. But when we need them to be like smart young adults, to teach a lesson, then we let them act older."

"Aces," I said. "But somebody said something about blackmail, which is a crime for kids from nine to ninety-nine."

Charlotte sighed. "What you have to know is, we just finished shooting another season of shows. Which means we had a wrap party, which we always do. Another thing we always do is, we put together a reel of outtakes and bloopers that were made during the entire year's production, and we show it at the party."

"Outtakes meaning mistakes." Stephanie addressed me. She was a dutiful young woman enlightening her feeble, knownothing grandfather. I let it slide.

"Well, a lot of it isn't mistakes," Charlotte Purdy said. "It's what the cast does between takes. Improvising and fooling around. While they're holding the puppets up for light checks and camera angles and whatnot."

I tilted my hat back and drilled Donnie and Charlotte with my best all-business stare. "This is quite fascinating, but I haven't heard yet why this is worth my time."

Donnie gave a dry little laugh. "Wait till you see the out-takes." He plucked up a smaller remote off the table, aimed it, and fired. A slim DVD player silently obeyed. We got another scene on the same set, with the kids deployed in different groups on the sand and on the benches. "Watch."

The camera was on Jimmy Farlow, the white kid. "Wow, Jenny," he said. His puppet arm gesticulated in explanation; his head turned, and the pupils in his eyes swiveled upward and his eyelids came down halfway, to denote concentration. "I never thought of it before, but Thangsgavivving . . ." He stopped, then banged his head with a fist. *"Thanksgiving."* The puppeteer sighed—and so did the puppet. "Sorry, gang."

The gal who played Jenny laughed. Then her puppet placed a hand saucily on her hip, cocked her head at him, and said, "Coked up again, Jimmy?"

The boy's eyes widened to a huge, hypnotized stare. His body started shuddering. He said, "Yeah, bitch. And that means I gotta have one thing . . . !" With a growl he pounced on Jenny, whose head went back in a fluttery-eyed faint of virginal surrender. Jimmy humped and slavered over her for a few seconds while she said, "Higher . . . not so hard . . . lower . . . that's good . . . harder . . ." until a voice from above, through what must have been a PA system in the studio, said, "Uh, kids? Cut. Cold showers for everyone. Starting with me."

The puppets went immediately lifeless. The heads dropped forward as though sapped by an expert. The eyes went half-shut and lost all focus. The arms fell limp.

The image froze. There was silence.

"It's all like that," Donnie said, wincing. "Which isn't bad. Usually. Everyone lets off steam and it can be pretty funny."

"Look." Charlotte got up and walked slowly toward her desk.

She sounded like she was pleading a case before a judge. "Everybody does this. *Abracadabra Avenue, The Dragon Gang, Kyle's Klubhouse*—whoever has puppets is going to have these kinds of dirty outtakes. It's part of the fun and keeps everybody sane. But they're never, ever meant for public display." She motioned us over. "So now look at this."

She was standing before her computer monitor. We walked over and flanked her, and watched as she moved the mouse and clicked here and there. "This came this morning."

An e-mail appeared. *One million dollars or this whole filthy mess ends up online. See attached for proof. Payment due this Thursday. On payment I will reveal my identity. Instructions to follow.*

"Here's the attachment." Charlotte double-clicked the little icon. A new little window opened and a new scene began.

Ramon, the Hispanic kid, wearing a T-shirt and chinos, was eyeing Latisha, the black girl, dressed in jeans and a football jersey. "Gee, Latisha," he said. "Is it true what they say about black pussy?"

I was stunned. But whoever was working Latisha took it in stride. She sounded black, which made her reply—a parody of a drowsy, seen-it-all streetwalker slur—maybe even a little more unsettling. "What dat?"

"Oh, man, you know. I hear that, like, if you eat black pussy, you get big and strong and can see through walls, and walk on water, and everything!"

"It *all* true, sugar," the other puppet said. "Brothers cain't do them things 'cause they be *afraid* a' eatin' a sistuh's pussy."

"Can I see for myself?"

Latisha sashayed over to him in an overdone, blowsy slink. "Dig in, Señor Rah-mone."

His eyes popped open and a great big smile lit up the lad's face. He turned to the camera and said, *"Ai, mi madre!"*

Then he buried his face in Latisha's crotch area and made lascivious gobbling noises as she waggled her head back and forth in ecstasy, head tilted back, eyes lightly shut, murmuring, "Yeah, baby . . . oooh, gimme more of that, honey. . . ."

The clip stopped. I was embarrassed for reasons that were obscure. I've always disapproved of spying on sex between consenting adults. Sex between consenting inanimate objects seemed more ambiguous.

"We assume that if he has this, he has the whole thing," Charlotte said.

Donnie added, "Assuming it's a he."

"How did anyone possibly get hold of this?" I was baffled. "Unless it was an inside job."

"It was, at least partly." Donnie thumbed the remote and eyed the machine. Still frames flashed by in a rapid slide show, showing the kids, the animals, different groups of puppeteers in jeans and T-shirts standing under the sets. He was running a search for something. "Somebody made a copy of the DVD we used for the wrap party. Either *they* sent this e-mail, or they gave the disk to someone else who sent it."

Charlotte looked suddenly stern. "Or they sold it to someone, who sent it."

Stephanie was gnawing her lower lip. She wasn't buying whatever was apparently for sale. "Is it that bad? Would it be such a big deal if it got out on the Web?"

"You tell me." Donnie sighed and thumbed PLAY. "Here's what parents and kids all over the country would be able to see on their computers."

We all turned toward the TV again. The dog, a floppy-eared beagle named Bounce, and the cat, a cross-eyed, persnickety little number called Pounce, conferred over a lunch box resting on a seesaw.

"Wuh, uh, gosh, Pouncie," the dog drawled. "What if I don't like peanut butter?"

A faint, barely visible diminution in brightness suddenly occurred.

"Yikes!" said the cat. "It's a solar eclipse, Bounce!"

"Hold it, guys," came the voice from above. "John, did we lose an instrument? They're plunged into darkness out there. Guys, can you stay in position?"

For a minute or two nothing happened, as Bounce and Pounce—their operators remaining in character and biding time—glanced around, ostentatiously patient, humming and, as best they could with their one-piece paws, drumming their nails as they politely endured the inconvenience. Finally it became apparent that they stood in discrete, overlapping rectangles of light, which became visible as the boxes of brightness shuddered and shifted. Some lighting tech was re-aiming lamps and focusing a new one.

"Sorry, folks," said the PA voice. "This'll take a while. Bounce and Pounce, stay up, please."

The animals looked around, mimed *Oh, no,* sighed deeply. Then, to kill time, the cat said, "Hey, Bounce. I hear ya got the dirt on Elmo."

"Uh, yeah, yeah, I got it," the dog said, nodding. "You want the dirt on Elmo, I'm the one that has it."

"So? Let's have it. What's his problem, anyway?"

"Fag."

A startled laugh burst from the girl playing Pounce. Then she recovered her character and had the cat say, "No! Really? Get out of *town*, dog!"

The pooch kept nodding, droopy-eyed, flop-eared, deader than deadpan. "Oh, yeah. Total fag. Big-time homo."

"Gee!" Rapt, the cat gazed at him with fascination. "How about Kermit?"

"Homo."

"Miss Piggy?"

"Lez."

"Bert?"

"Homo."

"Ernie?"

"Homo."

"Barney?"

"Killing himself with crack in a Comfort Suites in Dallas."

"Bear in the Big Blue House?"

"Homo."

"Baby Bop?"

"Crack whore."

"Howdy Doody?"

"Homo."

"Kukla?"

"Smackhead."

"Ollie?"

"Meth freak."

"Big Bird?"

"Juicer. Has his own wing at Betty Ford."

"*Fuck* me! Oscar?"

"Homo."

"Snuffleupagus?"

"Homo."

"Mortimer Snerd?"

"Coprophile."

"Charlie McCarthy?"

"Chicken hawk."

"Jerry Mahoney?"

"Homo."

"Knucklehead Smiff?"

"Homo."

"All four Teletubbies?"

"Wuh, uh, speedballs, angel dust, Robo, Valium, Paxil, Ambien, Vicodin, Nicotrol, Pepto, Bromo, Metamucil, Tums, cough drops, Tic Tacs, spearmint-flavored Altoids, and homo, homo, homo, homo."

The cat smacked her forehead with a paw in amazement. "Wow, Bounce-man! You know everything—"

"Guys?" You could hear ambient laughter from other people in the control booth. "Can we settle and do a take, please?"

Donnie stopped the disk and a pained silence descended. Or, rather, a pained silence would have descended, if it hadn't been shattered middescent by the audible noise of Stephanie Constantino, trying not that hard and failing to stifle wave after wave of gasping, body-doubling laughter. I looked at her wordlessly. She bit her lip, shook her head, and signaled don't-look-at-me with her hands. But she didn't stop. Finally, struggling for breath and turning purple with the effort, she reeled toward the door, threw it open, and staggered outside as though escaping from a burning building.

I shut the door behind her and turned to Charlotte and her husband. "Apologies, people. My associate usually displays more self-control than that."

To her credit, the broad waved it off. "We thought it was funny, too. Before all this started happening."

"You're very understanding. But let me ask you something." I moved back to the sofa and sat as they returned to their chairs. "Let's play devil's advocate, shall we? I'll be the devil and you be the advocate."

"I . . . um—"

"What *would* happen if some joker did put this up on the Web? How is it something worth a million dollars to avoid?"

Donnie took this one. "Are you kidding? It'd go around the world in a day. There'd be jokes about it on every talk show that night. In two days the characters would be ruined. And the network would have a heart attack. There's no way they'd continue broadcasting shows about kids who can be seen butt-fucking each other on every computer in the world."

"And on half the T-shirts in New York," Charlotte added.

"This show is our franchise," Donnie said. "This is what pays the bills."

I told them I would take the case. Then I invited Ms. Constantino to check her life-affirming sense of humor at the door and rejoin us.

After the usual boilerplate about rates, retainers, and confidentiality, I hit them with the standard introductory question. What enemies did they have?

Charlotte looked at Donnie. Something passed between them, something silent and intimate and known only to a man and a woman when they're married to each other and in business together. Finally Charlotte smiled and twinkled and said, "None!"

Then she conceded something. "I mean we've had our disagreements with people in the business over the years, surely. But not to the point where someone would want to do this."

"Let's say that's true," I said. "Or let's say I believe you. Or let's just say that the reason I believe you is that it's true, which may not be the case, but it's what we're saying."

"Wh . . . Excuse me?"

"I think what Pete is asking," Stephanie said, "is, How was the outtake reel made?"

"Oh. Okay." Donnie looked at her with something like relief. I could relate. We all want something like relief, if not relief itself. "Every shot is logged. Whether it's good or an outtake or whatever. The supervising producer keeps notes during production of segments she might want to use. Then she and the editor go through the footage and assemble the clips. We show it once at the party, and it's destroyed."

"Really?" Stephanie found this interesting. "Then where did you get the copy we just saw?"

Donnie spread his open hands out in an appeal for understanding. "I undeleted the file. And made this copy. I had to. Once this threat came in we needed a master copy to see what they have, what they don't have, if they've doctored anything. . . ."

Stephanie got up and wandered over to Charlotte's computer as she said, "Is it hard to make a copy of it? Who could have known how to do that?"

"The whole thing is done on the Videlex." Donnie thumbed vaguely toward out-the-door. "We have an entire post-production studio across the hall. This kind of operation used to be pretty technical. But the computers have made it easier. Anybody with half a brain who can handle a Windows program could figure out how to export that file to a disk."

"Hey." Stephanie was leaning over and staring at the monitor. "This kind of doesn't make sense. The deadline is Thursday—which could be, like, Thursday morning. Today's Monday. Let's say you freak out all of today and decide to comply tomorrow. Who can raise a million dollars in cash in two days? I mean, can you guys?"

Charlotte snapped, "Forget it!" and Donnie shrugged and said, "Well . . . let's just say it would be a challenge."

"But what's the rush?" Stephanie pointed to the screen. "And what is this supposed to mean: 'I will reveal my identity'?"

"Excellent point, Stephanie." I nodded in grudging admiration. "I was going to say something a lot like that. Why? I'll tell you why. Because which of us really knows his identity? Which of us really knows his so-called 'self'? Which of us can be sure we even *have* a self?"

"Pete—"

I waved her quiet and turned to the clients. "Ms. Constantino and I have discussed this matter before. She's of the opinion that we have a hundred selves."

"Um, Pete—"

"You ask me, that number sounds high. But I'm intrigued by the general concept. Let's split the difference and call it fifty."

Charlotte Purdy looked confused. "Do you mean . . . Are you talking about multiple personality disorder?"

"Lady, I don't know what I'm talking about, or who's doing the talking at this point. All I know is, an hour ago I was giving my associate the raspberry for talking about my head as though it were a department store, like Bergdorf's or Frisson. Now I'm dealing with a shakedown artist who wants to wave his identity in my face. If having a squad of Pete Ingallses upstairs will buy me a leg up, then put me down for as many as we can afford. Clear?"

The husband looked at the wife, and the wife looked at the husband, and then the wife said, "Not really, no."

"Put it this way," I explained. "What we're dealing with here is a demented kind of criminal psychopath with a taste for philosophy." I looked at Donnie and Charlotte. "Ring a bell? Sound like anyone you know?"

No one spoke. No one ever does. Then Donnie Dansicker spoke. "I've been thinking about that identity thing. I think I know why he said it." He took a deep breath and began a minilecture.

"It has to do with what happens when something is made digital. You take a picture, or a text, or a sound, or a film—anything. Once you make it digital, you can pretty much reproduce it perfectly, whenever you want. And store it forever. And send it wherever you want. A three-hour movie can fit on a DVD with room to spare. You don't need six reels and thirty pounds of celluloid."

"So you're saying the future is now." I wasn't impressed. "What else is new?"

"No, I'm saying, in a digital world, how do you blackmail somebody with incriminating images, when the images are infinitely reproducible? By a ten-year-old kid in his bedroom? Suppose we pay this guy. What's he going to do to complete his end of the bargain? Give us a disk with the footage on it? So what? How do we know he hasn't made a copy? How do we know what he's giving us isn't a copy? How do we know he hasn't copied it to his hard drive, where he can make a thousand *more* copies?"

Stephanie, for once, looked appropriately grim. "You're right. You pay him, and we think it's all over, and a week later he sends a new e-mail and says, 'Guess what?'"

"Donnie thinks that's why he says he'll tell us who he is," Charlotte said. "Once we know, we're in a stalemate."

"That's what we get for our money," Donnie said. "Knowing who he is. So if he does try to use the material again, we turn him in."

"And if you try to turn him in first, he gets a friend or his wife or his ten-year-old kid to release the footage," I said. "Smart."

"Maybe." Stephanie chewed her lip. "But I still don't get the short deadline. Would it kill him to give you a week?"

"He's in a hurry to make his first million," I said. I looked at Charlotte. "So how many people here knew about the outtake reel?"

"Everybody. Between cast and crew, and the people who work here on other projects, about fifty, sixty people."

It would be a challenge to interview that many suspects, follow up on their leads, and nail the perpetrator in three days. But life without a challenge is like death, which is no life at all. I thanked the concerned couple, signaled my associate, and we dusted the premises.

TWO

Ellen Larraby leaped up from her desk when we exited Charlotte's office, threw I've-got-dish eyes at Stephanie, and dragged her off to the side. The two huddled together and whispered like schoolgirls while I scoped the office and ruminated.

I thought about puppets, and sex, and about the kind of individuals who got their kicks watching puppets have sex—as though it were any of their business, yeah, and as though it were really sex, which it wasn't, because they were on TV, and all the parties involved were too young to do anything worth watching. And they were puppets. I thought about having sex myself, and not with a puppet either. I thought about it because, not that long ago, while working on an earlier case, I had actually had sex.

You say to me, "Pete, jeez. Really? Wow." To which I say, Yeah, really. You say to me, "What was it like?" I say: It was nice. It unlocked a door inside me that I hadn't known existed. The door opened onto a room in which a little Pete Ingalls had been waiting his whole life, which was my life, for the door to open, so he could leave the room and go somewhere else, like a different room, and have sex. Now he was out, and he would never go back in that room—the first one—again.

Finally Ellen shot me a little smile and returned to her desk. Stephanie and I waltzed down the way we had come.

"Charlotte said my sister can bring her kids here when they're in town next week," she said. "Maybe they can meet the puppets. They'll flip out."

I was about to wonder aloud if anyone could really "meet the puppets," when we heard a female voice rasp, "Son of a bitch!" This was followed by the sound of a heavy object—a human head, maybe, but more probably a book—hitting a resonant Sheetrock wall with a loud thud and slapping to the floor. We peered in the nearest open doorway.

Standing in the small room, an actual office with windows on the far wall, was a young woman fighting tears and losing. She was in her mid-thirties, with short, dark hair and big brown eyes. She wore tight jeans and a white blouse that didn't go out of its way to conceal some cleavage. Unlike the lithe college girls who drifted around the main work area, this one had some womanly heft. She held a single sheet of paper that she had half crushed in an angry fist. She sensed our presence and looked up and started.

"Sorry," Stephanie said. "Let's go, Pete."

The dame's eyes narrowed. "Who are you?"

I took a step toward her and introduced myself and my assistant. I said I was a private investigator. It elicited a familiar response. She rolled her eyes and sighed. "All right. Whatever. I'm not in the mood for jokes."

"He's not joking," Stephanie bristled. "And you are . . . ?"

"Natalie Steinberg. Special projects coordin—Private eye?

What for?" The idea seemed to vex her. "What's going on around here? People have been acting weird all day."

"Nothing's going on, Ms. Steinberg." I offered a soothing smile. "Or at least, nothing that need concern you. Although something is, in fact, going on, and it concerns the entire company." Then I added, "A word of advice. I wouldn't leave town if I were you." I say that to everybody. And I like to think that, most of the time, it sticks. You never know when you're going to need someone to be available for something.

"Believe me, I'm not."

I came alert. Something didn't scan right. "You're not what? Leaving town? Or not you?"

Natalie Steinberg shook her head, more to herself than to us, and held up the crumpled paper. "Neither. Both. I don't know. Can you—What do you want?"

Across the room, six feet away, the book she had flung lay on the floor, its point of impact marked by a streak of black on the eggshell wall. I strolled over and picked it up, then handed it to her. "Let's talk about enemies. You've met Donnie Dansicker and Charlotte Purdy?"

"They're my bosses." Then she looked sour and muttered, "For now."

"And DD Productions," I continued. "'DD' for 'Donnie Dansicker.' 'Productions' because they produce things. Am I getting warm?"

Natalie Steinberg looked at Stephanie and made a touching gesture of appeal. "Is . . . What—"

"Put it this way," I said. "Ever hear of anybody who might want to do this operation dirt? Who wouldn't bust into tears if it all blew up and silently stole away?"

"What?"

"He means," Stephanie said, with some condescension I didn't think was strictly necessary, "do you know of anyone who might want to damage the company? Do Donnie and Charlotte have any enemies?"

Natalie Steinberg reacted as though slapped. The hazy misery and unfocused pouting disappeared. She grew sharp-eyed and intent as she shouldered past us and, with an emphatic slam, shut the door. "Yes. As a matter of fact they do. Lots."

Stephanie gave me a silent look. Okay, all looks are silent. Let's just say this one was more silent than most. Then she looked at Natalie Steinberg and asked, "Are there that many?"

The woman laughed. "There's tons. You ready?" She cast her eyes to the ceiling, thought for a beat, and then rattled off names. "John Perkins. Marc Cohen. Elizabeth Marconi. Rick Fields . . ."

Stephanie held up a cautious hand. "Natalie—"

"Cleon Walker. TBD Transport. Midtown Theatrical Lighting and Sound—"

"So what are you saying? All these people hate them?"

Natalie Steinberg flipped the crumpled paper onto her desk, made her way to the chair, and sat. "Yes. That's what I'm saying. All these people hate them. And a lot of other people, too. Why? Have they received, like, death threats? Is that why you're here?"

"Not quite," I said. "But would it surprise you to learn that they told us they have no enemies whatsoever?"

She stifled a wicked smile and shook her head. "It would not surprise me in the least. They *would* say that. Go talk to Phyllis Zimmerman at *Abracadabra Avenue*. I've been here three years but she was here for six. She left last November."

"Why'd she leave?" Stephanie asked.

"*Abracadabra* made her a good offer, which Donnie and Charlotte said they couldn't match." She offered a stiff, patently phony smile. "That's how it works around here. They use you up." She picked up the phone. "Phyllis Zimmerman. She knows the history. Nice meeting you." She started punching numbers and turned away and we left her office, shutting the door behind us.

Stephanie hotfooted it back to Ellen for a minute; then we dusted DD Productions. It wasn't until we were standing at the elevator, in the narrow corridor under the dreary fluorescent lights, that Stephanie spoke. "What's her problem?"

"I wasn't aware that she had one."

"Oh, please. Natalie's pissed about something, Pete. Maybe on that sheet of paper she was throwing around. We're going to have to talk to her some more."

" 'We'?"

The elevator rumbled open and we got in. As we inched down, accompanied by the floor indicator's rhythmic bong, Stephanie dug from her purse a slip of paper on which she'd asked Ellen to write Phyllis Zimmerman's office number. "Of course 'we.' What, like you're going to interview that whole company in three days by yourself?" She produced her cell phone and started thumbing the buttons. "Maybe she can see us right now."

" 'Us'?"

"Hi, Phyllis Zimmerman, please? . . . Mr. Pete Ingalls." She handed me the cell, niftily ignoring my pointed query as to who was the detective and who wasn't.

Phyllis Zimmerman had a pleasant, well-modulated voice, which she used to deliver the pleasant, well-modulated news that she didn't know me from Adam and had no time for idle chitchat. I was halfway around the course in my explanation concerning certain parties and certain events, when Stephanie whispered, "Tell her you're a detective and you want to talk about Donnie and Charlotte."

I stared back. Stephanie was playing a subtle game. "But I am a detective," I told her. "And I do want to talk about Donnie and Charlotte."

"I know! Just tell *her!*"

". . . on the subject of Donnie Dansicker and Charlotte Purdy," I said into the phone. "Since, as happens to actually be the case, I'm a detective."

"Really?" The dame's interest level spiked. As we left the elevator I could hear her mentally bouncing the pinball of her schedule around. Finally she said, "Okay. I'll give you half an hour." She recited the address. We grabbed a hack.

Four hours later we exited a high-rise and paused, amid the late-afternoon rush-hour cha-cha, to review the bidding. I glanced around and realized, with an inward plummeting sensation, that I'd been here before.

Across the zooming avenue was the swank art bustle of Lincoln Center, its three kooky theaters framing that splashing wedding-cake fountain. It was a view I recalled from a previous case, when I'd stood outside a different building a block away, a place I'd staked out, entered, and where I'd even gotten fake-arrested. It was an evocative moment. But then, that's what happens in New York. Things suggest other things, and landmarks conjure memories like songs that, somehow, remind you of something. You're always running into your own past.

Poignant? Cry me a river. I think of it as a mixed blessing. Sure, it's nice that buildings stay put, so when you show up and look at them, they're there. They say, "Remember me?" and you say, "Now that you mention it, yeah," and they say, "That's because you have a past."

Yeah, it's nice. It's exotic and stirring and deeply moving. But here's my question: Who's talking to whom? Who's listening and answering? Who's putting the query to what party who maybe elects to evade the issue? You say to me, "Well, heck, Pete, Stephanie's given you the skinny. You've got fifty parties of the first part screaming at each other trying to get a word in edgewise in the canyons of your mind. Doesn't that explain it?" My answer: Not by a long shot, brother.

"Look, Pete, what's going on?" my assistant said. "You're staring kind of funny and freaking me out."

"Get used to it, sugar. I'm trying to grasp how I can have many selves. It would help with the case. But I can't buy it. Because how can I? I've been living with myself since time immemorial. How can I be so wrong about something so intimately involved with the reality that is me, and vice versa?"

She held up her hands palm out, in surrender. "Look, I can't convince you it's true. But if you read the book you'd really see how there can't be some little self up in your mind that takes it all in and puts it all together. Because where does he come from? How does he do it? Who puts it together for *him*?"

"Take it all in and put it all together? I don't see the mystery. Isn't that what a PI does every day of the week?"

"Fine. You win. There's just one you, and the guy who wrote this book is wrong. Happy?"

"Delighted."

"Now can we talk about this case we have to solve?"

"With pleasure."

"Okay. Now what do we know?"

We started reviewing the facts of the DD Productions black-mail case, but even as I spoke and listened and made a significant contribution, I knew I was living a lie. Because I wasn't happy. I was still haunted by Stephanie's theory. It remained in my imagination, beckoning like some seductive ghost in a movie that featured such things, promising an answer to an important question even while it refused to spill what the question itself was. I had to drag my attention to what Stephanie—and I myself—were talking about. But I did it, because it's my job.

We recapped: Of the two women we'd spoken to, both had been cooperative. In fact, they'd been eager. All we had to do was mention Donnie and Charlotte, and they sang like soused canaries.

We had started with Phyllis Zimmerman, a tall, elegant broad who was a producer of the perennial preschool hit *Abracadabra Avenue*. She had background dirt she was happy to share.

It seems that Donnie Dansicker and Charlotte Purdy had met at university, started out doing small-time corporate "media" gigs, and then nailed a PBS franchise with *Playground Pals*. That's when they started raking in the green from licensing and merchandising fees for the six kids and two animal characters.

"Good for Charlotte and good for Donnie," Phyllis Zimmerman said. "And good for Stephen O'Neil." This latter citizen proved to be the puppeteer who worked Jimmy Farlow, the current heartthrob of the pre-K set. Put Jimmy's mug on anything from lunch boxes to pajamas, and you were moving merch and doing biz. The same was true, to a lesser extent, of the other characters. DD Productions was in clover—or so Zimmerman assumed.

But did they have any enemies? we asked.

Zimmerman didn't exactly say, "Yes, everybody," but allowed as how most people in the industry "had a Donnie and Charlotte story." They all had one thing in common: the couple's tendency to hug you to its bosom in the beginning, then hand you your hat and indicate the door when you'd served your purpose.

"Talk to Sheila Pasternack at Gyroscope," she said. "Ask her about Marc Cohen." Zimmerman made the call to arrange a sit-down with this lady while I tried to remember where I'd heard that name before. Stephanie reminded me: from Natalie Steinberg. We then thanked Zimmerman and cabbed it over to where we now stood.

Twenty floors up, we had sat in stylish misery on little padded block banquettes while Sheila Pasternack held forth. She was a with-it exec from Gyroscope—what Stephanie knowingly called "the hip kids' network"—and looked the part, in a bright yellow mock-teenage jumper, yellow knee socks, and saddle shoes. She had worked at DD Productions for two years, and had plenty to say about Marc Cohen.

He was a writer and a producer who "collected and displayed grudges the way other people had tattoos." In fact, Cohen had recently had something in development at "Gyro" that had ended badly. "We may have led him on a little," Pasternack conceded. "We kept saying, 'We love this,' and everyone was excited. So Marc put some of his own money into it, commissioned some scripts and some character designs. Then there was a palace coup upstairs and we were told to pass."

How did he take it? He screamed and threw coffee mugs and threatened lawsuits and made one secretary burst into tears. "But that was nothing compared to what happened at DD."

About eight years earlier, Cohen had been on staff at DD as a director of some home-video educational series. And at a certain creative meeting one day, a writer named Ted Mills, inspired by the jovial warm-up chitchat, suggested an idea for an entirely new show. Everyone was thrilled for ten minutes, then put it aside and got back to work.

A week later Cohen quit the company and disappeared. A month passed, and then word arrived via the jungle drums that Marc Cohen had pitched that very idea to WNET, the New York PBS station, which had taken it to the network and gotten a deal. "Well," Pasternack said, "naturally Donnie and Charlotte were perturbed."

She elaborated: The Dansickers, because the idea had been germinated while everyone was on their payroll, thought they had a legal, never mind moral, right to first crack at it. The couple had their attorney send a friendly mash note to Cohen, suggesting that they be allowed to match WNET's deal with Marc, that DD be brought in to produce the show, and that WNET present it on PBS. Everybody would have a slice and nobody would have to go to bed hungry.

And everyone was happy—the network, the station, even Ted Mills—except Cohen. Instead, he withdrew the project from consideration. He picked up his toys and went home. When Mills and the Dansickers went to PBS to try to salvage the project, they were told it was now radioactive with potential litigation, and should be quietly smothered in its crib.

Whatever Pasternack was expecting by way of stunned and appalled reaction from us, she failed to elicit from Ingalls, who had sensible observations to make about business being business and things being tough all over. But she got it on stilts from Stephanie.

"Jesus," was all the gal said, but you could see she meant it. Then she turned to me and explained, "You don't turn down a chance to get a show on the air. *Ever*. What spite. What a baby."

Pasternack agreed. "It was Marc Cohen throwing the biggest hissy of all time. As only he can."

Now the youngster and I stood at the entrance to Gyro's building. I thought we were trying to add it all up. But what my assistant offered by way of a conclusion was, "Fuck, Pete. I need a drink."

I ignored the language and offered to buy a round. But she threw me a slider that nicked the outside corner. "We're not done yet. We have one more guy to talk to."

THREE

Marc Cohen's office was in a narrow, ten-story building on West Twenty-third street, the kind of building you normally don't even look at, because it's hemmed in tight between two larger, more important buildings, like a perp in custody, or it's too small to accommodate a storefront, or you're on your way somewhere else entirely. So your eye skips over it and your heart doesn't care, and your mind never dwells on the lives being lived inside.

And that's too bad. Because these are the places where the real people live and work, where they don't say, "Good morning, Harry," to the doorman, because there isn't one. It's where people save the uneaten half of their tuna on rye to take home for later, and then treat themselves to the modest luxury of a single-dip cone at places with names like This Can't Be Yogurt as they walk to the train. And if the contradiction never occurs to them, maybe that's because the part of them that saves the sandwich isn't the part that craves the treat.

The building smelled faintly of ammonia. It always does. The lobby was just bigger than an elevator and the elevator just smaller than a phone booth. Constantino and I got out on the sixth floor and found the door marked EMCEE PRODUCTIONS. We knocked.

A slim gent, looking puzzled, amiable, and just a little psycho, opened the door. I put him in his early forties, of average height, with a long face and short brown hair and big, horsey teeth. He wore a wrinkled white dress shirt and new-looking blue jeans. The shirt wasn't tucked in. It bothered me.

Then again, a lot of things bother me. But it doesn't mean I complain about them. Although I do in fact complain about them. A lot. But the complaints are strictly optional—yeah, optional, and in vain.

So I kept mum about the shirttail and introduced myself and my associate. We dispatched the preliminaries and got down to business. I said we'd been retained by Donnie Dansicker to look into a certain matter at DD Productions, a firm with which, word had it, Cohen had had some history.

"Oh. Them. Well, yeah. Years ago." He turned and headed into his loftlike office and we followed.

The place was one big rectangular space with a single expanse of windows along its length. To our left was a kitchenette fronted by a counter and four tall stools. On the side was a door that must have led to a bathroom.

To our right was a wall entirely covered with bookshelves. Some of the objects on the shelves were actually books. Most were other things: trophies, plaques, objets d'art, electronics, and office supplies. A tall, flaring statuette proved, on closer inspection, to be an actual Emmy.

And there were many puppets.

"What's going on up there at DD?" Cohen asked. "I mean,

why did they hire you?" There was a living room space carved out of the center of the loft with old, mismatched furniture arranged on a faded Persian that had once been deep red but had decomposed into a wan maroon. Cohen flopped himself down onto an angular moderne sofa covered with aged, stretched pink canvas. He gestured vaguely to a pair of low sling chairs, covered in black leather and reaching up at us like amorous starfish. We entered their embrace and sat.

"They're being blackmailed," Stephanie said. "We wondered if you knew anybody who'd want to do something like that."

"Wow, no shit." His eyes were brown, under dark brows, and flitted over Stephanie and myself as though constantly monitoring our reactions. "Real blackmail?"

I spoke up. "As real as the day is long, pal."

He nodded. "Superb. 'Pal.'" He revealed a toothy grin and widened his eyes at me. "And you're really a private eye?" He looked at Stephanie. "And you're . . . what? The plucky gal Friday? Who answers the phone and types up the letters and flashes her legs at the bad guys who show up with blackjacks?"

I started to reply but Stephanie beat me to it. "Yup!" She was chirpy as a tour guide. "That's about the size of it! Those bad guys love my legs!"

Then she bounced onto her feet and strode over to the wall on the right. She gestured to the items on display and said, "And you're . . . what? The borderline sociopath who gets his rocks off dressing up kiddie characters in whips and chains?"

Our mouthy Ms. Constantino stood perusing a five-shelf gallery of figures covering about a third of the wall. I took a slow stroll over and perused the display.

They were all there: Kermit, Gonzo, and Miss Piggy. Charley McCarthy and Mortimer Snerd. Howdy Doody, Flubadub, and

Phineas T. Bluster. Elmo, Oscar the Grouch, and Bert and Ernie. The kids from *The Puzzle Place*. Kukla. Ollie. Jerry Mahoney and Knucklehead Smiff. A few marionettes. Gangs of characters I didn't recognize and clusters of figures I had seen before but couldn't place.

Several of them appeared to be working puppets, the ones you'd actually see on television. They had oversize heads, and armatured joints, and controls and rods hanging off them like faulty prostheses. And they had that banged-up, used appearance you get, whether you're a puppet or a man, when you've been on the job. Of these, none looked familiar, and it occurred to me that they could have come from Cohen's own shows.

The rest were commercially available copies, toys you buy in a store: hand puppets Daddy could manipulate, miniature renditions of ventriloquist dummies, small stuffed figures baby Timmy could take to beddie-bye, big, plush, cushiony monsters little Britney would squeal with delight over when she saw one under the tree on Christmas morning, and then scream with terror at when the streetlight hit it just so as it sat in stuffed, massive menace on the rocking chair in the bedroom at night.

Yeah, Marc Cohen's Puppets on Parade made for a nice, happy display of stylized faces. Some were familiar, others were strange, and all showed a wide range of cartoon emotions, from sly mischief to dopey joy, from shy coyness to misanthropic crankiness. It was a rogues' gallery to delight children from six to ninety-six, and adults under the age of five. Or it would have been, except for one little detail.

Every single creature, animal, and character was dressed in a costume of sheer depravity.

You say to me, "Pete, wow—'sheer depravity'? Isn't that kind of harsh?" But you tell me: What would you call it when the scenario plays out as follows. Assemble the beloved puppet stars of screen and television and, yes, radio. Take these revered childhood icons, and then systematically strip them of their familiar clothing. Then recostume them in leather vests, studded collars, crotchless panties, thigh-high boots, spiked heels, nipple clips, whips, cat-o'-nine-tails, masks, hoods, and the like.

Not that it wasn't impressive. No, you had to applaud the curator's attention to detail. Everything was to scale. Those chains were tiny but complete. The little knouts had been lovingly hand-tied to their little handles. The vests had zippers that zipped and, of course, unzipped. It all gave proof of the kind of dedication to craftsmanship you just don't see anymore. At least I don't. Yes, we were looking at the fruits of a patient application of considerable expertise.

And it stank to high heaven.

There was only one thing I could say and I said it. "Cute."

"It's a hobby," Marc Cohen said, the bright-boy grin all gone and replaced with a look of deadpan cool. "You don't work with these things. You have to do something like this to stay sane."

Stephanie wasn't buying it. "A *hobby?*" She laughed. Her laugh had an edge and didn't suggest much mirth. "You mean you do this for 'release'? For 'escape'? That's probably what Jeffrey Daumer said when they asked about his gourmet recipes, Marc." She shrugged airily. "But fine. To each his own. Now will you answer our questions?"

Cohen stared back at her from under heavy lids. "If I can."

"Who do you think is blackmailing Donnie and Charlotte?"

Cohen turned and walked away—not back to his couch, but farther on, to a massive, cluttered worktable. "I don't know," he said loudly, as though to clear the air and regain some kind of control. "I can think of a lot of people who'd *want* to. But, I mean, what kind of blackmail? What is there you can blackmail them *with?*"

"Puppet porno, friend," I said. "The outtake reel of this year's filming."

"It's not filming. It's video. We say shooting." He toyed with some sheets of paper, gathered up a sheaf, and headed back toward us. He looked amused. "So, what—someone got hold of the out-take file? And is threatening to send it to PBS or something?"

"To put it on the Web," Stephanie said.

A great big grin appeared on Marc Cohen's face. "Oh, my god, that's *brilliant!* I wish I'd thought of that."

"Did you?"

Stephanie's question took us both by surprise. Cohen leveled a chilly stare at her. "No. I don't have to do that. I haven't worked with those people in years."

"Maybe you're still mad," I said. I looked over toward Stephanie for some tag-team backup. But she had spotted something of interest at the far end of the second shelf. I turned back to Cohen. "Maybe you figured out a way to get the outtakes because you want the money."

"How much money are we talking about?"

"A million. In cash."

Cohen made a face of contempt. "Donnie and Charlotte don't have a million in cash. Whoever's doing this doesn't know his, uh, audience."

"Whereas you do."

Cohen looked mildly put off, his heavy-lidded eyes fluttering. "Oh, come on. I got over being mad at DD Productions six years ago. And anyway, it's the business. Everybody screws everybody else. You get used to it."

"Pete?"

Stephanie waved me over to the far end of the second shelf. There they were: the six kids and two animals of *Playground Pals* in their scaled-down, stuffed-toy incarnations, with immobile faces and only slightly movable limbs. Still, there was plenty of drama and excitement among the group: Latisha, with a little rubber phallus strapped around her waist, was approaching, from the rear, Ramon, whose head was buried in the crotchless panties of Tamiko. Jenny, in a scant black undergarment, towered in spike heels and with an upraised whip over a cringing Victorio. Jimmy Farlow, decked out in leather and studs, beamed as Pounce and Bounce posed, pushing what looked like little rubber plugs into each other's anuses.

"This kind of thing costs money, doesn't it?" she said to Cohen. "These custom-made costumes and all these props?"

"Exactly. Which is another reason I don't need to blackmail anybody. I've had three shows on the air."

"But none lately."

Cohen approached, brandishing the sheaf of papers. "That's right. None lately. Because I've been busy. Because I'm developing something much bigger than any of these. . . ." With a gesture he dismissed the wall of figures. "Puppets are history. They're finished. You know why? They suck. They're retarded. They're a medieval form that's outlived its usefulness. It takes half an hour and two cameras and four people to arrange for one puppet to hand another one an apple. You can't show a floor when you do puppets. You need a special setup just to show a pair of feet. They can't eat or drink. They can't throw or catch. Some of them can't even fucking *hold hands*." He thrust out the pages. "Here's what I'm doing instead."

Stephanie took them in spite of herself. I looked over her shoulder.

They were color printouts of a series of characters—jungle animals, with big eyes and appealing faces and persuasively hairy, glossy coats and manes. But they weren't just an artist's rendering. They weren't just pictures. They were rounded and had the kind of solidity only a real object had.

"Big deal." Stephanie sniffed. "Computer graphics."

"No, no, not at all." Cohen's manner shifted from sneering and aggrieved to quietly, intensely devout. "Computer-enhanced puppets. You record real puppets with motion capture, and you smooth out the bad parts and you enhance the motion, you improve the hands and add the feet—and you have this library of moves. And it's all in the computer. So you can put somebody in a jungle or a lake or a savanna, and have them run and dance and swim and fly. And play baseball and throw a Frisbee and fucking thumb wrestle!"

Stephanie stared at the drawings. I wanted to move things along. "Then who do you like for the DD blackmail?"

Cohen grinned. "I love that. 'Who do you like.'"

"Are you going to answer?" This guy rubbed Stephanie the wrong way and she itched to rub back. "Or just show how right everyone was when they said you were obnoxious?"

"Yeah, I'll answer." He tossed a sort of bored glance at my assistant, then looked at me. "Who's the blackmailer . . . well. Obviously somebody who works there. That's who hates their guts *now*. Once you get out, you move on and you get over it. Anyone with motive is going to still be there." He reached out and gently took the pages from Stephanie, with a soft, "May I . . . ?"

She handed them back with a look that could have roasted almonds at twenty paces. "Best of luck with your future endeavors," she said.

He smiled. "I wish you what you wish me."

I thanked him and corralled my assistant. We were just about out the door when Cohen called to us from the wall of puppets. "Hey. I just thought of something." He walked up and said, "Another suspect could be Donnie and Charlotte themselves. They have access to the clips. They could be staging this whole thing."

"And why would that be?" I said. "To destroy their own company?"

He shrugged. "How are they doing? How's the *Playground Pals* merchandise doing? What's their balance sheet look like? Where's their stock at? I don't know, but you can find out."

"And who do they get to pony up the million?" Stephanie said.

"Wish I knew." He flashed her a fully phony smile. "Bye-ee." He shut the door.

Stephanie steamed. "Prick."

I stepped in front of her and held up a hand. "Just a minute. Why the heat? Why snap at a guy we're trying to get to open up and give us some dope?"

Her thin, wide mouth was clamped tight with irritation as she reached past me and jabbed the elevator button. "Because I don't like it when jerks like that make fun of you."

"Of me? Or of you?"

"It was of you, Pete. Well, yeah, me, too. With the legs. Oh, never mind. It's the same old shit."

"Please? The lingo?"

"Sorry." She sent a sharp glance back toward Cohen's door. "It just pisses me off. People see this"—she gestured to my suit, the double-breasted jacket with the padded shoulders, the ample, pleated trousers, the broad and stylish headwear, the gleaming wing tips. Modesty forbade me from bowing—"and they start that whole are-you-for-real thing."

"Just like you did, kid. At first."

She sighed. "Yeah, I did, didn't I? But what kills me is, it wouldn't happen if you showed up in a sport coat and chinos. Even with all your weird talk." The elevator door opened with the sound of a bowling ball rolling down a very short alley, an alley at the end of which there were no pins at all. Stephanie shook her head as we got in. "You'd think I'd get used to it."

"You'd think a lot of things," I said.

She laughed. "Man, you got that right. Sometimes all at once."

Back at the office I had Stephanie call Charlotte Purdy and announce a staff-wide meeting for the next morning. Then I sat at my desk and reviewed what we had learned in school today.

I was well into this reverie when I heard a discreet knock on my door. Since it was Stephanie's custom, when we were alone, to barge in and gas off without the slightest observance of the formalities of rank, office, or who was paying the bills, this display of delicacy could mean only the arrival of a third party, possibly a client. "It's open," I called. Of course it wasn't open. It was closed. But I was speaking metaphorically. I do that.

Constantino ushered in a young woman whom I put in her late twenties. She was slender and nicely done-up in a tailored one-piece dress or suit or whatever it's called, in a modest gray. Her hair was a handsome dark brown, abundant but pinned up and out of the way. Her legs were nothing to write home about, but that was jake with me. I wasn't writing many letters home these days.

"Uh, Pete? This is Chris Page. Ms. Page, Pete Ingalls."

I rose. "Thank you, Ms. Constantino. Ms. P—"

"Shall I remain? And take notes?"

"No, thank you, Ms. Constantino."

"I can fetch another chair."

Fetch. Always the actress. "Thanks, Stephanie, but we'll take it from here."

Stephanie rolled her eyes like a teenager and then bounced. Chris Page and I shook hands. Hers was cool; I have no idea what mine was. Can a man know how his own hand feels? Let's say he can. Let's say he can if he shakes hands with himself. Yeah, and let's further stipulate that that was the kind of thing I didn't go in for.

Chris Page sat in the customer's chair. "I saw your ad in the *Village Voice*." Her voice was a nice deep alto. She was one of those dames whose face seems to have two strikes against it—a hooked nose, a too-small mouth—but that somehow manages to get on base more often than not. Call it carriage, call it poise, call it an ineffable something that you can't really call anything. "Actually I hope this job isn't too small."

"No job is too small, Ms. Page," I said, and then felt a stab of panic when I realized it wasn't true. Say a kid wanted to hire me to find his missing hamster. Would I take the case? The question haunted me. I tried to ignore it. "How can I help you?"

She picked up her purse and placed it on her lap. "I was at a restaurant last night. The Silver Dove. I left my tote bag at the coat check, and when I retrieved it after the meal, something was missing." From the purse she withdrew an envelope. "It was a necklace. It's rather valuable. I was taking it to be cleaned. It was in a Tiffany's box, which of course anyone can recognize right away. I'd like you to go to the restaurant and see if they found it, or if they know who might have taken it." She pulled a photo from the envelope and handed it to me.

The pic showed an informal head shot of Chris Page, wearing

a black cocktail dress and smiling coyly at the camera. Around her neck was a stunning noose of gold links and deep blue set stones. "Beautiful," I said. "Mind if I ask a few questions?"

"Please."

"Good. Because your story's got more holes than a piece of cheese—not Swiss cheese, but that other one. The one with the holes."

"I . . . you mean Jarlsberg?"

"Let's say I do. Let's say I mean Jarlsberg."

"What . . . um—"

"First: You say you were taking it to be cleaned. But level with me, Ms. Page. How dirty do necklaces really get?"

The question seemed to take her by surprise. "Well, it's not a question of 'getting dirty,' Mr. Ingalls. . . ." She struggled. "From use, from the oil on one's hands . . . from smoke at parties . . ."

"Fine. So we've got this dirty necklace. Why did you have it with you? It was evening. You were at dinner. Did you plan on going to the jeweler's at night?"

"Oh." She looked relieved. "That's at least a good question. I never got to the jeweler's. Various things came up, so I still had it with me at dinnertime." She reached for the pic. "Is this not your field? Should I ask someone else?"

I snatched it back. "Oh, it's my field, all right. One more thing. Let me try to put this gently." I thought for a second. "This item has great sentimental value to you. If someone demands a ransom, are you prepared t—"

"Actually it has no sentimental value at all."

"What?"

"The necklace. It has no sentimental value." The woman looked me smack in the eyes. "I want it back because it's beautiful and expensive and I like to wear it." She gave me a chiding look—a thing I'd normally decline to accept, but coming from this dame it wasn't so bad. "Not everything has to have sentimental value, does it, Mr. Ingalls?"

I leered. "You mean sometimes a cigar is just a cigar."

"I, no, I don't think that's what I mean—"

"I think we understand each other, Ms. Page." I summoned Stephanie and summarized the client's case. "Stephanie will take your particulars. Would a retainer of five hundred strain your checkbook?"

"That will be fine." Chris Page rose to join my associate. "Please keep the photograph."

"Hey, Ms. Page, can I ask you something?" Stephanie said.

She and the client stood two feet apart, neither moving. The Page woman glanced at me, then back at my associate. "Of course."

"Why do you need a private eye to get a necklace back? Why not just call the place or go there yourself?"

Chris Page smiled. "Because someone at the restaurant may have stolen it. And I want them to see I have allies and resources. It's like having your lawyer send a letter threatening legal action. You can send one yourself, but his is better."

After she left I caught a glint of dissatisfaction from our gal Stephanie. "You look vexed, sugar." I sat on the edge of her desk. "Shake it up and pour it out."

"Something's weird with that Page. I can't put my finger on it."

"Do tell."

"I mean, why *not* ask them herself? If the guy at the restaurant knows who took it, he can blow you off just as easily as her." She waved the woman's check like a hankie. "Why pay five hundred bucks for that?"

"File it in the folder marked 'Human Nature,' angel." Cynical?

Maybe. But maybe a cynic is just a realist who insists on paying cash. "People don't value what they don't pay for."

She nodded absently. Then she got clever. "You know, you may have a point there, Pete."

But I had shifted with the pitch, and was in position to field it off the bat. "No, you cannot have a raise."

"Oh, come on—"

I headed for the door. "See you tomorrow."

She called after me, "It still doesn't make sense!" And those were the last words of hers I was ever to hear. Until the next day.

FOUR

The office at DD Productions was buzzing when I arrived—alone—at nine the next morning. Charlotte had assembled all hands on deck without explaining to them exactly why. It made for an interesting atmosphere. School was out but the kids were paranoid.

And yeah, I said "alone." Stephanie and I had warmed up for the day's challenges by engaging in one of our usual turf spats. Her position, in brief, was that she was entitled to join me up-town. Mine, succinctly put, was, "Sez you."

"Yes, sez me!" she insisted. "You can't interrogate fifty people by yourself!"

"Thirty, counting the freelancers and puppeteers."

"Still! Plus I already called Jeff." He was her Web designer pal, our go-to guy on computer issues. I declined to point out that, just because you go to, doesn't mean they come through. "I asked if he could trace the blackmail message. I have nothing left to do!"

I had retrieved my hat from the rack in my office. I put it on, signaling the conclusion of the debate. "We've got two clients. The floodgates have opened. I need you to hold down Command Central. Now man the horn and I'll check in later." With that I'd walked out. If she huffed and pouted and threw a pen down on her desk in a fit of pique, I certainly didn't hear it, or certainly pretended I didn't.

Now I was at DD and surveying the milling mob of producers, writers, designers, secretaries, tech types, executives, and everyone else who contributed to the company's "quality family programming." Charlotte stood nearby, fending off queries. I held up a hand. The noise continued unabated, so I went over to a workstation and leaped nimbly up onto a desk. Now the boys and girls settled down. I greeted them, announced my name, and then tried to set the stage.

I used a formal tone and a hypothetical angle to keep things professional and contained.

"People, I'm here to talk to you about a situation that has arisen. Now, in a company, or in a family, or even with an individual, sometimes certain things happen. I don't think anybody will disagree with that. And when these things happen, when they take place, well, you naturally want to ask, Why? Why has this thing taken place? What is the provenance of this so-called thing that has happened? And so you initiate certain proceedings. You do certain things. Some people do some things and other people do other things. And, much as we hate to admit it, that is how the world works. By people doing things. So let's just face that fact and get on with it. Are there any questions?" The crowd seemed sluggish. No one knew what to say. I tried to prod them a bit. "I mean, of course there are questions. We know this. So let me try another tack. Is there anything *besides* questions?"

It seemed to do the trick. One young woman in the middle

of the room raised a tentative hand. I pointed. She said, "What are you talking about?"

I gave a dry little laugh. "Angel, if I knew that, I wouldn't be here." Then a voice inside me said, *Careful, Ingalls. That may not be strictly true.* It was a valid point. But I didn't have time for philosophical hair splitting. I told the voice inside me to pipe down. How? With a different voice. Then I turned my attention to the people looking up at me from the floor.

"Someone is trying to destroy this company," I said. That brought a response: whispers, some mock cheers and applause, Charlotte playfully slapping one wiseguy offender, a general spirit of boisterousness. I took that as an opportunity to jump down off the desk and make my way through the jocular, oblivious crowd to the conference room in the rear. When I reached its door I turned and called for silence. "Yeah, it's all a joke," I said, "until the blade falls and you look up and it's your head in the basket."

Somebody yelled, "Ew! Gross!"

I took it in stride. "Perhaps. But if anyone has anything pertinent to say, about themselves or other people or anyone else who might want to harm this company, I'll be in here. Give me a minute to get settled." I walked in and shut the door, sat at one end of a long, gleaming conference table, and gave my plan time to work.

I reviewed its artifice and cunning.

Somewhere out in that office was the person who had made the illicit copy of the outtake reel—and who, for that matter, might be the blackmailer. Such a person, when presented an invitation to step forward and squeal on his fellow man, would be tempted to do just that to deflect attention away from himself. In fact, he'd be first in line.

But the criminal mind is devious, and he would start to

reconsider. He'd suspect a trap. He'd become reluctant. *Ingalls is making it too easy,* he'd think. So he'd decide to avoid my pointed questions and just lie low. He'd get out of line and quietly retreat to his workstation or office or console.

But then he would think: *Ingalls will notice who comes forward, yeah, but how much more will he take note of who* doesn't *come forward—who seems to have something to hide? Ingalls will make a list of such no-shows, and he'll check it twice. So I'd better get in line.*

But what of everyone else? They'll each have their share of office carping and complaining to do, about colleagues they hate and injustices they've suffered, and none of it having anything to do with the outtakes or the extortion. They'd all get in line.

But an office is a family, where you have to get along with others until either you or they "commit suicide" or "are disowned." They'd wonder: Do I really want to finger so-and-so, who's three feet behind me in line? Whom I'll have to look in the eye and work with when this is all over?

The answer, of course, will be: No. Better to live in a stable, if imperfect world, than rip to pieces the fabric of society.

Then those people, the ones not guilty of any criminal act against the company, will get out of line and discreetly go back to work.

Result? The only person in line would be the one who'd made the outtake reel. I had transformed the office of DD Productions into a vending machine for the delivery of my bad guy. All I had to do was open the door to reveal a single, embarrassed, culpable, and thoroughly nailed individual.

I got up, walked to the door, and, with a silent prayer of thanks to the gods of deduction, opened it.

A small mob surged in. I struggled within the mass of humanity, uttered an audible curse, and reached in my suit coat pocket for my cell phone. I turned away from the laughing, jostling throng and punched a preset number. The party answered.

"Pete Ingalls, PI."

"Hop on up here, angel." I had to shout to be heard. "I've got work for you to do."

Stephanie snickered. "Are you sure, Pete? Because y—"

I pressed END.

Four hours later Stephanie and I had spoken with and questioned the entire full-time staff of DD Productions, with the exception of its founding couple. Of course, most of the personnel who created *Playground Pals* were contract workers or freelancers; they visited the offices rarely and they'd have to be pursued one by one on the outside. But we asked the hard questions of everyone else: the researchers, the producers, the tech gang in the postproduction studio across the hall, the financial people, the custodial staff.

And, as usual when you trawl with a big net, you land a lot of boots and tires.

The assigned topic may have been, *Tell us who might want to harm the company,* but what we got was a numbing litany of petty grievances.

People asked why the company didn't pay for lunch. People asked why the Christmas party last year was so "cheesy." People asked why holiday bonuses were so lousy. People asked why the health plan kept costing more and providing less. People asked why they didn't get a raise. People asked why the raise they got was so small. People asked why the company wasn't being more aggressive. People asked if I knew if there were any jobs open in the industry. People asked if there were any jobs open in my "agency."

As for the blackmail plot against the company, some people

knew about it—or different versions of it—and some didn't. Shelley Ezrine, the pretty, ponytailed child-development specialist, whispered she had heard that "someone at Scholastic" was behind the plot, the purpose of which was to destroy *Playground Pals*, thus removing it from the PBS lineup and "opening up the slot for one of their shows."

I had to laugh. And I did laugh. I laughed because the purpose of blackmail is to coerce the transfer of money from the good guy to the bad guy, not to bully your way onto the PBS kiddie lineup like a villain in Shakespeare killing the king to move up the ladder to the throne.

When Shelley left the conference room I said as much to Constantino. I got a cursory nod and a sour look for my trouble. "Maybe," she said. "But there's something interesting about her theory."

"Like what?"

"I don't know. Something." First she knew, but didn't know, what was off-kilter about Chris Page. Now this. Our Stephanie was cultivating a talent for the higher esoteric wisdom of the East, and it was as appealing to me as a stubbed toe. "Next!"

Next was Steve Wentzel. How do I know? Because I did what detectives do—or what they used to do, back before the world became digitized and we began to pay machines to remember things for us. I used a pen and paper and I took notes. Some extracts:

Steve Wentzel—Here 6 mos. Fld prod BB 4 yrs. Lks D/C. Attn. W. Party—saw Vid. Who hurt co.? Ntl Stnbrg b/c pilt no sale, ld off.

After Wentzel left the room I scanned this material to be certain I'd nailed the salient points. According to my jottings, before coming to DD Productions, Wentzel had filed produce for a bed-and-breakfast for four years and lacked direct current (in his home? his office? It wasn't clear). He brought to the attention of someone named W. Party the fact that he saw ("saw"? was dating?) Vid (a person unknown to me), and, with respect to who might be hurting the company ("Who hurt co.?"), suggested the National Strindberg (Festival? Company?), because "pilt" wasn't selling with "the lid off."

No, it didn't make sense. And that's what bothered me. Because the little chat we'd just had with Mr. Wentzel had struck me at the time as being pleasant and informative. What, then, could these cryptic notes possibly mean? I asked Stephanie if she had any theories.

She squinted at the notepad, nodding and pursing her wide, thin lips, until the veil dropped with an audible clang.

"Oh! Okay, yeah. Jesus, Pete, what did you write this with, your foot? What it means is, he's been a field producer for *Book Brigade* for four years, he likes Donnie and Charlotte, he attended the wrap party, where he saw the dirty puppet video . . . and when you asked him who might want to hurt the company, he said Natalie Steinberg, because the pilot for the show she's producing hasn't sold or been picked up by anyone, and she's being laid off."

Memo to self: Develop less ambiguous note-coding style. Meanwhile I allowed myself a brief smile. "That explains the little drama we saw yesterday. That piece of white paper in her hand might have been the pink slip."

My assistant nodded. "Which also explains how hot she was to tell us who Donnie and Charlotte's enemies were. Talk about motive . . ."

We heard a timid knock. The door to the conference room

opened slowly and a short, boyish-looking man stuck his head in. "Am I next?" he asked.

"We'll talk about Natalie later," Stephanie muttered, and waved the mug in. "And you are . . . ?"

He was Norman Tibbler, and he ran the studio across the hall. He was in his thirties, probably, with a clean-shaven face and a swarming mass of unshaped dark curly hair. He crept in with the shy, tentative manner of a lad who had long ago discovered he preferred the reactive responses of machines to the assertive demands of actual people.

He sat in the hardwood-and-chrome chair we'd been using for entertaining, and promptly folded himself in two and began nibbling a thumb. After some preliminaries he asked us what was going on.

"Like I said, someone's got DD Prods in his sights." I smiled. "Any theories?"

He frowned. The little boyish face looked terribly vexed. "What do you mean? What kind of problem is there?"

I put on a poker pan. "Who said anything about a problem?"

"Uh, you did. You said someone is attacking the company."

"Did I?" I looked visibly entertained. "Did I say who it was?"

"What . . . you . . . uh, no. Who is it?"

I sat back. "You tell me."

The young man shrugged. "I don't know."

"And what if I said I don't know?"

He looked blank. He turned and faced Stephanie. "Do you know?"

"Guys . . ." She took a deep breath. It had the effect, paradoxically, of clearing the air. And yet if something had just been avoided, it wasn't terribly clear what. "I have a question. Norman, you run the Videlex next door?" Tibbler nodded. "Okay, so how easy is it to run off a copy of a file? Like, say, a video file, ten, fifteen minutes long. To copy it onto a CD or whatever. Is it really a specialized task? Or can anyone walk in off the street and do it?"

Tibbler shrugged. "It's not so hard. If you can copy a file on a computer you can do it on the Videlex."

"Would you show us?"

He shrugged again. "Sure. Okay."

We followed him out of the conference room, past the three or four concerned citizens milling around near the door, and out the main entrance. Six feet down the hallway, across the corridor, was a single red door with a sign reading DD POST, INC. Tibbler opened it and we followed him in.

"Is it always unlocked?" Stephanie asked.

He shook his head. "We usually keep it locked. But I knew I'd be coming back soon so I kept it open."

We were standing in a little waiting room, ten feet to a side, tops, under ugly fluorescent lights. There were plastic stacking chairs against all three walls, a corner table holding a lamp, a phone, and some tech magazines, and that was it. But we followed him a short way down a hushed, carpeted corridor and came to the door—thick, heavy, shut—of the first studio.

Inside was a command room of a spaceship, lit for romance. A tall, thin geek in a white short-sleeved shirt sat at a huge console bristling with sliders and knobs, on which three big TV monitors glowed in the spotlighted dimness. The black boxes of loudspeakers angled down from the ceiling. There were racks of gear, wall-mounted pegs holding dozens of coiled-up cables, and innumerable small boxes, of varying size and colors, with a multitude of meters and gauges and logos, all attached to one another and to the master unit. Tiny red and green operational lights glowed all around us, like Christmas decorations.

The tall bird deferred to little Norman and ceded to him the captain's chair. And then the lad was in his element. He showed us how to find a file, configure it for copying, and burn the file onto a CD. If you'd done it once you could do it blindfolded; if you had never done it at all, it would take five minutes to figure out.

"So," Stephanie summed up, "if someone had run off a copy of the wrap-party outtake reel—"

"They did?" Norman's color, pale at best, lost several more degrees of tint, visible even in the studio gloom. "Oh, boy."

"Yeah, look, just between us? They did."

Stephanie turned to me and made a gesture of futility. "I mean, are we serious? Do we really think we can keep a lid on this?"

"We can try." I leaned in over Norman and let him feel the impinging mass of my presence. "You won't tell anyone, Norm. Right?"

He looked duly intimidated. You say to me, "Oh, sure, Pete— but who wouldn't? It's the suit. With the big padded shoulders and that more-than-ample hat. The kid is intimidated 'cause you're cowing him with the symbols of authority and guts." Guilty as charged. But if you don't mind I'll take a thin sliver of credit for myself. It takes a certain kind of man to wear the suit— a certain kind of man that the world has been running out of since Guinevere two-timed Arthur and they turned Camelot into a musical.

"Uh, no," Tibbler managed to say. "I won't tell anyone. Who am I going to tell?"

"So." Stephanie reclaimed the floor. "You could have run off that copy. Right?"

"But I didn't. I mean, yeah, I could. But I didn't."

"Do you know who might have?"

The little man stopped and thought hard. "It could be any-body. Everybody who works here hangs out sometimes and watches editing or mixing or stuff. So they could see how it works. And freelancers? Like, talent? I mean, who knows where they've been and how much they've worked on things like this?"

Stephanie snorted. "Great. That narrows it down to six billion people. Let's go, Pete." Then she snapped a finger. "Wait. Norm? Who has a key to this studio?"

Tibbler frowned and then ran down the roster. Besides him-self and Donnie and Charlotte, Eddie the maintenance man, Tony the scarecrow we'd just met, Deborah the company comptroller, and possibly others.

The picture was as clear as a punch in the nose: Lots of people had motive; lots of people had method; lots of people had oppor-tunity. We walked back to the conference room on feet light as lead.

Natalie Steinberg was waiting for us. She didn't look happy to be there. Not that she didn't please the eye. Her brown hair was gleaming and her cleavage was invitingly visible, the ways guys like it. She was ready for seasonal fun or interrogation in a tight black skirt, a bloodred blouse, black pumps, stockings, and va-va-voom makeup. She didn't rise when we entered the room.

"Can I be next?" she said in a put-upon voice that hinted that "no" was not a feasible answer. "I have an appointment down-town and I don't want to be late."

"Easy, sister," I said. Stephanie and I sat. "We all have an ap-pointment downtown." Okay, I wasn't sure if it was literally true. But sometimes that doesn't matter. "But okay, fine. Let's have a chaw and a talk."

"Jesus, where did they find you?" she muttered. "Look, there's a rumor. Somebody's blackmailing the company with the outtake footage."

Stephanie muttered, "Shit. Great."

I said smoothly, "Let's play a little game. Let's pretend that's a rumor."

"It *is* a rumor," Natalie Steinberg said.

"Then it's working, isn't it? Our little game. Okay, so—"

"You want to know who's behind all this?" Steinberg looked sour and impatient.

I smiled. "Please."

"Donnie and Charlotte."

She stared at us in defiance and paused for effect. Stephanie snorted, "Yeah, right!" and I touched my fingertips together and murmured, "Do tell. . . ."

"Think about it," she went on. "What's the blackmail for? A million dollars? They get the money from somewhere, they pay themselves—"

Stephanie wasn't buying it. "What do you mean, they get the money from somewhere? Like where?"

Steinberg shrugged. "I don't know. Insurance."

"Why?" I said. "Why take the chance? They're running a successful company. Last time I looked, crime was for criminals. The ones who can't make it legit."

"I don't know how successful it is," Steinberg said. She faltered but held her ground. "I mean, who knows what their books look like?"

"How did you know it was for a million?" Constantino asked.

"I just said it. Hypothetically."

"And you're telling us this theory has nothing to do with your own situation?"

Steinberg recoiled, offended. "What situation?"

Stephanie rolled her eyes. "Come on. You're being laid off. Which is why you're so dressed up. You're probably going to a job interview, right? You hate Donnie and Charlotte, so you're trying to make them look like criminals."

For her reply, Natalie Steinberg stood up. "You wanted my opinion about what's going on around here, and I gave it to you. Frankly I don't give a fuck about what happens to this place."

At the door she said, "Have a nice day." But I didn't think she meant it. That was okay. Yes, that was just fine. There are more important things in life than having a nice day.

It was late afternoon by the time we left DD Productions. Stephanie went back to the office while I cabbed it downtown to the Silver Dove, in the East Twenties.

It was a nice place, swank, deluxe, and swell, with a single dining room that still held a few late lunchers, while all around, the brisk and efficient staff made ready for the dinnertime rush. I stood at the entrance, near the lectern, where a sleek gal in a tight purple sheath was fielding the phone and writing reservations in a big book. She looked up.

"Yes?"

I handed her my card and told her I represented someone who had lost a necklace in her establishment the night before. She studied the ticket, and me. "I'll get Eve." She marched off toward the rear of the place with that ice-skating stride that thin women adopt when their block-heeled shoes make them bottom-heavy. A minute later a suave little joker in a tux drifted out and glided up to me in a manner I wasn't quite sure wasn't dirty.

"Mistaire In-gulls?" His accent was French.

"Speaking," I said. I glanced past him. "But make it fast, friend. I'm waiting for a dame named Eve and it's about business."

"This is me. Voilà." He held out something between fingertip and thumb like an insect he was forced to study against his will.

It was my card. I drilled him in his Gallic brown eyes. "Check your number and dial again, Ace." I indicated the card. "This is *me*. Not you."

"We." He nodded.

"We what?"

"No. We. Yes." He flapped my card at me. "This is you, we."

I don't like brain teasers. On most days of the week my brain is teased enough by life as we know it. I don't mind crosswords and the jumble, but I steer clear of anagrams, riddles, and all those other mental karate drills that some people's minds can't live without. And I was on a case. The last thing I needed was a per-fumed French fancy boy lobbing me verbal conundrums. So I snatched my card from his delicate fingertips and tore it into pieces. "This is me," I said, thumbing toward myself. "And this is you." I flung the pieces in his face. "Now excuse me, I'm looking for Eve."

"No. Ah. Please. But . . . I see. Mistair Ingalls . . ." He reached into an inside pocket and produced a card of his own. He handed it over. "Voilà."

I took it warily and scanned the text. It said, under the logo of the restaurant, YVES COMARD. MAÎTRE D'HÔTEL.

"So you see"—he beamed—"I am Yves."

I absorbed this information, expressed a reasonable bit of sur-prise to learn that the place that was obviously only a restaurant was also trying to palm itself off as a hotel, and then made my pitch. I told him what I'd told the reservations gal, that I repre-sented someone who had lost a necklace here the night before. I produced the photo of Chris Page wearing the item and said I had come to collect the jewelry.

Yves Comard took the pic and eyed it with an expression of resigned boredom. He looked like a man for whom turning over a lost necklace to a stranger was a daily occurrence. "I must telephone Mademoiselle Page first, of course, to confirm your legitimacy," he said.

"Of course." I pulled out my notebook. "The number—"

"I have the number, sir."

He bowed slightly and withdrew. Ten minutes later he emerged from the rear bearing, with ceremony and care, in both hands, a light blue Tiffany box. He handed it over to me along with the photo. "I have spoken to Mademoiselle Page and she confirms who you are."

I took the box, opened it to ascertain that it contained the ice in question, then thanked the man and started to leave. He had a last-moment inspiration and put a slim, smooth hand on my arm. "*Un moment, s'il vous plaît,*" he breathed. "Might I have another of your business cards, Mistair Ingalls?"

I couldn't imagine what he'd want it for. But then, I can't imagine a lot of things. "Sure thing, pal," I said, and handed him another card.

He took it and smiled. Then, in a gesture of half working-stiff solidarity and half creepy French perversity, he winked. "*Merci.* For my collection."

FIVE

I let Constantino join me the next day at DD Productions for the talk with the puppeteers. They worked freelance and didn't have offices in the organization, so Charlotte had to wrangle them from all over town. Everyone showed except two. Stephen O'Neil was, according to Ellen Larraby, "in Boston doing Jimmy stuff." Bob Borger was on a job somewhere.

Maybe it was just as well. They could have been both sitting quietly nearby with their hands neatly folded on their desks, and I wouldn't have been able to question them. By the time I'd debriefed two of the gals, my head was full and my mind was on empty.

First up was Shirley Takahashi, the Japanese-American skirt who played Tamiko. She had a boyishly thin body and short, jet-black hair, and wore a kind of black cotton pants/T-shirt ensemble that would have worked as pajamas or a stagehand's outfit. She spoke like a native of Cincinnati, which she was.

While Stephanie, in the next room, interviewed Maurice

Carnes, I asked Shirley Takahashi if she had any theories as to who might be behind the blackmail. She thought for all of half a second and then hit me with, "Donnie and Charlotte." That's what sourpuss Natalie Steinberg had said. A consensus was forming. "Sez who?" I queried.

"Some asshole named Arnie Feldman at T. K. Gromyko," she replied. When I volleyed back with a pointed, substantive, "Huh?" she delivered the full tutorial:

T. K. Gromyko was the securities company that issued the stock in DD Productions, stock that she and every other DD employee within the sound of my voice made sure to buy as soon as word of DD's winning the *Playground Pals* franchise came through. Everyone got in at three or four and had a happy ride to twelve or fourteen. Over the past year, though, the honeymoon had ended and the stock gracefully swan-dived into the shallow end of the low threes.

Why?

Because, the gal explained, the merch was sitting on the shelves and not moving. The T-shirts and stuffed toys and reader books and board games, the figurines and pajamas and toothbrushes: They were backed up in the warehouse and not finding favor with America's youngest youth.

You had to wonder how this could be. The show was a hit. Stephen O'Neil and Jimmy Farlow were on tour to the applause of thousands.

Shirley granted that. She said they'd all expected a long-time, high-return kidvid institution, like *Abracadabra Avenue*. But what undid them in the stores was the very thing that made the show virtuous and worth showing on TV.

Playground Pals was reasonably popular, but it offered no single beloved icon to represent it. On the contrary. Its six kiddie characters were, by definition and per mandate, scrupulously similar to one another. They had to be; the show was about respect for differences and tolerance of everyone's looks, culture, family, holidays, religion, snacks, hair, songs, and everything else that life is supposedly all about, when it's not about earning a buck or trying to get lucky in the sack. No one was the star. No one character predominated from one show to the next. The puppets even looked a lot like each other.

As a result, the kids didn't know who to long for, and the parents and the grandparents didn't know who to buy.

So licensers declined to renew, the profits went down, and the stockholders got sad. Meanwhile, as Arnie Feldman told Shirley, "management" unloaded a million shares and faced "a big tax hit" next year. It didn't take a financial planner to convert that information into a motive for blackmail, even if it meant blackmailing oneself.

That, Shirley added, also explained why Jimmy Farlow had recently become so popular. Donnie and Charlotte, and their partners at KLAE, the PBS station in Philadelphia that coproduced the show, made a conscious decision to subject young Jimmy to a massive dose of famousness gamma rays. "They needed a Kermit or a Barney," Shirley said. "So they picked the white kid. I mean, that's the audience with the money, right?"

I probed. It's what I do. I asked if I detected a note of jealousy. She shook her head. It looked credible. She said, "God, no. I'd hate to have to do what Stephen O'Neil is doing. Traveling all over with Tamiko? Doing all those morning talk shows? It's exhausting and stupid. They don't care about you. They just want to interview the puppet. They think it's so clever and cute. You feel like a jerk, sitting out there while they ignore you."

This sobering lecture ended on an ominous note. If the merchandise didn't start selling, then the show would cease to exist. PBS picked up only a fraction of the tab. The rest came from deficit financing, which worked only if there was money at the other end. These days the prospect for that looked dicey.

I asked Shirley if any of the other puppeteers coveted Stephen O'Neil's new role as handmaiden to the star. She had to think about it. "Not really," she finally said. "I mean, Bob Borger seemed a little put out. But he always does. About every-thing. It's hard to tell what bothers him, because he's *always* weird."

Susan Bollinger confirmed all this and more.

"I love Bob," she said as we sat at the big conference table. Susan was the dame who played Jenny, the Jewish girl, and Pounce, the cat. "He's totally dedicated to the craft." She laughed. "Of course, he's totally weird and a complete nerd, too. Which can be kind of scary sometimes."

"Scary?" It was a telling word. It meant "frightening." "Scary how, Ms. Bollinger?"

"He gives you notes between scenes, and it's like he's channel-ing the spirit of the puppet god. He doesn't make any jokes and he can't stand it when you do. Everything is dead serious, like the puppets are his children and we've been hired to take care of them."

She was tall, and had a short shock of blond hair and a face on which a longish nose and a strong chin served notice that this was no fluffy girlie-girl playing make-believe with dollies. She wore jeans and a man's white oxford shirt with the sleeves rolled back. Also no makeup and no brassiere, and white Keds over white shortie socks: in a word, pure functionality and all business. "Bob takes puppet performing more seriously than everybody else put together. Donnie and Charlotte know this. That's why they made him the head puppeteer. He has responsibilities the rest of us don't have."

This caught my ear. "Responsibilities, eh?" I played it circumspect and ultradiscreet. "Would one of these responsibilities include having a master key to the postproduction studio?"

She shrugged. "I don't know. It's possible."

"How about Stephen O'Neil? Could he have had one?"

She shook her head. "Nah. He's never around. He's out of town half the time. Plus, what for? It's not his job to work on post. Bob, maybe. Sitting in for looping and editing. But not really."

I played my trump card, which I'd been hoarding ever since Stephanie had mentioned it in the cab uptown and said, "It's your trump card."

"You know, Ms. Bollinger," I said, hinting at reserves of sympathy and fellow-feeling. "O'Neil gets all this star treatment—the press coverage, the interviews, the swinging, groovy parties at the jet-set hot spots, where the bad girls wear skimpy clothes and the bad boys laugh at things that aren't very funny. . . ."

"Um . . . what?"

"I can see where something like that might rankle the sensibilities of other puppeteers. Such as yourself and your colleagues. O'Neil's character gets popular, goes national, and suddenly he's the belle of the ball and the talk of the town and the king of the cowboys. Meanwhile you and Maurice and the rest of the family are stuck at home on a Saturday night, playing Parcheesi and hoping the phone rings. Someone might say it's not fair."

Susan Bollinger looked rueful and ironic. "Tell me about it."

"You tell *me* about it, if you would."

"You tell *me* about it. You're the one who knows everything."

"Am I?" It was a seductive idea. "Let me put it this way. Has anyone been jealous of O'Neil's success? Have you?"

She sat back, looked down, toyed with a ballpoint. "I guess. I mean, sure. Who doesn't want to make all that extra money? Or be that famous?"

"And this big success is all due to Stephen O'Neil's talent? Or do the writers give him all the good lines?"

"A little of both, I guess." She suddenly stopped and tossed the pen onto the table, then sat forward and replaced a curl of hair behind her right ear. "No. You know what it is? They give him all the bad lines. They give him all the clueless lines." She shifted her voice and became high-pitched, innocent Jimmy Farlow. "'Gosh, Tamiko, what's so special about having a silly old tea party?'" Now even-toned, quizzical Tamiko. "'Jimmy, haven't you ever heard of the Japanese tea ceremony?' 'Tea ceremony? Wow, what's that?'"

Bollinger smirked and looked away, then turned back to me and spoke with a sudden explosiveness. A long-suppressed secret feeling had finally burst into the light, and it was squinting. "Jimmy Farlow is the most boring character on the show. He's the most boring character on television! He's the ordinary white kid. He's the one we don't mind making look stupid, because there's no white guys' association to complain about it. He's the one who asks all the dumb questions and gets everything wrong, so the other characters have to explain things to him, which is how we explain things to the audience."

"What you're saying is, he's the straight man."

"Right. And for the first time in showbiz history, the straight man has become the star."

"Which the rest of you resent."

"I don't know. Maybe. A little. Wouldn't you?"

"He plays the white guy, angel." I spoke with some knowledge. "That's where the money is."

"Fine. Whatever. Meanwhile, Stephen plays him on one note. The rest of us are killing ourselves to be funny, and dramatic, and sad, and touching . . . and old Jimmy just keeps lookin' to the camera and sayin', 'Wow!' and, 'Golly jumpers!' "

"Ever complain to the brass upstairs?"

"Who? Oh, Donnie and Charlotte." Susan Bollinger let loose with what seemed like a sincere laugh. "We don't have to! Charlotte jokes about it all the time. Besides, what is there to complain about? The show's a success! We're all working! This is what a puppet performer dreams of."

Bollinger had no theory as to who was shaking down the organization, but she left my thoughts provoked with one thought-provoking point.

"Why does this have to be about getting back at the company?" She shrugged her lean, bony frame. "Why can't it just be about getting money?"

"I hear you, doll. Money as a statement of superiority—"

"Oh, come on. No. Money to buy stuff with. Or to pay somebody off with." She stood up. "Can I go now?"

I nodded and thanked her and plunged into thought. She had a point. Money to buy stuff with: It raised issues I hadn't fully considered—issues like drug habits, mob loan-shark debts, gambling losses, or even a prior blackmail that had to be paid off. Call it algebra, call it physics: X blackmails Y; Y turns around and puts the touch on DD Productions. Motion—in this case, the act of extorting dough from someone—was transferred from one subject to another, like a set of gears, or those clicking silver balls on an executive's desk.

Or like people working puppets.

————

The news about the stock, and the merchandise, and the push to make Stephen O'Neil and Jimmy a star, was a bombshell I had the pleasure of dropping on Stephanie after the day's interviews were complete and we regrouped back at the office to compare notes.

The bomb was a dud. It hit the ground and just sat there as Stephanie nodded, unsurprised. "Oh, yeah. The merch. Donnie and Charlotte sold shares and owe the IRS gazillions."

"And you know this how . . . ?"

"Maurice told me." Maurice Carnes, one of the few African-American puppeteers working in the business, also owned shares and also had been badgered by Arnie Feldman. "I asked him what he thought about it—the idea that Donnie and Charlotte are behind the whole thing. And he laughed and said, 'Impossible. Charlotte, maybe. She's all practicality.' I love that. Crime is what's practical. 'But Donnie's too moral.'"

"Everybody's too moral," I said. "Until temptation sidles up and asks them to dance."

"Maybe. But Maurice said he wouldn't be surprised if it's *Natalie!* Don't you love it?"

"What about Bob Borger?" I opened the bottom desk drawer and brought out the house bottle and two plastic cups. "Chivas?" She declined; I poured just one. "*The Man Who Wasn't There.*"

She idly picked up my cup. "He's working. He wasn't not there because he's hiding. He's on a job." She took a quick snort and shuddered. "Or how about Susan? She's jealous of O'Neil's stardom."

"Which she wants for herself." I nodded in something like sympathy. "For herself, and for Jenny, the child."

"Pete. Jenny's a puppet. But yeah, maybe she does. Because get this: Stephen even has an exclusive contract with DD Productions. He's getting paid to stay on call all year, even when they're not in production. Just so they can send him around the world with Jimmy. Shirley doesn't care for that kind of thing, but maybe Susan does."

We looked at each other. I felt that quickening, that high-energy vibration that sometimes signaled the arrival of a break-through theory. "So, what are we saying?"

"We're saying it could be her. Or Natalie. Or Donnie and Charlotte, who, of course, are our damn clients. Or someone else." She got up. "We're saying I'm starving, and I have to stop off and buy cat food and get home."

It was getting dark outside. The late summer gold of sunset glare off the taller buildings had faded. The city was now in shadow as, overhead, the sky still glowed a faint metallic blue. "Well, we'll find out tomorrow," I said. "After the payoff the blackmailer is going to reveal his identity."

"Or hers."

"Or theirs."

She looked at me. I elaborated. "If it's Donnie and Charlotte, they'll have to reveal their identities to *themselves.*"

"Um—"

"Yeah, I know: Is such a thing even possible? We'll either see, or we won't see."

She gave an exhausted wave and walked off.

SIX

The blackmail note hadn't mentioned what time on payoff day the fun would begin. That meant I was facing a sixteen-hour stretch of pacing the floor at DD Productions. Sure, it came with the job. But for every voice inside my head urging me to do that, there was another urging the first to shut up and listen to a third voice, which suggested that I find Bob Borger.

He and Stephen O'Neil were the only two principles we hadn't questioned over the past two days. O'Neil was still out of town, but Borger was around.

Or so everyone thought, but nobody knew for certain. He had few friends, no wife or girlfriend, and no agent. Either he didn't own a cell phone or no one knew its number. The other puppeteers had told us that they never socialized with him and had no idea where he might be. I made a few fruitless phone calls. Then, because Stephanie was due in late from an audition, I decided the hell with it, and took a run up to the Upper West Side.

Borger lived on West End in a doorman building. The gent on duty called up to announce me but got a large portion of nothing in reply.

By then Constantino had returned to the office, so I called her from the street to convey the results.

"Bob Borger is fundamentally inaccessible," I said. Some big-picture philosophizing seemed in order. I wanted the kid to appreciate what a significant anomaly I was reporting. "You'd think that wouldn't be possible. I mean, in today's world as we know it. With our modern wireless communicational networks of tele-com connectivity, and the unparalleled, awesome power of the Internet, with its backbone nodes of hardwired software. But Bob Borger is off the grid. I'm not saying the man is a criminal genius, and I'm not saying he's not. I'm saying he's gone until further notice, period, end of sentence, full stop. It's as though he doesn't exist, until he decides to rematerialize. He is a nonpres-ence, an un-man, partaking of a negative being."

"Uh–huh," Stephanie said—a bit unhelpfully and, if you ask me, unsympathetically. "Listen, hang up. I'll call you back."

I leaned against a brick wall and observed the passing caval-cade of contemporary New York life. Eight minutes later my cell played its *1812 Overture* ring tone.

"Ingalls."

"Okay," she said without so much as a greeting. "Call this number and ask for Bob Borger. Got a pen?"

I wrote it down. "And you obtained this information how?"

"I called AFTRA and asked if there were any kids' TV shows in production around town. Look, just call the number."

I called the number. It had a 718 area code. A fast-talking dame answered with what sounded like "Astoria" and I asked for Bob Borger.

"Is he with Klonky?"

I was in no mood to be cosmopolitan. I lashed out. "He may be, lady," I said. "But I don't speak Yiddish, so I wouldn't know. Try again."

"No, I mean, is he shooting *The Klonky Show?*"

It turned out that Borger was with Klonky; in fact he *was* Klonky—Klonky himself, or itself, or however a fantasy puppet character should be designated. My call was transferred to the set. A young man told me to hold. I held. Ten minutes later someone picked up the phone at the other end.

"Yeh."

"Is this Bob Borger?"

"Yeh." He spoke as though he'd been born with a gun to his back.

"My name's Ingalls, Bob." I went on to tell him how I had been hired by Donnie and Charlotte to find out who was black-mailing the company with the outtake footage.

"How do you do that?" he said. His voice had the minimum amount of inflection; all feeling had been damped and suppressed. He must have saved all his expressiveness for his puppets.

"How do you do what?" I said. "Blackmail them with the footage? You threaten Donnie and Charlotte with putting it up on the Internet unless they fork over lots of cash. Sound like fun? Know anything about it?"

"I hate that thing."

"What thing is that, Bob? The Internet?"

"That outtake thing. I wish they wouldn't do that."

"Why's that, Bob?" I normally didn't address people by their name like that. It's phony and irritating and the stuff of bad movies and TV shows. But I wanted to goad the man. "Why do you hate it?" I said, and then added, "Bob."

His voice suddenly got closer and more intimate. He may have cupped his hand around the phone, so people all around him wouldn't hear the passion and near-despair in his whisper. "Because puppets aren't meant for that," he said intensely. "Puppets aren't meant to be just as terrible as people. They're meant to be better than people. Those outtakes . . . those cheap sex jokes and drug jokes with the puppets . . . they're funny the way sex with children is erotic. It's bogus and disgusting and obscene."

I had to pause. He'd started out dazed and distant. Now the man's fervor came over the wire like a blast of scorching radiation. "You've thought a lot about this."

"Yeh. I have."

I looked at my watch. I wondered how much time a trip to Queens and a sit-down with this tormented genius would cost me. "Bob? Are you going to be there for the next hour? I wonder—"

His voice now sounded normal. He'd removed his hand and was speaking for attribution. "No. My scenes are done for today. I'm leaving here."

"Okay, great. Maybe we can have a drink—"

The line went dead with a decisive slam. I looked at my cell as though hoping it could summon him back on the line, then flicked it off. I had no illusions that I'd be able to track down Bob Borger for the rest of the day. I hailed a cab and went over to DD Productions.

The place was as calm as an emergency room on New Year's Eve. If anyone on staff was not aware of the big events pending and the large issues at stake, I didn't see him. Outwardly everyone seemed to be making an effort to do their jobs, yes—but every ring of a phone, every walk through the office by Charlotte Purdy, and the mere appearance of Pete Ingalls, PI, brought a sudden tension to the atmosphere and a simultaneous craning of every distracted head to see what land mine would blow up next. When Charlotte came out to receive me, the whole vast loft fell silent, like a saloon in a Western when the bad guy clinks in through the swinging doors.

"I'm on two Valiums and barely breaking even," Charlotte muttered. "Have you learned anything?"

"Not much," I had to say. "Where's Donnie?"

"Out. On a mission." She flashed a prefab smile at all the elves and motioned for me to follow. "Let's talk in my office."

I traded looks of significance with Ellen Larraby as I followed Charlotte into her lair. She shut the door and fell into an armchair as I settled onto the couch.

I got right down to business. "You have enemies around town," I said. "And certain parties here at home who don't love you as much as you might like."

She waved that away. "I know that. What else?"

"I don't know who copied the outtake footage, and I don't know who sent the blackmail note."

"Great."

"I assume you haven't heard any more from the blackmailer. Or you would have called me."

She sighed. "Nothing. I check my e-mail about every ten seconds." I started to speak, then stopped. She caught it and looked at me sharply. "What?"

"I hear Stephen O'Neil is on the road, doing publicity appearances," I said.

"In Boston." She furrowed her brow and squeezed between her eyebrows. It read *stressed*. "A talk show on WGBH and an interview for the *Globe* Sunday magazine."

"I also hear that the purpose of this PR blitz is to make Jimmy Farlow a star, to help focus the sale of the merchandise."

Charlotte Purdy looked surprised, then impressed. "You have good sources. Yes, we're trying to give the show a single iconic representative."

"And all the other puppeteers are happy about that? No one's had his or her feelings hurt? No one is jealous of the attention and the extra money?"

She shrugged it off. "Maybe. Susie Bollinger isn't thrilled. The girl who does Latisha? Shareena Hill? She has some attitude. I don't blame them. But it's a business call, and business is business." She shifted in her chair and suddenly froze, struck by a thought. "Why? You think one of them is behind this?"

"Isn't it possible?"

Charlotte laughed. Maybe the Valiums were working after all. "To the point where they'd want to destroy the show? I seriously doubt it. Look, who have we got . . . ?" She ticked them off on her short, plump, burgundy-tipped fingers. "Susie? I don't think so. She's a nice girl. Shirley Takahashi? Forget it. She's a sweetheart. Maurice? Out of the question. He's a mensch. Shareena? I can't see it. She may be a bit prickly, but she's almost pathologically honest." She opened her hands and spread her arms in triumph, as though she'd just proven something. "These are sweet kids. How else do you want to become a puppeteer when you grow up?"

"What about Bob Borger?"

A silence fell, a silence so profound that, if it had been a noise instead of a silence, it would have been an earsplitting, loud noise. Charlotte looked thoughtful. "Well, God knows he is peculiar."

"Peculiar enough to do this?"

She looked away. When she spoke it was as though she were

arguing with herself. "But he hates those outtakes. He never takes part in them. Victorio. His character. As soon as someone gets cute, Bob lowers the puppet and just waits it out."

"So . . . ?"

"He'd rather eat glass than spread those images around the world."

"And yet . . . ?"

"Of course, you could say he's a puritan, right? Which means big repression and lots of issues."

"Aces. So—"

"And it's true, we never see him with a girlfriend, or a wife . . . or a boyfriend. Maybe that means something."

I smirked. "Everything means something. You ask me, it—"

A noise caught our attention. It was the sound of Donnie Dansicker out in the main office, laughing and saying, "Nothing! No comment! Go back to work!" Charlotte and I had just enough time to look at each other before the door banged open and Donnie blew in.

He was carrying a large satchel, a fancy leather number with a lockable brass closure and heavy handles. It looked full of something. He shut the door and slammed the bag down onto the glass table between us. He looked at his wife. "I got it!"

She looked baffled. "What—"

He whispered, "The M-O-N-E-Y!" He leered at me. "Ever see a million dollars before, Pete? Voilà."

He opened the bag and there they were: stacks of band-wrapped, nice, new hundred-dollar bills. We all stared at them. Charlotte said, "Where—"

"From our Wall Street friends."

"No!"

He held up both hands placatingly. "As an advance. Against the insurance claim."

"Donnie! How—"

"No points. No interest. Just to keep the ship afloat. Okay? They're not *all* scumbags, Char."

I nodded in full comprehension. "From Kropotkyn."

Charlotte looked slapped. "What?"

"Sorry. Potemkin."

"Who?"

"Gomulka. Krevchenko. Nabokov."

Donnie Dansicker rolled his eyes. "Gromyko. Yeah." He sighed. "I was so nervous. Walter calls my cell while I'm in the cab; he says, 'I may have good news; I may have bad news—'" He stopped and stared at Charlotte. "Have we heard? Has he written back?"

With lips tight she shook her head no, then got up and marched to her computer. "I haven't checked in a while. . . ." She clicked the mouse a single time and squinted at the screen. Then her eyes went wide and she fell into her chair.

We ran over and gathered behind her. Flapping her hand on the mouse, she found one of six e-mails that had just downloaded. Its subject line read INSTRUCTIONS. She clicked and it opened up.

> Two red nylon sports bags. Bring to NW corner Broadway and Eighty-sixth at ten P.M. Wait at pay phone for further instructions. Just DD. Any police, plainclothes people, etc., and deal is off.

"Oh, my God," Charlotte breathed.

"Christ," Donnie said. "I guess this is really happening, isn't it?"

———

Donnie Dansicker asked me if I would agree to shadow him when he made the payoff, and I said yes. All three of us wondered about the inclusion of a warning against "plainclothes people." Did it refer to me? Was the blackmailer indeed someone on the inside who knew I was involved?

Donnie and Charlotte decided there was enough time before the payoff to make it worthwhile for them to return to their home in Dobbs Ferry. Charlotte would stay there with their son and daughter while Donnie drove back later in the evening to meet me fourteen blocks from the appointed corner.

At the office I found Stephanie gazing at a whiteboard on which she'd written every name that had arisen in the case so far. The names were coded in blue, red, and yellow, by job; the lines connecting them were in thick, urgent black. The thing was a magpie's nest pretending to be a flowchart.

"I can't make any sense of this." She sounded surprised. "Fuck it. We just don't know enough."

"Please?"

"Sorry. To heck with it."

"They got the e-mail," I said. "Tonight at ten. We'll go with plan A."

"Right." She glanced at the whiteboard and suddenly frowned. "Wait a minute. . . ." She leaned toward the tangle of names and symbols, eyes darting from one to the next.

I wanted to get as far away as possible from that chart, so I went back into my office and made a phone call. When Chris Page answered I told her I had her necklace.

"Yes, I spoke to the maître d'," she said, sounding pleased. "Did anyone give you any trouble?"

"Nothing that a quick course in English as a Second Language couldn't fix."

She said she was going out of town for the weekend. That's when it hit me: I hadn't told her not to leave town. And now it was too late, although it didn't matter in the slightest. Then she said she'd call me when she returned, to reclaim the ice. I said that was fine and we hung up. I felt good. It was a pleasure to accomplish something for once. I hoped it was the start of a trend that would continue.

By nine thirty I had gone home, showered, changed into a dark suit. I ate a light dinner of leftover rice pudding and a cup of coffee and took the subway uptown. It was a cool, dry, pleasant evening, a late-summer gift before the rains and chills of fall. Broadway and Seventy-second was swarming and jumping as usual. I loitered on the designated corner for a few minutes until finally Donnie Dansicker appeared, walking moodily out of a garage. He wore chinos and sneakers and a blue dress shirt under a maroon windbreaker, and moved with the wary self-consciousness of a man who expects at any moment to be shot.

Two red Nike bags hung from his shoulders. They looked heavy.

"All set?" I asked.

He was pale and nervous. "How do I know? I've never done this before. What if we get mugged?"

"We won't. Not at this hour on Broadway. Not with two of us." I gave him a direct stare, man-to-man. "Do you want me to carry the bags?"

He shook his head. "Let's follow directions."

I agreed, then voiced a thought I'd had more than once over the past few hours. "What if this phone call gag is a blind? What if while you're waiting for the phone to ring, the guy shows up and snatches the merchandise?"

He shrugged. "Would that be bad?"

"I could try to take him down."

Dansicker squinted, thinking. "It wouldn't help. If he's got an accomplice, the accomplice will release the footage, and we're fucked. Let's play it straight and hope for the best."

The plan was for me to arrive first, stake out the phones, and wait until Donnie hit his mark and the fun got under way. As I walked up Broadway I stopped occasionally to look behind me. I didn't see what I was hoping I wouldn't. Everything was jake and on schedule.

At the corner of Eighty-sixth I strolled into a movie multiplex and, from the lobby, eyeballed the phones outside until Donnie arrived, one bag on his shoulder, the other in his hand. He loitered with obvious intent, like a first-time shoplifter. Suddenly he started, lunged at a phone, and answered. He listened for five seconds and hung up. I banged out of the doors and joined him.

"Now we have to go to Seventy-ninth and Columbus. At eleven o'clock." He sighed. "What's the point of this fake-out?"

"Probably to see if you follow directions."

"Which means he's watching us right now. And you're not supposed to be here."

I realized he was right. I had to think fast. I slapped my forehead and cried, "Of course! Times Square is in *Brooklyn!*" I pulled out my wallet and shoved a buck down inside his jacket. "Thanks, buddy!" Then I scrammed, briskly, announcing loudly in body language, *I don't know that guy and I have nothing to do with his two bags.* I killed time until about a quarter to eleven, then legged it to the next pickup point.

The only decent space near Seventy-ninth and Columbus from which a guy could watch in concealment was a butcher shop three doors up. I ducked into its entry and pretended to scrutinize the wares in the window.

They consisted of a number of postcard–sized signs on little silver platters, announcing, in handsome calligraphy, PRIME ANGUS BEEF and PORK LOIN TO ORDER and ASK ABOUT OUR U.S. CHOICE SKIRT STEAK FOR ¡¡¡FAJITAS!!!

It was then that it hit me: The rice pudding hadn't been enough. I was starving.

"Can I help you, sir?"

The bird in the doorway was my height, stocky, bald, and wore a spotless butcher's apron and a neat little black bow tie. "Kind of late to be open, isn't it, Jack?" I said.

"Open till eleven on Thursday nights," he said. "For folks planning Friday getaways. Can I get you anything?"

Donnie wouldn't show for ten minutes. I could give this mug the brush-off and stand my ground until the party started. But it was possible that the blackmailer, or an accomplice, was himself (or even herself) planted nearby, scoping the area to keep things kosher. And now I'd been openly addressed by the butcher. I could no longer simply linger. I had to rally back and talk about meat.

I said, "Maybe you can at that, soldier," and followed him.

I took one step inside and felt that spurt of hot panic when you're caught leaning too far off first. Because there was a customer on the premises, and this customer wasn't just any civilian stopping by an upscale meat store on the way home late one Thursday night. The customer was a cop.

The cop looked at me and we traded crime-pro nods. At least I did. The butcher shut the door and took up a position behind the counter to the right.

The place was small, with glassed-in refrigerator cases on either side of a narrow space. Inside, under tiny glamorous halogen spots, slabs and cuts of beef, pork, chicken, and lamb lay glistening on silver trays, each surrounded by a festive garland of parsley. Everything had a name tag and nothing had a price tag.

The cop asked the butcher for two pounds of loin pork chops. The butcher replied that he'd have to get that from the back room, and disappeared through a doorway.

I gave the cop a just-folks smile. "Think the rain'll spoil the rhubarb?" I said. I always do. You throw up a cloud of cornpone and neighborly gab, and nine times out of ten the other guy gets comfy and doesn't ask any questions.

"Who's asking?"

Okay, this was the tenth guy. I could see his trained eye giving me the once-over. That's when I started to think. The thoughts came as a series of items, as though each had been spoken by a different voice inside my head.

Item: It was important that the cop not linger in the area outside the shop after he left. His presence would spook the blackmailer and jeopardize the payoff.

Item: The only way for me to possibly affect the cop's behavior outside the shop would be if I left first, and sent him off on some bogus mission.

Item: And yet I could not, right now, just leave. It would look bad. It would look suspicious. It would look as though I were fleeing the presence of a duly sworn police officer. I might as well hand the lad an engraved invitation to tail me, question me, and generally get even more enmeshed in this event than he already was.

Item: The only legitimate way for me to get ahead of the cop, to get him out of the play and keep the field clear for Donnie, would be to buy something before he did and leave the store first.

The butcher emerged from the back, his plump hands bearing a small mound of light pink chops on a sheet of thick, creamy paper.

"Say, Officer," I said. "I just realized, I'm really late. I have various people coming over for dinner." I thumbed toward the butcher. "I wonder if it would be okay if I asked this mug to serve me first."

The cop shrugged. "Be my guest. I'm in no hurry."

I thanked him and turned to the butcher. I just had to buy something. It didn't matter what. "So, listen, what's the cheapest kind of steak you have?"

"That would be chuck steak."

I nodded. "Perfect. Chuck steak. So let's see, I've got six people coming over. . . . Let me have six pounds of chuck steak."

"You got it."

The butcher reached into the glass case and hefted two thick slabs of deep red, marbled beef, and slapped them onto a scale. "Six and a quarter. That okay?"

"That's just great. Wrap it, bag it, and I'll run."

He printed out the price sticker, then covered the meat with the creamy paper and taped it shut.

I reached for my wallet. "What's the damage on that, chief?"

He squinted at the sticker. "That'll be a hundred and twenty-three dollars and sixty cents."

I looked at him. Then I looked at the cop. For a demented second I thought this entire event was part of the blackmail, or a bad, bad dream. I heard myself say, "For two steaks?"

"It's U.S. prime," the butcher said. "This beef had a happier childhood than *you* did."

I was in no position to contest it, and I didn't have time to argue. All I could say was, "I don't know about that. But it's sure having more fun right now than I am." I dealt him a credit card and signed in the little box. He gave me the bundle in a nice plastic bag, with the shop's logo on it and a drawstring, and said, "Enjoy it."

Donnie Dansicker was manning his post when I got outside, standing by the phones and looking visibly burdened by the cash. My watch said it was one minute until eleven. Dansicker glanced up and saw me with the bag of meat, started to say something, then thought better of it and turned away. It was then that the cop emerged from the store with his own drawstring bag. I had my lines down cold.

"Listen, Officer," I said. I acted agitated. It wasn't hard. "A guy . . . I think a guy just mugged a person. An old lady." I pointed uptown. "He ran that way."

"Really." Deadpan, he glanced up the street, then back at me. "Where's the old lady?"

I pointed downtown. "She ran that way."

He shrugged. "Sorry. Not exactly my jurisdiction."

"A crime's a crime, friend."

He gave a little smile. "Let's put it this way, honey. The only reason I put on this costume is to take it off."

I wanted to take issue. I wanted to say, *So what?* I wanted to say I didn't care whether he liked his job or not, and no matter how eager he was to get out of the blue and into civvies, that didn't buy him a permit to blow off a crime report and call a material witness "honey."

But before I could speak he stepped past me into the street and hailed a cab. A yellow Chevy pulled up immediately, he got in, and it drove off. I looked at my watch: it was exactly eleven o'clock. I joined Donnie at the phones. They were all free.

We waited for one to ring. For an excruciating minute the seconds ticked by, each full of the sound of no phones ringing. Then another minute inched past. While Donnie stared at the phones I began scanning the immediate area, but no one looked even slightly like a person who would blackmail you over puppet pornography.

More minutes elapsed. The butcher, now wearing jeans and a gray windbreaker, turned off the shop's lights and locked the door and made his way up Broadway. I withdrew to the darkness of his store's entrance and took up my position there. Buses came and went. Good-looking dames, some with dates or husbands but some alone, or with other good-looking dames, strolled the avenue, laughing and speaking with that thrilled lilt you acquire when you're out on the town. Older married couples poked past, trading their quiet, well-worn comments or saying nothing at all.

It went on like this for an hour: no phone call, no in-person visits, no further instructions. Finally I went up to Donnie.

"All dressed up and nowhere to go," I said.

He nodded grimly. "Ask me how much I like standing here holding all this money."

"Then the hell with it. He got cold feet. Or he got detained. Or he got killed. Let's go home."

"But what if he calls?"

"Tough. First rule of ransom demands: Obey your own

rules." I had no idea if that was true, but I wanted to say something reassuring. "Didn't we obey his?"

"Actually, no. You're not supposed to be here."

"I'm not leaving you alone with the dough," I said. "Look, give me the bags and I'll take them to my place. You go home and get some sleep."

Dansicker protested a bit more, but his heart wasn't in it and he knew I was right. I took possession of the red Nike bags, stowed the meat-shop bag in one of them, and told him good night. I watched as he got into a cab to go back downtown to his garage. I glanced around to make sure I didn't see something, and was pleased when I didn't see it.

I took a cab to my place, and got a meatball sub from the joint on the corner. It was twelve thirty by the time I shuffled into the apartment. I put the money bags on the sofa, put the sandwich on a plate, opened a bottle of beer, and collapsed into a chair in the kitchen. I had managed two bites and a bracing gulp when I heard a knock on my door.

I padded, in stocking feet, to see who it was. A glance through the peephole revealed an individual in a spangly, glitter-encrusted harlequin mask. Naturally I opened the door.

"Pete Ingalls?" he said in a goofy, cartoony voice.

"The same."

"Cool!"

He pointed a weapon at me and I felt a dart stab into my shoulder. I reeled back from the doorway and the harlequin pushed past me. He seemed far away. The room itself seemed far away. I heard a kind of roaring in my ears that I knew wasn't real. A chair in my living room seemed to stare at me and to ask what my problem was. "Nothing!" I said out loud, or at least I thought

I did, or at least I intended to. The next thing I knew I was on my knees, crawling to the chair. It was far away. That struck me as unfair. It was an unfair chair. The harlequin walked past me with a cheery, "Good night!" and shut the door. He didn't seem to care if the chair was far away. Different chattery voices took up the chant in my head: *There is an unfair chair over there, but does anybody care?*

Then I went to sleep.

SEVEN

I woke up on the floor of my living room with my head in a vise and my neck stuffed with lumps of pain. The dart was still stuck loosely in my shoulder. It was daytime; by my watch either nine thirty or three and a half o'clock. When I tried to stand up the floor somehow tilted, but after I walked carefully into the bedroom it managed to steady itself. I showered and shaved, ignoring the phone when it rang three different times.

I got dressed slowly and methodically; I was going to have to deliver some bad news and I suppose I was stalling. Then I realized I was light-headed from hunger. I couldn't face the cold meatball sandwich, so I went to a coffee shop near my place and had the Wild Man's Breakfast. I didn't feel like a wild man. Halfway through the waffles I realized the enormity of what had happened the night before.

The guy in the harlequin mask had not only boosted the ransom money.

He had taken the six pounds of prime chuck roast.

Stephanie was on the phone when I got to the office, wearing
a white blouse and tight blue jeans and looking harried. As soon
as she saw me she mouthed, *Charlotte,* and pointed to the phone
and rolled her eyes. I shook my head. "As soon as he gets here,"
she told the caller. "Absolutely. Right." She hung up and sprang
out of her chair and ran to me.

"Jesus, Pete, you look horrible. What happened?"

I described the events of the previous night, leaving out only
the detail about the cost of the meat. "No wonder you didn't answer at home," she said. "Charlotte has been calling all morning.
Oh, and by the way: Whoever robbed you last night, it wasn't
Donnie."

Stephanie was the tail I'd looked for last night, the one I was
glad I didn't see. "You followed him?"

"All the way to Dobbs Ferry. Good thing I rented that car. I
hung out near their house for an hour and then came back to the
city. I don't think they're behind all this."

I shrugged. "It could have been an accomplice."

"I don't think so. Check this out."

She motioned for me to follow her and positioned me in front
of the whiteboard. It looked less cluttered than the day before,
and a number of urgent red lines now converged, with frantic ar-
rowheads, around a single name.

"I noticed this yesterday. I think this is our guy."

I squinted. "Marc Cohen?"

"Look at all the clues!" She made sweeping gestures toward
the chart. "Those pitches at Gyro and whatever that went
nowhere. All that animosity toward the Dansickers. And, like, his
total general weirdness as a person."

"That's it? General weirdness?" I shook my head. "No sale.
Put him on the watch list and keep going."

"To who?"

"Bob Borger? He hates the outtake reel and would fit right in at the funny farm."

"I haven't met him. Maurice said he's nuts but not a criminal."

The phone rang. Stephanie said, "Oh, Jesus, it's probably Charlotte again," and scrambled to field it. "Pete Ingalls, PI . . . One moment, Charlotte."

I legged it into my office and picked up. "Sorry, Charlotte, I just got in. I had an unexpected visitor last night." I told her about the harlequin mask and the trank dart and the theft of the ransom. When she asked if the thief had revealed his identity, per the original e-mail, I had to tell her no. "You might want to think about contacting the police," I said.

"Oh, God." She sighed. "That's just what we need. The stock's already in the toilet."

"Maybe. But the money's gone and we have no guarantee they won't put the touch on you again in six weeks. Or six hours, for that matter."

She said she'd discuss it with Donnie. Then I thought of something else. "You know, we're assuming the bird who heisted the cash is the blackmailer. But what if he isn't? What if the blackmailer couldn't make it, let it slide, and this third party took an active role? In that case the blackmailer still has the footage, and may be inclined to use it." She wasn't crazy about that scenario, and I had to agree. I said I'd continue the investigation at my end and I'd be in touch when something developed.

Out in the front office, Stephanie was gazing at her chart. "There's still something I don't get." She folded a stick of gum into her mouth and spoke around it. "That short deadline. What's the rush?"

"Maybe they had a deadline of their own."

Stephanie looked at me. "You know, Pete, that actually makes sense. I never thought of that." The phone rang. She answered with the spiel, then put the caller on hold. "Some lady to speak to you. Someone new."

I took it in my office. "This is Ingalls."

"Mr. Ingalls?" Her voice was cultivated and pleasant in its musical range. "I have a certain problem I think you can help me with."

"I'll do my best, Miss . . . ?"

"My name is Giselle Blanchard, and . . . well, briefly: I was in a restaurant the other night—the Silver Dove, maybe you know it?"

I smiled. "As it happens, I do, Ms. Blanchard."

"Good. Well, I went there after a day of shopping, and I had in my packages a thin blue box from Tiffany's. And inside was a very pretty necklace. . . . Anyway, I checked my bags at the coat check, and when I got home that night I realized that the necklace was missing. I don't know if I lost it, or if it simply fell out of the bag, or . . . well, you know. Something worse."

I felt like I'd been hit in the head with a pillow. It didn't hurt, but it wasn't supposed to happen. "You . . . um . . ."

"I'd like you to go to the restaurant and see if they have it. Do you do that sort of thing?"

"Uh, yeah, sometimes—"

"The reason I'm asking you, Mr. Ingalls, instead of doing it myself, is that if there's been any . . . you know . . . hanky-panky at the restaurant, I think they'd be more inclined to respect your inquiries than mine. Does that make any sense?"

I made an effort to regain my composure. It was successful. "Lady," I said, "it makes so much sense it reminds me of a very similar case I just completed. In fact, they're identical. Same restaurant, same Tiffany's box, probably the same necklace. So my question, not to put too fine a point on it, is: What gives?"

At first she said nothing. She must have been as puzzled by this as I was. Finally she said, "I can assure you, Mr. Ingalls, that the necklace is mine. If someone else had you fetch it for them, I can only assume they were involved in its theft."

"They might say the same thing about you."

"Yes, they might." Her voice got cooler and cagier. "But I happen to have proof. I have a photograph of myself wearing the necklace. Would you like to see it?"

I told her I would indeed, and that if her necklace was different from the one I'd just retrieved, I'd be happy to take her case.

"Why don't you come to my place now?" she said. "I can show you the photograph and we can move forward."

I said that sounded fine to me and she dictated her address. I told Stephanie I'd be back in an hour or so. When I left she was still staring at the diagram.

Giselle Blanchard lived in a high-rise apartment building off Sixth Avenue in Chelsea. I'd told the plump security guy at the desk I was expected; he'd called up, checked, and waved me through. Nonetheless, when I got to the door I had to rap hard with the knocker before I got a response.

When the door opened I could see why: A maid was piloting around the place a stainless-steel upright vacuum cleaner that made slightly less noise than a Harley. Giselle Blanchard, meanwhile, was a tall, thin knockout, five-ten at least, in a pretty taupe dress that did nothing to conceal her slim runway figure and everything to reveal a pair of gams as sleek as barracudas. Her chestnut-brown hair was full and shoulder length, in a kind of forties Katharine Hepburn 'do.

"Mr. Ingalls?" She had to shout over the whine of the appliance. "Giselle Blanchard." She held out a slim, shapely hand. Her blue eyes sparkled. Maybe she was wearing makeup and maybe she wasn't, because she looked like she didn't need to, because it looked like she already was. "Thanks for coming on such short notice," she yelled.

I shook the hand. It was dry and cool and I had to think hard for a reason to let it go. "My pleasure, Ms. Blanchard."

"Please. Giselle."

"Giselle." Somewhere nearby the vacuum cleaner snagged something loose and thin, and its whine revved up louder, to a higher pitch. I smiled and said, "I assume that's French? For gazelle?"

She hollered, "What?" and I repeated the comment.

"No." She led me into the apartment, away from the noise, into a book-lined study. She shut the door and the din fell to a distant drone in the background. "I'm sorry. Carla likes to use that machine but it's terribly noisy."

I scoped the room. It was furnished in expensive good taste, with a leather couch along one wall, a desk near the windows across the way, and plenty of handsomely framed photographs of Giselle with what I assumed to be her parents, sisters, and school chums, all smiling and cutting up and enjoying the good life, the kind of life where you get to lounge on the beach, and sail on boats, and cut a fine figure on horseback, and beam brightly from ski lifts, and there's always some poor bastard standing by to take your picture.

One pic in particular caught my eye—three young ladies with their arms around one another. Giselle was in the center. The gal

on the left was a stranger, but the one on the right looked familiar. Maybe she was a movie star—because somebody has to be. All
three stared at the camera in sullen resentment—or worse. You
say to me, "Gosh, Pete—is there anything worse than sullen resentment?" I say, Don't even ask. You don't want to know.

I pointed. "You and friends in happier times?"

Giselle glanced at the photo and gave a forced, bitter laugh.
"Me and my sisters."

"You don't look too glad to be there."

"We're not. My father took the picture, and we hate him."

" 'Hate'? Strong language, angel."

"How about 'detest'? Will that do?"

I said it would do just fine. Then I asked about the necklace.
She walked to the desk, opened its big top drawer, and pulled out
a photograph. "Here. That's me, obviously."

The photo caught her turning toward the camera in an allur-
ingly spontaneous way. She wore a minimal black dress and
seemed to be standing in front of a restaurant at night. Her hair
had been pinned up and she looked like a million bucks.

And the necklace was the same as Chris Page's.

Which is to say it was either the identical item, or its deliber-
ately produced twin. The stones, the settings, the pattern: All were
the same. Just like this dame's story of having left it at the Silver
Dove was the same as my client's. "Nice bauble," I murmured.

"Thank you." She took a step closer. A faint scent, something
floral and heady, began to envelop me. I began to wonder if, for
the second time in twelve hours, I was about to pass out. Maybe
that's how those things work. You spend a lifetime not passing
out, and then it happens once and you barely get on your feet before it happens again. It's murder on the clothes but it keeps the
statistics in order. "Do you think you can get it back for me?"

"That isn't really the question, is it?"

She stepped closer. The nice wide forehead, the straight nose, the handsomely sculpted cheekbones, the wide, deep eyes, the generous mouth and perfectly proportioned chin: Whatever it was that made a dame conventionally beautiful, this one had it in wholesale lots. "What is the question, then?"

I stood my ground, if only physically. "I can ask at the restaurant if they have it, yeah. And when they say, 'No, sir, you already have retrieved the aforementioned ice once already, Mees-tair Ingalls,' then I'm stuck in a dilemma, Giselle. Because—"

She moved closer still. "I'm stuck in a dilemma, too, Mr. Ingalls. May I call you Pete?"

". . . because—What? Yes. Sure. See—"

"Because I've never met anyone remotely like you and I find you overwhelmingly attractive."

". . . because that necklace, I have another client who also has a picture—"

Her head tilted in that way that heads tilt when they come in for a landing. And then her mouth was on mine and, sue me, mine was on hers. She moved into my arms as though we'd been practicing, and for a period of suspended time I was adrift in the swells and currents of a kiss. Then, from a distance but drawing nearer fast, a fighter plane—a MiG, say, or a Zero—approached. I held Giselle Blanchard tighter as though to protect her from being strafed, or as though to just hold her tighter. The noise, a whining, snarling, high-torque drone, suddenly burst upon us.

" 'Scuse me," a woman said, and I was dimly aware of Carla, the maid, pushing the vacuum cleaner into the room. She said, "Oops, sorry," and retreated and shut the door, and the noise subsided.

Giselle pulled back from me, but languidly, grudgingly, without really separating from me all that much. She took my hand

and led me to the leather couch on the side of the room. And I let myself be led. Why? Because she was a woman and I was a man, and because she wasn't a client—yet—and because when a knockout skirt drags you to a sofa in this lousy, corrupt world, you go, if you want to. And I wanted to, brother. I wanted to like nobody's business—except my own.

We got to the sofa and I sat. She pulled me to my feet, then slid her hands inside my jacket and, her eyes on mine, in a single move, like a magician, whisked the garment off. I undid my tie. She dispatched the first few buttons of my shirt until I took over and removed everything except my hat. That freed her to reach behind her neck, unclasp the dress, and let it fall to the floor.

All women are beautiful naked. At least the only other one I'd ever seen was, and now here was Giselle Blanchard, similarly beautiful and naked. Okay, maybe I've had a limited exposure to the world of naked women. But maybe that's a blessing. Because I'm not sure it's a world where I'd like to live.

Shocked? Think about it. Sure, one of your selves (if you're a heterosexual male, and if you had more than one self) would find it endlessly arousing. Plus, why are they naked? Answer: Because the weather's nice. So you can be naked, too. Although there's probably a saying, something like, "In the world of naked women, the guy who keeps his pants on is king."

But what about your other selves? What about the selves inside you who aren't all that interested in naked women? Say those selves exist. Then they matter. What about the self who likes to have a drink and read, whether there are any naked women around or not? Or catch a movie? Or bowl a few frames?

Or what about the self that takes on a client and goes out into the world and handles a case? Think you don't have that self pacing the floor and checking its watch in your head? Because don't kid yourself. You do. I don't know how they do it in the world of naked women, but over here, in the real world, most of us have to work for a living.

Although it so happens I don't have to work for a living. I happen to have been the recipient of a stipend, or an endowment, or some kind of underwriting fund, for my detective services, courtesy of a dame whom I did some work for (and whom I saw naked) and who later came into a landslide of dough. But I do it anyway. I put on the suit and go out into the world, and work for clients who just happen, sometimes, to want me to take off the suit and get, like them, naked.

I don't know if I was thinking these thoughts as Giselle Blanchard and I fell together onto the couch and found the right ways to entwine with each other as the heat ramped up and we started to do those certain things. Let's just say some thoughts, about something, were in the back of my mind. In the front of my mind was the realization that the sofa was covered with that thick, stiff, chilly leather, like the kind you find in the waiting rooms at train stations and on the chairs at barbershops. The furniture itself was too short to contain me without my bending my legs and making other contortions that threatened to distract me from the business at hand.

Giselle, meanwhile, thanks to that perfume, smelled like a garden in which something naughty but thrilling was taking place. We both began to breathe harder and make various sounds. So I could barely register the fact that that fighter plane, which earlier had buzzed us and flown away, was returning.

And then the door opened and the fighter plane arrived in the person of Carla and her whining, revving vacuum cleaner. She said, "Whoa! Sorry," which struck me as inadequate. "But I can't wait. I gotta leave at three."

But Giselle said nothing and just kept on going. So I did, too. And Carla did, as well, with the vacuum. And I thought, *Ingalls, take a lesson from this. This is what* civilized *means.*

Then Giselle began to breathe fast and talk strange, and I began to move strange and breathe hard, and even as the maid wheeled the snarling monster out of the room, Giselle and I exploded, each in his or her own way.

We settled, relaxed, and cooled down. And then, when the frenzy had passed, and we reencountered each other on the far side of passion, on the opposite shore from desire and its fevered imperatives, I said the necessary thing, the important thing, the thing I knew she was yearning to hear.

"I'll take the case."

As if cued to arrive from offstage, I heard music. It was simple, yeah, like a music box or a kid's toy piano. But I knew the melody. It was the *1812 Overture,* magically arriving out of thin air to herald and celebrate what this primo skirt and I had just experienced.

"I think that's your cell phone," Giselle said.

Gently, and with some effort, I disentangled myself, peeling my sweaty skin off the leather couch, reclaiming the use of my knees and lower legs, extricating myself from her cooling, recumbent body. I groped around for my jacket until I found the phone, pulled it out, and answered, "Ingalls."

"Pete? It's me. I'm at DD Productions. Get your ass over here fast, man."

EIGHT

I had plenty of time, in the cab uptown, to think about what had just occurred. And what had just occurred was sex. Now, like you, I happen to think that having sex is a pretty big deal—unless you're one of those citizens who thinks having sex isn't so big a deal, in which case I'm not like you at all, brother.

No, I'm like me, and I was starting to like it that way. Because this wasn't exactly my first sexual encounter. It was my second, so pardon me if maybe I was just a little impressed with myself. *Ingalls*, I thought, *the floodgates have opened. Ever since you put the gumshoes on you've been a devil with women. You're getting more action in six months than in the previous thirty-three years.*

Then I offered a silent prayer that I never become jaded or bored with this thrilling, exciting activity. Because it can happen. I heard an interview once with a gent in one of those holistic macrobiotic groups, who said that having an orgasm was "essentially like blowing your nose."

I didn't know what to make of it at the time, but I damn well knew now. Now I knew it was the statement of a guy who had never had an orgasm. Or maybe he had never blown his nose. I wasn't too sympathetic to him either way.

It was Stephanie who answered when I knocked on the door to the DD offices. She looked grim. "You won't believe this," she said.

I stepped into the reception area. There was no one at the main desk. The entire office seemed deserted. "What gives?" I inquired.

"They sent everybody home. Charlotte called me after you left. Everybody was here, but nobody could work. They were just sitting around freaking out. So Donnie told them all to just take a day off."

"Freaking out about what?"

"You'll see." Then she frowned, paused, and sniffed. "How come you smell like Bloomingdale's?"

The phone rang at the desk. Nobody caught it. "They've got a machine taking messages," my assistant said. "It's been ringing all day. Come on." The ringing stopped. A second later it started again.

She led me through the big, open loft space, past the door to the conference room, past the little offices of the producers and the open workspaces of the writers and researchers, to the rear. Ellen Larraby was at her desk, like a stout colonial soldier manning an outpost under siege. I nodded hello. She made a gun of her fingers and held it up to her head and pulled the trigger.

"Mr. Ingalls? In here."

Charlotte and Donnie were in Charlotte's office, sitting—or, rather, collapsed—on the sofa. Stephanie dragged me past them toward Charlotte's desk and her computer. "Check it out." I sat in the chair and turned to the monitor.

There, within the browser frame, in a little window above the QuickTime control bar, were our old friends Ramon and Tamiko. Her head was at his crotch and she was pumping it back and forth while, eyes shut in ecstasy, he reared his head back and smiled a great, big puppet smile.

I looked over at the Dansickers. Donnie sighed and just waved a limp hand in defeat. Charlotte said, "It's been on the Web since last night."

Stephanie bumped me off the chair. "Move. Watch this."

I let her sit. As she tapped the keys I said to Charlotte, "How do you know it's since last night?"

"That's when the phone calls started."

"From everyone," Donnie added. "Parents. PBS. KLAE in Philly. *Kids themselves.* 'I saw Jenny and Jimmy on the computer and they were doing something and it was nasty.' It's a nightmare."

"Pete."

I leaned in. Stephanie had entered *puppets, sex, porno* in some search box, and the program had responded with, it claimed, 53,744 sites in .03 seconds. *Got puppet porno?* read one, in blue letters, underlined. Another read, *See Jimmy F and the* Playground Pals *gang get it on!!!*

"We've been thinking," Donnie Dansicker said, sprawled like a corpse on the couch and barely moving. "We never heard from the blackmailer today. Which means either he's dead, or he's the one who robbed you last night."

"I say it's Marc Cohen," Stephanie said. "He's the blackmailer, he's the guy in the mask, he's behind the whole thing."

The Dansickers looked at each other. Donnie's shrug signaled: *Could be.* Charlotte turned back to us. "Really?"

All eyes turned to me. I held up a calming hand. "Why?" I asked astutely. "The game board is covered with suspects. Natalie Steinberg. Bob Borger. Even Shareena Hill. What about Phyllis Whatshername?"

"Donovan?" Donnie said.

It didn't click. I said, "No—"

"Regan?" Charlotte asked him. "Didn't a Phyllis Regan work here once?"

"Alice Regan. You're thinking of Phyllis Levinson."

"How about Paul Craye? He hates us!"

"He's dead. He died of AIDS two years ago."

"Oh. Too bad!" It wasn't clear whether she was lamenting his death, or his elimination as a suspect. She thought again. "Larry Speziak! Remember that fight we had?"

"Yeah, but I thought we all apologized."

"Wait a minute." Stephanie had stood up from the chair and now confronted the rest of us, hands on hips, full of actressy confidence. It made her look good, yeah, but I knew from experience things were going to get demanding. "I'll tell you why it's Marc Cohen. Spite."

You could have filled the silence that followed with a symphony orchestra's rich, symphonic sound. Finally I said, "Meaning what?"

"Come on, Pete! Think about it. He steals the money last night, and then he puts the footage up on the Web *anyway*! Just to be nasty! Isn't that just like a guy who would cancel his own show, rather than have to share it? With people who actually deserve to share it in the first place?"

I made a conciliatory gesture. "Let's say."

"Of all the suspects we have, he's the only one who has a history of acting this way."

Donnie pulled himself up to an actual sitting position. It was like a declaration of revived hope. "That's plausible."

"Plus"—Stephanie turned to me—"remember what he said when we asked if he was mad that Donnie and Charlotte had sent their lawyers after him?"

I took a flier. " 'They have a fool for a client'?"

"No. He said something like, 'What's the big deal? It's the business.' "

"Yeah. He did. So?"

"So, if he's so blasé and professional, why'd he get so pissy and spiteful? 'It's the business.' Bullshit. He doesn't really think that. He takes everything personally." She looked across at the Dansickers, who were following this exchange with rapt fascination. "Am I right?"

Charlotte seemed thrilled. "Absolutely!"

"I'm telling you, he's either lying about something, or he's lying about everything."

Donnie shrugged. "I'll buy it. The little shit."

I nodded, put-upon, like some kind of beleaguered father. "It plays, yeah. But let's all take a deep breath."

"Fuck a deep breath," Stephanie said. "Let's go visit Marc Cohen."

I walked over to the Dansickers, who seemed slightly revived by our conversation. I leaned down and spoke confidentially. "I apologize for my associate's poor choice of language." Then I added, "I'm going to play a hunch and visit Marc Cohen. You have my cell number. Keep me posted."

"Why?"

The question hit me like a snowball in summer. I stopped and stared at Charlotte. "What do you mean, why?"

"Why bother doing anything? Isn't it too late? The money's gone, the outtakes are all over the world. . . ."

"The money isn't gone. It's out there, and I'm going to find it. When I do, I'll bring back the joker who's behind all this. Isn't that what you want?"

She blinked as though awakening from a brief nap. "Oh. Well. Yes, of course."

"And one more thing. You may really want to bring in the police now. The cat's out of the bag. Your stock is going to suffer regardless of whether the cops are on hand or not."

Charlotte nodded. "We'll take care of it. Good luck."

Outside, the phone was still ringing.

In the cab downtown I openly mused on how to play it. Clearly, if Cohen was our man, he wouldn't welcome us into his office and display, with understandable pride, the two bags of cash. The most we could hope for would be an in-person, unsparing series of questions, with him knowing that we knew that he knew that we knew that the payoff and robbery took place the night before, and he knew it. So we'd look for signs of guilt. Our very appearance at his door might be enough to spook him into doing something revealing.

"Follow my lead," I said as we rode the tiny, dented elevator to Cohen's floor.

Stephanie looked unusually grim. She was lightly made-up, in a white blouse and jeans, and the severe set of her expression didn't sit well on her. "I think I'd better," she said. "I don't like this guy."

"Because he's a sexist pig?" I smiled. "Aren't we all?"

She shook her head. Her reddish brown hair, in a short, shiny pageboy cut, executed a tight swirl, first one way, then the other. "No. Because he pretends to be a sexist pig. To be 'provoking.' It's all dreamy irony with him. Like anyone else is a jerk for taking anything seriously."

"Then let's teach him a serious lesson—in seriousness," I said. The elevator doors rumbled apart.

We walked down the narrow, quiet corridor to the door marked EMCEE PRODUCTIONS, and I pushed the little beige button. The buzzer sounded dimly inside. No other noise followed. I knocked. The office remained silent.

"So he's out." Stephanie sighed.

"Out, at home, on a job, on the lam . . ."

We looked at each other. She eyed the door lock, pounded on the door. "Mr. Cohen! It's us!" Still no sound could be heard.

Stephanie suddenly whipped her little shoulder bag off, dug for her wallet, and hissed, "Cover me." She pulled a credit card out and went to work inserting it above the lock mechanism. It fit easily and she slid it down. Nothing. "Shit. I've done this at my sister's place." She took the card out, reinserted it, slid it down sharply while leaning against the door—which lurched open. "Yes!"

I took her arm. "Are we sure we want to do this?"

"We're just looking around. Maybe the money's in plain sight! We owe it to the client to look."

I followed her in.

There were no hallways, no entry areas bordered by walls, no separation into rooms. The place was just one big, bright, open box full of daylight. So of course we saw him immediately, limp on the floor near the desk at the far wall of windows. "Jesus," Stephanie breathed. We approached.

Marc Cohen was more or less on his back, in an unnaturally contorted posture, and covered in blood. It had oozed down off his once-white T-shirt and beige corduroy pants onto and across the floor a foot or so. But what really seized our imaginations was the murder weapon.

There can't be that many murder weapons in the world inscribed to the victim by name. You say to me, "Well, but wait a second, Pete. I bet a lot of guys have been killed by their own guns or swords or ceremonial knives with their names engraved on them." Maybe. But how many include the citation, *For Best New Preschool Series: Ronnie Rat and the River Rascals?* I say this because there can't have been that many occasions in history when a man has been bludgeoned and stabbed with his own Emmy.

The base of the award had been used to bash Cohen in the head—we could see blood from the wound under his hair at the back of his skull, which rested on the floor—and then the wings of the figure had been plunged into his breast.

"Wow," Stephanie said. Her voice sounded shaky. "Oh, boy. Okay, uh, first, let's not touch anything."

"Right," I said. "Second, we phone the buttons."

"Not yet, Pete."

"It's a homicide, doll."

"I know it's a homicide!" She turned down the volume to a whisper. "Sorry. But we're on a case. First we look for stuff we can use."

"Like what?"

"How do I know like what? Like two red bags of money!"

She spun away from me and the body and, as though not wanting to disturb the sleep of the dead man, began tiptoeing and pussyfooting around the loft, intensely scrutinizing whatever she came to but assiduously avoiding touching anything. She made her way to the wall on our right and, as she had during our previous visit, stood there and gazed in fascinated repulsion at the gallery of puppets and dolls with their sex-play clothes and fetish props. Then, recoiling with a little shudder, she turned and crossed to Cohen's big worktable. She looked at the computer.

"Hey."

She tugged her shirttail out of her jeans and used it to prod the nearby mouse. The screen saver disappeared, revealing the usual fruit salad of program shortcuts. She peered, searched, and said, "All right!" and clicked on one: A calendar program bloomed. "Bingo," Stephanie breathed. She scanned the top of Cohen's desk until she found a pen and a memo pad, then peered at the calendar. "Here's something: next Wednesday. 'Two thirty. LJ at Gyro.'" She wrote it down, tore off the sheet, then put the paper and the pen in her purse and dropped the pad on the desk.

That's when we both saw it, lying on the desk, tethered to the thin umbilical running down to the floor and into an electrical outlet. "Hot dog!" Stephanie said, then grabbed the item, disconnected it, and shoved it, too, into her purse.

I held out a hand. "That cell phone is evidence, angel. Not to mention private property. There are laws against taking it."

Too late. She had already circled the desk and unplugged the recharger from the wall. This, too, she put in her purse, as she said, "I know. But we need a break, and this could come in handy." She snapped her fingers and said, "I'll be right back. Don't touch anything." She hustled out the door.

As soon as she left I used my cell to call 911, and reported the homicide. I gave the address and said I'd stay until they sent someone. Then I walked around the loft and looked for things

that might tie Marc Cohen to the recent events, such as the harlequin mask or the dart gun. I came up empty.

Stephanie burst in with a bag from a drugstore and produced
a disposable camera. When I told her I'd buzzed the johns, she
got exasperated. "Then we only have a few minutes." She
snapped photos of Cohen's body and parts of the loft, until suddenly we heard a voice outside in the corridor.

"Mr. Peter Ingalls, PI. But did he come with his comely assistant?"

The door swung open and a big, heavy, shuffling lug in a
crushed, slept-in beige trench coat flopped in. "Oh, great,"
Stephanie muttered.

"Just as I hoped," Detective Henry Thoreau said. "Miss
Stephanie Constantino. Fate conspires to bring us together, precious. Still single?"

"Go to hell, Thoreau. Still married?"

"Not in my heart."

"Fuck you."

"Ever the flirt. I approve." He turned to me. "Ingalls. You
made the call? Good man. Very civic." He made his ponderous
way across the floor and stood above the corpse. "Friend of
yours?"

"No. Meet Marc Cohen." I kept it short and to the point.
"Television producer. Not a client, either."

"Shall we assume neither of you killed him? Oh, let's."
Thoreau craned his long, ovoid head around, eyeing the body from
a couple of angles. "Therefore, how'd you folks enter the premises?" He then looked to the side and spoke to his invisible friend.
"Or was the door *uncharacteristically ajar* when they arrived?"

"You got it," Stephanie said. She and I traded a look.

"Don't I always," Thoreau muttered. As usual, he looked half-asleep and entirely unwilling to be there. "Please tell me you two didn't touch or take anything."

"Didn't touch, didn't take," Stephanie said.

"And just happened to be shooting holiday snaps when you arrived." Thoreau nodded toward her camera.

She shrugged. "Why not? We're celebrating the moments of our lives."

"Ingalls—any theories?"

He'd been on the scene for a minute and already the floor under me had turned into thin ice. I couldn't just lie and stall; this was now a homicide and it was illegal, let alone morally suspect, to conceal evidence. But I was entitled—nix; I was *required*—to protect my clients, and to shield them as much as legally possible from implication in a murder case. So I answered carefully.

"He was in show business. There are a lot of people in show business, and most of them don't like each other."

"But most of them don't kill each other. At least not physically." Thoreau snickered as though at a smutty joke, then resumed his scrutiny of the body. "Thanks, Marlowe. And you're here, why?"

"On business, Detective."

"I see." The more his beaklike mouth flapped, the more inert and unfocused his watery gray eyes became. "So, to sum up: You represent someone, who shall remain nameless, whose affairs require you to visit this producer, who, for reasons I'm supposed to guess and that you say you have no idea about, has become a dead guy. Super." He stood up and stretched. Or at least that was what I assumed it was. He was like a water buffalo who performs some odd, deforming action, and you wonder what it is, and the guide at the zoo says, "Oh, that's how they stretch!"

Thoreau's attention had fallen on the right-hand wall and the shelves of leather-clad kiddie characters. "Hello. What have we the fuck here?" He strolled over to the display like a tourist at the Met. "Our boy had a hobby." He walked down the wall, studying the figures. "Isn't that nice. Very folk-arty, very craft-oriented. You guys have hobbies? I do."

"I'll bet." Stephanie snorted.

"Yes, what I do is, I like to send away for postage stamps from foreign lands." He turned back toward the rest of the room, spied Cohen's worktable, and wandered toward it. "Then, when they come in the mail, I put 'em all in a little pile on a table, and I sit there, and I whack off to thoughts of Miss Stephanie here. It's fun! And, of course, educational." He surveyed the table, frowning, his big white hands clasped palm to palm, like a concerned minister. Stephanie gave me a quick look of apprehension. "Busy boy. Lots of 'projects.'" He turned to us. "You two can go. Stay in town. I may have an urge to question you later. In fact, I almost certainly will. Right, Steph? 'Cause I know you know all about my *urges*." He reached for a memo pad on the table and picked it up by its edges and frowned at it.

Stephanie suddenly went pissy. "Hey, eat me, Thoreau."

The cop looked up at her and grinned abominably. "I thought you'd never ask."

"You're such a pig."

Thoreau gave a wan little smile. "Pigs are people, too."

"Asshole," Stephanie snarled. She marched to the door and flung it open. "Come on, Pete." She stomped out.

I hurried after and caught up with her at the elevators. "What's the problem? Since when do you let him get to you like that?"

She laughed as she pushed the DOWN button. "I didn't want him to look too hard at that pad until we got out."

"It was blank."

"Yeah, but with the impression of the note I'd written about Cohen's appointment at Gyro. Meanwhile, the desk was covered with papers with Cohen's handwriting. I didn't want him even close to comparing the two. 'Cause I'd told him we hadn't touched anything. So I let him have a cheap thrill teasing me."

As we rode down in the elevator, I paused yet again to marvel at the boundless depths of women's insights, and resourcefulness, and calculation, and guile, and sneakiness. I wondered what this world would be like if women ever involved themselves in criminal acts. Then I remembered that they did, and that the world would be almost exactly as it already is. The thought was reassuring—and yet terrifying. I remained deep in thought in the cab back to the office.

NINE

"Something's weird."

Stephanie was at her desk, examining the photos she'd taken at Marc Cohen's loft. I stood behind her and reviewed the pix, dealt out like a hand of solitaire: apart from the fact that the domicile's tenant could be seen collapsed on the floor, soaked in blood and in a state of advanced death, nothing looked amiss, and everything, apart from the man's Emmy, seemed in place.

"How so?" I pointed to views of the body, the kitchen, the worktable, the windows, the doorway, the S-and-M gallery of beloved characters. "No B and E?"

The gal looked impressed. Score one for the boss. "Well, yeah, now that you mention it. Which means he knew his killer. Maybe. Or he let in the pizza guy, who saw the money and went nuts."

"No signs of a struggle," I murmured. "That means that a struggle didn't take place."

"Well, okay. But he was bashed in the head. Whoever did it

sneaked up behind him. But that's not what I meant. Something's either there that shouldn't be, or isn't there that should."

I had to laugh. And I did laugh. I laughed—*ha, ha, ha*—and said, "Tell me about it, doll. Isn't that the human condition?"

With theatrical patience she said, "No, Pete." And that was aces with yours truly. I happen to enjoy being spoken to patiently. And I don't care if the patience on display is theatrical, sincere, forced, faked, saintly, robotic, low-cal, or extra-crispy. As long as it isn't rushed. When people are patient with me it calms me down and makes me feel like I exist. And there's no feeling on earth like that, brother. "The human condition is either having not enough money, or having too much."

"Do tell," I said. It was possible she was leading up to something. I saw the play developing and decided to disrupt it with the blitz. "Then let's make a deal. You don't ask for a raise and I don't reduce your take-home."

"But, Pete—"

"I'm holding the line against inflation, angel. Too few secretaries doing a normal amount of work chasing too much money. End of topic."

She sat back from the pictures in defeat. "Yeah. Whatev—*Hey!*" She dived for her purse, which was on the floor at the foot of her desk, and fished Marc Cohen's cell phone out. "Shit, we gotta use this fast. By now they probably know he has a cell number, and Thoreau's gonna be looking for the phone." She switched it on. "Hmm." She studied the little screen. " 'Names.' "

"Get his known acquaintances, his relatives, whatever biz contacts are on there." I headed for my office, adding, "In fact, get everything. Enter it all into the main DD file."

I shut the door and sat. On my desk, a number I'd used recently was scribbled on an envelope. I dragged it over and dialed. I had no idea what to expect.

A smooth-voiced woman answered. "Good evening, the Silver Dove, how may I help you?"

I ID'd myself and gave the spiel: how I'd visited a day or two before, claimed a Tiffany necklace for a client, etc. Now, I said, I had a new client who seemed to have misplaced a similar necklace at the same establishment.

Some muffled words were exchanged as the dame covered the receiver. Then a familiar voice said, "Mis-tair In-gulls? I am Yves. How is this further necklace to be 'similar'?"

"Okay, pal, let's just say identically similar. Very, very similar indeed."

"Ah, *oui,* this business again. No, monsieur, we do not have an additional necklace like the one. We have the one necklace, we give it to you. *C'est tout.*"

I played ball; the guy had me at his mercy and it wasn't much to ask. "Two," I said. Then I waited. There was the sound of a lot of nothing taking place. Finally I said, "Now what?"

"Now what how?"

"You said, 'Say two.' I said it. Now why would you tell me to say that? My theory: There are two necklaces."

"*Non,* monsieur, we have just the one necklace, which we have give to you."

I'd had trouble with French restaurants before. I once spent an entire day casing a French joint that turned out to be the wrong place. You say to me, "But jeez, Pete, that's not their fault. That was your fault for getting the name wrong." Point taken. But it was French.

I finally got the guy to come clean, that the necklace I'd already picked up was the only one they had. That meant that

Giselle Blanchard was playing a baffling, devious game with re-
gard to a necklace that belonged to Chris Page—a game that I
was losing.

"*Pete!*"

Stephanie banged in from the outer room with Marc Cohen's
cell phone in her hand and a look of triumphant joy on her
young looker's mug.

"Whattaya got, kid?"

She held up the unit. "I'm looking through the names, and
then I remember—call log! They all have them. So I'm looking at
calls missed, and calls received—and then calls made. Which all
have the date and time! So I look to see if there were any calls
made last night at around ten o'clock. There's one number. So I
call it. And guess what happens!"

I spread my hands and played the helpless ignoramus. It's a
stretch role, but within my range.

"Some stranger answered," she said. "I said, 'Where am I calling, please?' He says, 'A phone booth on the corner of Eighty-
sixth and Broadway.'"

"Which means . . . ?"

"That's where Donnie got the pickup instruction. The first
place you staked out. This is the phone that made that call. Marc
Cohen *is* the blackmailer!"

I pointed at her. "Home run, doll. Hit the ball and touch 'em
all. Now: Is he the one who wore the mask and heisted the
dough?"

Her smile froze, reverted to a pensive frown. "Good question.
We don't know. Maybe Thoreau found the mask in Cohen's loft.
Although we didn't see it. Or Cohen could have just thrown it
away, which is what he should have done. Or the guy who
robbed you could be someone else."

"In which case, why kill Cohen?" I reached for the phone, punched in a number, and asked for Charlotte Purdy. She came on fast.

"Mr. Ingalls! Do you have any news for us?"

"Some, Ms. Purdy. I hope you're sitting down."

"Really? Why?"

I had to pause. It struck me that I didn't really care whether or not she was sitting down. What did it matter whether she received momentous news sitting down or standing up? Or even in a kind of half-kneeling position? Yeah, I know what the *assumption* is: that if it's really bad news, she'll faint, and it would be better if she's sitting rather than standing, so she wouldn't have to fall as far. But first: She's a short woman. How far, really, would she have to fall from a standing position? And anyway, that's not my real point. I hear this sit/stand argument and I want to reply: Do people really faint? At bad news? Sure, they pass out—from oxygen deprivation or low blood pressure, and so forth. But from the verbal conveyance of trouble? Suddenly I was filled with doubt about that.

Besides, what I had to say wasn't all bad. So I canceled the sit-down order and just told her I had news. She got her husband on the line and I told them about Cohen, his death, our reasons for thinking he was the blackmailer and the guy who knocked me out last night, and so on. Then I said, "The blackmailer is dead and the porno has gone wide. But the money is missing. Shall I assume you want me to stay on the case?"

"Oh—" Charlotte started to say, with an upbeat, encouraging tone—you could almost hear the "of course" about to burst out. But she stopped, and then said, "Honey, what do you think?"

"Definitely," Donnie Dansicker said. "Find that money, Mr. Ingalls. But, ah, do you think the police will want to talk to us?"

"I don't see how it can be avoided," I said. "But I can promise you the cops won't get to you through me unless I absolutely have no choice."

"Then why would they at all?" Charlotte asked. "If you don't tell them about us, why would they think of talking to us?"

"They'll find your name in Marc Cohen's address book, or on his résumé. They'll talk to someone else, who will mention you. It's not a question of if, but when."

"Oh, God." Charlotte Purdy sounded punched. "I can't wait."

"Don't wait," I said. "Go to them first. Voluntarily. If not now, then once the story hits the news. Why not? You have nothing to hide."

"That's true," Donnie said. "Char, we have nothing to hide."

"But once they hear about the blackmail, they'll want to get involved *here*," his wife persisted. "With the company."

"They're the police!" Donnie shouted. "They're investigating a murder! We have no choice!"

It was time to blow the whistle—the whistle of reality. I said, "Ms. Purdy, the blackmail resulted in the money, and the money is probably why Cohen was killed. It's the central fact in a homicide investigation."

"Oh, God, I hate this!" she cried. "Everything is flying out of control."

"Look, Ingalls," Donnie said. "Go look for the money. Meanwhile Charlotte and I will talk about how to deal with the police. Just don't tell them about us yet, okay?"

I agreed, and was just about to say good-bye when Stephanie handed me a note she'd just scribbled. I read from it into the phone, " 'Ask to speak to Ellen L. Ask re LJ at Gyro.' "

Charlotte, bewildered: "What?"

Me, to Stephanie: "She says, 'What?' "

Stephanie took the phone and asked to speak to Ellen, then asked her who "LJ" might be at Gyroscope. Then she hung up.

"She thinks it's probably Lackland Jessup," she said. "He's a development guy there. I'll get us an appointment."

She went back to her desk, leaving me to have certain thoughts about a disturbing trend I detected in the DD case. I thought the thoughts and then decided to share them with my associate.

"Jessup gave me the runaround," Stephanie said as I joined her in the front office. "Then I told him Marc Cohen was found dead this morning, and he said to come up in half an hour."

"Which I will." I spoke firmly. "Solo."

"Pete!"

"I didn't go into this racket to do a Fred-and-Ginger act, or to feel like when I'm out on the street that every day is Bring Your Daughter to Work Day."

"First of all," she said in her crisp, all-facts tone, "you're only eight years older than me." But suddenly she stopped and composed herself in her chair. "Okay. No problem. Here's the address and the office number." She wrote out the details and handed me the paper.

"So we're square?" I asked. "I hit the pavement and you run HQ?"

"Sure. You bet."

"Aces."

I got my hat and headed uptown.

I went back to Gyroscope, on Broadway in the Forties, where we'd spoken with Sheila Pasternack what now seemed like a year ago. I sat nice and still and waited in the cockeyed, brightly colored waiting area, surrounded by TV screens and giant toys, until a young man in black jeans and a wild orange Hawaiian shirt came out to greet me.

"Mr. Ingalls? I'm Lackland Jessup." We shook hands and he led me around two corners into a small, windowed office. The desk and chair and half-size sofa took up most of the space. The rest was taken up by a file cabinet and a vertical bookshelf unit crammed with videotape boxes, stacked scripts, and books, all watched over by a scattered array of goofy Gyro character figurines. There was an open laptop on his desk.

This annoyed me. It all seemed rather smugly "sleek" and "cool." I found myself wondering why he couldn't have a big, heavy desktop computer, like everybody else. We sat.

Jessup was smooth-faced and bright-eyed and at least twenty-three years old. He gestured to me, and then my suit, and made a series of gee-whiz expressions of amazed delight. "Wow," he said. "I mean, yeah!"

"Come again?"

"I mean, all riiiight!"

"Look—"

"I mean"—he gestured to my clothes—"I've never seen a real detective before."

"That makes two of us. Just tell me, Mr. Jessup—"

"Hey. Jessie."

"Okay. Mr. Jessie—"

"No, I mean, that's what everyone calls me. Just Jessie."

I took this in and nodded. "Because it's better than Lackey, eh?"

He looked slapped. "Huh? I mean . . . what do you mean?"

"Jessie to everyone and lackey to none. Good policy."

He shrugged, then looked delighted. "Thanks!"

"But let's quit shuffling and deal from the top, shall we?"

"Sure! Huh?"

"Talk about Marc Cohen. My sources tell me he had an appointment to see you next week."

"Oh. Ooh. Yeah. Marc. Wow. What a . . . what a tragedy. Do they know why he died?"

"He died because somebody killed him."

"I know *that!*" He laughed. Then he got serious again. "I mean, who?"

"I'm working on it. Which is why I need to hear what you can tell me about him. What was he going to see you about next week?"

"Oh. Huh. Let's see. . . ." He twiddled his fingers over the laptop keys, which made rapid little clicky sounds as he called up and paged through his calendar program. "Here it is. Wednesday. Marc Cohen, TBD."

"TBD," I murmured. "Sounds Spanish."

He pointed to the screen. "The note I wrote to myself says, 'To be determined.' "

"Yeah, sure, Jessie." I adopted a fatherly tone. He was young and it might get results. "We all want 'to be determined,' " I said understandingly. "And we all want to be vigilant, and resourceful, and focused, and all that good stuff. And yeah, we all write little inspirational notes to ourselves. You should see the Post-its I've got on my bathroom mirror."

"Really? Cool!" The kid frowned at his screen. "The last thing Marc pitched here was something called *Henry the Horse at Home*." He paused, distracted by a thought. "But that wasn't just his. This puppeteer was involved in creating it, too. Stephen O'Neil? Do you know him?"

"Not yet. But I plan to talk to him."

"We had to pass on it. *Henry*. It wasn't right for us. Marc was coming to talk about something different."

Cohen and O'Neil: Both had worked for DD Productions. Coincidence? *Wake up, Ingalls,* I told myself. *There are no coincidences. And if there are, there's always a hidden cause behind them.* "Did Cohen work with O'Neil a lot?" I asked.

The kid opened his eyes wide. "I don't know." He frowned and thought hard. Then he brightened. "Hey, you want to see their leave-behind?"

"Come again?"

"Marc and Stephen. I can show you their leave-behind."

I had to look away to control my revulsion. This was a kiddie network, so it didn't surprise me at all that its employees spoke to each other, and to visitors, in baby talk. To my ears, *leave-behind* sounded like a juvenile euphemism for excrement, like *poo-poo* and *caca,* only for today's generation of smarter, more sophisticated toddlers. Improbable? After the depravity of Cohen's S-and-M gallery of toys, anything was possible. "Why would you even have their leave-behind?" I asked. "And why would I want to look at it?"

Jessup looked confused. "Well, uh, because it's . . . it's my job, and it's . . . it might help your, uh, what—"

"And where would such a thing be kept? In a refrigerator? In some kind of laboratory freezer?"

"Right here!" He turned around to face the file cabinet behind him and pulled open a drawer. I didn't know whether to stand and walk out or reach over and slug him. But I did neither and was too late: He pulled something from the drawer. As if by instinct I shut my eyes. "Here! Check it out!" I heard a light slapping sound on the desk in front of me. In spite of myself, and against my better judgment, I looked.

It was a small pile of papers, a document, about twelve pages long, with a lot of white space and different headings and some text. At the top of the first page, centered, was:

Henry the Horse at Home

Proposal for a Half-hour Preschool Program
Created by Stephen O'Neil and Marc Cohen

I looked up at Jessup. "What's this?"

"The leave-behind. You know. People come in to pitch ideas, and they leave behind this, like, proposal. So everybody in the company can look at it and discuss it."

I absorbed this and added it to my expanding understanding of the children's television business. I picked up the document and skimmed it. It was exactly what Jessup said it was, a rundown of the show's premise, characters, sets, stories, and so on. I asked if I could have a copy. Jessup disappeared to a Xerox room for a minute.

He came back with a copy of the proposal and handed it to me. "I heard Marc was setting this up at Ronson," he said. "It's too bad he was killed."

"It's too bad everybody is killed," I said. Then I realized I hadn't actually said what I had meant, which was that it was too bad when anybody is killed.

But it didn't matter. Lackland Jessup nodded grimly and said, "Wow. Yeah."

On the street I called Constantino and filled her in on the meeting. I ended with the suggestion that I speak to Stephen O'Neil, now that he was back in town.

"I already spoke to him," she said.

"Is that a fact? And was it a fruitful conversation?"

"Oh, please, Pete. I didn't question him. I just set up a meet-ing for us with him tomorrow morning at his place."

"Well—"

"And I'm going. Jessup didn't matter, but O'Neil is impor-tant. You need me there and I'm going, period."

"Sold," I said. She gave me the address and the time. "See you there tomorrow."

Maybe I was too tired to argue. Or maybe some part of me was smart enough to realize that I'd need all the help I could get.

I was about to go one-on-one with a puppet superstar.

TEN

Stephen O'Neil lived on the Lower East Side, where they ran out of numbers for naming the avenues and there was nothing left but the alphabet. I met Stephanie at the appointed time on a gritty street that didn't have much green. The skinny trees looked tired and their foliage drooped. All around, auto-body shops and machine-parts stores alternated with bodegas, Laundromats, and the occasional newly spruced-up eatery. The steps of O'Neil's building were a dirty matte maroon that came off in potato chip–sized flakes.

But the lad who answered our buzz was bright-eyed and alert, tall and rangy in jeans and a blue workshirt. "Pete! Stephanie! I'm Stephen." His gaze lingered on my associate, and why not? She looked good in a tight black skirt and a red-and-black-striped blouse. I wore my dark blue suit, the cordovan wing tips— although remind me to discuss, at another time, my thoughts about just what "cordovan" is supposed to mean—and the wide-brimmed fedora, because this was business, and that's what I wear.

O'Neil had the whole first floor, and the place he ushered us into was potentially a cave with very little daylight. But he didn't need it: The joint was skillfully illuminated by track units on the ceiling, and had the cozy, romantic, controlled feel of a recording studio. He herded us toward a big handsome sofa dully shining in dark brown velvet upholstery. We sat, and sank onto a spongy, yielding bed of ancient stuffing that finally stopped at a lumpy, knobby substrate. You had to shift and squirm to find a decent spot, and fend off prods to the posterior. At least I did.

Frankly, this is my beef about antique settees and sofas and divans: they look plump and noble and welcoming, but the inside is often as tired as the outside. Like with people, yeah. So you take your chances when you try to get comfy. Like with people.

O'Neil winced sympathetically at my reaction. "Sorry. It's an old couch. How about something to drink? I've got coffee, fifteen kinds of tea, and I think ginger ale." He had an open, clean-shaven face, pockmarked from teenage acne, and a head of thick, untamed dark curls. With his bright blue eyes and dark, expressive eyebrows, he radiated the kind of nervous creative energy I associate with that type of individual. "Oh, and vodka." We asked for joe and he tripped off toward the kitchen in the rear. We settled onto the sofa, in front of the white-curtained window, and scoped the pad.

There were a couple of big easy chairs; they were old and overstuffed, with faded brocade upholstery and scarred wooden feet. I found myself in a big hurry not to sit in them. In a corner was a stand with a TV and the usual cluster of support boxes. The bookshelves on the main wall were fully laden with books, but also with puppets and their related paraphernalia: old marionettes, little sock jobs from beginner roles years past, familiar *Abracadabra Avenue* figures, unfamiliar characters from kiddie shows that had failed to catch fire, and various mechanical devices and armatures like free-form metal sculptures. The other walls featured many framed posters, some modern, some antique, all about puppets: troupes, movies, marionettes, even a French ventriloquist. The table at our knees held neat piles of *Variety*, *The New Yorker*, and a single shopworn copy of *People*.

Stephanie got up and strolled the shelf, smiling at the figures. When O'Neil returned with a tray bearing three mugs and a pot of coffee, she held one up.

"What happened to Jimmy?"

It was a Jimmy Farlow toy, about a foot tall, a miniature version of the puppet character. And it was naked—or, at least, unclothed. Jimmy's head was recognizable, with its trademark crew-cut yellow hair, bright blue eyes, upturned pug nose, and cheery, gap-toothed smile. But below the neck the kid's body was a lumpy, stuffed sack of gray muslin attached to two legs and two arms, also naked, stuffed, and gray. O'Neil set the tray on the table and looked up.

"I spilled coffee on his clothes and I'm trying to soak it out." He gave her the eye. I kept mum. We were his guests, and it was his eye to give. "I'm just glad he didn't sue me."

She laughed. "He wouldn't dare. You made him and you can break him. He was *nothing* before he met you."

"Don't let him hear you say that. He's under the impression that he made me."

Yeah, it was witty and diverting. Everybody was enjoying a flirty little chuckle—everybody except Ingalls, who glowered like the lunatic uncle and thought dark thoughts about murder and extortion. Then Stephanie sat down, and we all got our coffee orders straight, and O'Neil pulled up an old black paisley-patterned wing chair and settled in.

O'Neil started as though he had read my mind. "We're sitting here laughing, and meanwhile Marc's been killed. It's unbelievable." He was upset, and his face was expressive, frowning, eyebrows angled down. "Plus this blackmail thing at the office. Jesus." He slurped from a black mug that read PUPPETEERS KNOW HOW TO MOVE YOU WITH THEIR HANDS. "Is there a connection?" He looked at Stephanie. "But there must be, right? You don't have these two horrible things happen at the same time without being connected."

She spoke softly. "The connection is Marc."

"He was being blackmailed, too?"

"He *was* the blackmailer."

"What?!"

"We think he was," I said. I explained the events of the past couple days, climaxing with our discovery of Cohen's corpse. I omitted mention of the cell phone that my associate had filched and just alluded to "evidence" that Cohen was the blackmailer. "We also think he tranked me and boosted the payoff dough," I said, more in sorrow than in sadness. "And then somebody else got wise and popped him for it."

He put the mug down, visibly upset. "Jesus Christ. Who?"

Stephanie said, eyeing him over her steaming mug, "We were hoping you could tell us."

"Me? God." He looked away, shifted in the chair, licked his lips. "Okay. Look. He and I were working on a project together. A preschool show called *Henry the Horse at Home*. We took it to Gyroscope a week or so ago and they passed."

"I know. I spoke with Jessie Lackland," I said. "Nice leave-behind."

Then Stephanie asked what the show was about, and I had the floor.

"Well, apparently"—I chuckled—"Henry is a horse who lives at home. And he has two special friends: Mimi the Mouse, and Katie th—"

"Pete?" Stephanie said, all smiles. "No offense, but we're sitting here with the creator. Mind if I hear it from Stephen?"

I acceded and O'Neil summarized the premise of the show. He was just beginning to describe the pilot episode when my assistant interrupted. "So how would that have worked with you and Marc? He'd produce? And you would what?"

"Play Henry!" O'Neil couldn't decide whether to look thrilled or bereft. "And I've got the voice all figured out! Part Mister Ed, part Bullwinkle, with a little bit of Nixon." He held up his hand with fingertips all touching, flapped his fingers against his thumb, and spoke in a guttural, cantankerous voice: " 'Mimi, I'm not talkin' about another thing till we eat them carrots.' "

I smiled. Stephanie said, "Fabulous. In a big walkaround suit?"

O'Neil nodded. "One man. Sort of *Equus* meets Big Bird." He spread his hands in helplessness. "Marc came up with some great ideas for the design. We had a meeting at Disney next week . . . and we were talking to Ronson . . . although Marc said he wasn't sure how welcome he was around there anymore. Jesus, you know, I just talked to him two days ago. I called him from Boston."

"So," Stephanie said with some delicacy, "you worked with Marc lately. Any idea who might have wanted to do this?"

"Oh, my God, no." O'Neil groped for a theory. "Couldn't it have just been a robber?"

"We think he knew the person who killed him. And if Marc was the blackmailer, and if he did steal the ransom money from Pete, who else would have known he had it?" She shrugged. "There's a lot of 'ifs.' That's why we're here. Donnie and Charlotte have hired us to find the money, so we're talking to everybody."

"And they probably all said the same thing, right? That Marc was obnoxious and temperamental . . ." He gave a little laugh. "Which he was."

"Why would he do this blackmail thing?" Stephanie drilled her gaze into his. "Did he really need the money? Was it for some kind of revenge? Or what?"

"I have no idea." The puppeteer looked grim, then tried to shake it off. "I didn't know him well. I'd never worked with him before. I just kind of knew him from around. And I knew his reputation. But I met him at a party, I mentioned Henry, and the general idea, and he was interested. I thought, Shit, he's had stuff produced, he knows everybody, so why not?" He paused and sipped his coffee. "But it is true that a lot of people hated him. *Hated* him."

"Did you?"

Stephanie's question went off like a grenade, although O'Neil took the blast in stride and kept on marching, and I wasn't all that stunned, either. "No. I mean, we weren't friends. But I didn't care about his personality. I didn't depend on him for anything personal. So when we disagreed and he got . . . you know . . . *prickly*—I just said, 'Look, that's not okay; let's figure it out.'"

The memory must have spurred some sadness reflex in the guy, because he suddenly sat back and clammed up. It left a vacuum of feeling in our little group. That's when Stephanie spied the *People* magazine on the coffee table, frowned at its cover, and paged to the contents. She gave me and then O'Neil a little look, and dropped the mag onto the table, where it stayed open to a spread that had obviously been perused many times before.

Under the headline NEW KIDS ON THE BLOCK were Stephen

O'Neil and Jimmy Farlow, the puppet, in a nice black-and-white photo, both of them beaming and delighted. The caption read: *Jimmy Farlow and friend: Not since Kevin Clash brought Elmo to life has one character so dominated PBS kidvid.*

Stephanie said, "You're, like, the hottest puppet guy on the planet these days, aren't you?"

Stephen O'Neil made modest, minimizing shrugs.

"I mean, come on!" Stephanie persisted. "*People* magazine! How cool is this!?"

Stephen O'Neil looked . . . well, let's just say he looked like a lot of things, and all in about one second: surprised, pleased, dismayed, wary, and amused. "It's somewhat cool," he said carefully. "But you know how that goes. It's not because I'm so great and Bob or Maurice or Susie or the others aren't any good. It's this weird zeitgeist thing. Everybody's crazy about Jimmy. Next year they'll be crazy about Tamiko. Or next week!"

"Or they might just stop watching the whole show entirely!" I contributed helpfully.

"Pete—"

"So they send me all over the country doing PR, and it's all Jimmy, all the time." He added, "It's self-fulfilling, isn't it? I'm the one they send, so I'm the one people see."

"You mean now that production's over," Stephanie said.

O'Neil rolled his eyes in a puppetlike manner, and for a moment the puppeteer had become the puppet, in a sense. "Constantly. Now. Last week. Next week. During preproduction. During *production*. Weekends, breaks . . ."

"Yikes!" Stephanie looked sympathetic. "How does that work? Doesn't AFTRA get mad?"

O'Neil shrugged. "They would if I told them. If I complained. But I don't."

"Neither would I." My assistant waved off the tiresome details. "As long as you're making the big bucks."

O'Neil forced a laugh. "I wouldn't go that far. I mean, it's better than scale. But Donnie and Charlotte had an option on me after the first season, so I basically had to take what they were offering."

Stephanie shrugged, one pro to another. "And it's work, right?"

"Yeah. Although sometimes it's not just work; it's *work*. The malls. The bookstores. The school assemblies and the local morning shows. You can only be Jimmy Farlow for so long before you want to kill yourself. Plus traveling can be such a nightmare." He finished his coffee and set the mug down on the tray, then leaned back and grew reflective. "Then again, I was out of work for a year when this came along. I went into puppets because I wanted a variety of jobs, not just to collect unemployment and do free shows at children's hospitals my whole life. So I took what they gave me."

He suddenly sat up, jazzed by a new thought. The blue eyes burned and the dark curls quivered. "Hey. You know who you should talk to? Samantha Rosen. The show Marc won the Emmy for? *Ronnie the Rat?* She was his head writer. They have real history." I asked him where we could find her and he suggested we call the Writers Guild.

It felt like enough, if only for now. I stood up and the other two followed my lead. "Out of work for a year," I said, and pointed to the magazine. "And now this. Now you're a big star."

Stephen O'Neil laughed. "Hardly. No, Jimmy's the star. I'm just the schmuck with my hand up his ass."

———

By Monday morning it was clear that the pool of suspects for the heist of the blackmail money was limited to the people who knew and disliked Marc Cohen, and that it was an Olympic-sized pool. Now, like you, I don't really know what that means. Is "an Olympic-sized pool" a pool as big as Mount Olympus? But it can't be. Mount Olympus is a vertical structure, while a swimming pool is a flat—or let's say a negatively vertical—structure. A mountain goes up, and a pool, which is a big hole, goes down. No wonder I was stymied.

That's why the first thing I did on Monday morning was phone Donnie Dansicker and tell him I wanted, once and for all, to find the person or persons who made the copy of the outtake footage. To accomplish this I proposed to reinterview the entire staff of his company.

He welcomed the idea like a vegetarian welcomes a T-bone. "It's too disruptive," he said on the phone. "Things are already a fucking mess here. Pardon my French."

"French pardoned."

"Besides, sooner or later the cops are going to trace Marc Cohen's associates and whatnot and end up here. Then we'll really be fucked. The footage is on the Web, the phones won't stop ringing, and I've got some insurance guy asking questions. Meanwhile we've got to try to get business done. I've got twenty-four new shows to edit and mix and complete. Can't you do something else?"

I accepted his argument. I asked what he knew about Samantha Rosen. "Who? Isn't she a writer? She worked on *Ronnie the Rat*? Yeah. I don't know. Nothing. Have you spoken to Bob Borger? Everybody knows he hated Cohen. He's plenty weird enough to be involved in this. Ingalls, look, I gotta go."

And I thought, That's why, in the literature, PIs rarely use the phone. They travel to the location and confront the individual in person. Because they can't hang up on you when you're standing there. They can slug you, but then you know you've got their attention.

The only time I had spoken to Bob Borger had been on the phone, to a number with a 718 area code, where I got a dame who said "Astoria." By using my investigative resources, I asked Stephanie and learned this was a reference to Astoria Studios, one of several movie and TV production facilities across the river, in Queens.

I hit the street and headed for the subway. In one of those inexplicable coincidences that often happen to remind us that such things do happen, the gent who followed me down the stairs and through the turnstile got on my car, and disembarked at my stop. He wore a dull tan suit and a yellow shirt and a black tie and a hat, one of those gray felt snap-brim hats men wore in the fifties, before JFK didn't wear one and everything in America changed forever.

The train let me out a couple blocks from a huge, ornate old structure, once either a warehouse or a factory. I stood at its entrance and admired it as the man from the subway walked on past me and up the street. Then I went inside. I found my way to Studio B, where a guard at the double-door entrance gave me the once-over and asked, point blank, if I was "talent."

I was flattered. In my business, "private eye" and "private talent" are synonymous, and I silently gave the mug credit for reading the signs of my attire and hitting the target first try. "You bet, brother," I said.

"I thought so, in that getup." He laughed and opened the door. I went in.

It was big and dark and largely empty, in essence a vacant box with a ceiling lined with mounting rods and festooned with lighting equipment. The set of a kids' TV show stood, brightly illuminated, in the center, an island of color and brilliance in a black sea. People hovered in little groups on the periphery of this sacred central space, which was framed by tall, false walls made of two-by-fours and sheets of plywood. Three video cameras, each attended by a slouching tech wearing headphones, aimed their big glass eyes at the action in the middle.

A short, plump woman in a lumberjack shirt and jeans and a utility belt bigger than a cop's, wearing headphones and a telephone operator's mouthpiece, hollered "Okay, settle, people!" and everybody and his brother took a collective breath. A gal emerged from the darkness with a jazzy, flouncy puppet riding her right arm, a shimmering blue-and-purple creation of feathers and boas and costume jewelry. She took up a position behind one part of the set, held the character aloft and into camera range—and then did one of the most extraordinary things I'd ever seen.

She began to watch television—yeah, then and there, on the job, while working.

Someone said "action," and this performer, while moving the puppet and reading her lines into a head-mounted microphone, had her eyes glued to what I saw was a tiny black-and-white TV on a stand right next to her.

You had to ask yourself: What was she watching? What kind of programming, at this hour, was worth this kind of distraction from her job? Some daytime soap drama she couldn't live without? A beloved old movie? Breaking news with immediate consequences? It seemed impudent and unprofessional.

Still, I thought, what cool. What absolute confidence in her abilities. I observed and admired until someone yelled, "Cut!" Then the puppeteer lowered her character and handed me my next shock: She completely turned her back on the TV and walked off the set.

I considered and nixed the idea of mentioning something to someone. Stepping repeatedly over pythons of cable and conduit taped to the floor, I made my way to the stout dame with the head mike and the clipboard.

I inquired whether Bob Borger was around. "Somewhere . . ." She turned toward the set and hollered, "Bob Borger! Visitor!" Then she froze, listening to the voice in the headphones. "What? . . . Okay." Then she called out, "That's it till after lunch, people." Way up on the ceiling, the white fluorescent work lights blinked on, the rich gold and rose set lights died a slow, lingering death, and the magic drained away.

I strolled around the edge of the backdrop onto the set itself: It was some kind of playroom or shop, with bright yellow walls, and pink-and-blue woodwork trim, and an abundance of toys, tools, and unidentifiable gizmos arrayed throughout. It was only then that I noticed that the walls, the shelving, the tables and chairs—the entire room stood on stilts and uprights, and began only about four feet off the floor. On the shelves were toys, dolls, animals, and other characters that looked like they came alive when a puppeteer worked them from the rear.

In the center of the space was a kind of home base or dais that stood at the focus of all three cameras. I approached it warily as the crew stood in little groups, conversing, or drifted toward the far end of the big room, where I could see a lunch buffet and a scattering of tables.

"Hellooooo!"

It was a voice, yes, but it wasn't human—or, rather, it was part human and part alien, unearthly, of a tone and timbre from another world, another species. It spoke again. "Helloooo! Are you my visitor?"

Some creature had popped up from behind the central dais and was addressing me. It resembled no animal I had ever seen. Its lightbulb-shaped head seemed bald, but the pelt or coat of the creature was tangled and purple, as though made of shag rug or layers of matted yarn. Its eyes looked like half Ping-Pong balls painted with black pupils; thin violet eyelids occasionally shut over them and reopened, batting comically long and thick black eyelashes. The creature's hands, at the ends of two long, floppy purple arms, were unequal in dexterity. One was almost human in its shape and articulations; the other seemed fixed to his body, and looked essentially unusable. I saw no ears to speak of, and a flat, piggish nose.

"Hi!" it said. "My name is Klonky! What's your name?"

I took a few cautious steps toward it. "The name's Ingalls. Pete Ingalls, PI."

"Cool!" Its voice was a kind of ultranasal chirp. Its mouth was wide and moved rapidly, the jaw making exaggerated flaps. "Are you looking for Bob Borger?"

"Maybe." I paused. "Know him?"

"Oh, sure! He's my friend!"

"Aces."

"Isn't it great to have friends?"

"Until they stick the shiv in, yeah."

"What's a shiv?"

"A homemade knife."

"Ooh! That would hurt!"

"Yes, it would. And it does, pal, believe me."

"Why would anybody do that?"

I had to laugh. And I did laugh. I was talking, of course, with a puppet, explaining to him the finer points of back-alley and jailhouse weaponry. *Okay, Ingalls,* I thought. *You're big on philosophical introspection. Let's see you explain your worldview to this Klonky character.* "Why would your friend slip the blade in?" I posed. "Because the world gets us jazzed on expectations—expectations it has no intention of meeting. So your friend gives himself permission to do the other guy dirt to make up for the shortfall." I added, "And sometimes the other guy is you."

For a solid five seconds Klonky gazed at me with big round eyes and an open, gaping mouth. Then he said, "Wow! That's the smartest thing anybody has ever said, ever!" Then he tilted his head and gave a big, broad frown, and said, "But it makes me sad, too. Does it make you sad?"

"It breaks my heart," I said.

Klonky brightened. "Then you must be a good person!"

I have no trouble admitting that I like praise. I like it when it's sincere, and even when it's insincere, when I can see through it and tag it for what it is. Why? Because then people praise me by saying, "Good for you, Pete Ingalls. You saw through that insincere praise."

And I liked it even when it came from a puppet creature named Klonky. But this wasn't the time to pat myself on the back because a purple puppet liked my analysis of the human condition. That could come later. For now, I had a job to do. "Thanks, kid," I said. "But what can you tell me about Mr. Borger?"

"Everything! Maybe," Klonky said. "What do you want to know?"

"I want to know a lot of things," I said. "For starters I want to know what Bob thinks about a guy named Marc Cohen."

"Ooh, Bob doesn't like Marc Cohen. Bob thinks Marc Cohen is a bad person." Klonky looked away and shook his shaggy head in disapproving sorrow.

"Why is that?"

"Because Marc Cohen is nasty, and too big for his britches, and does bad things with puppets."

"What kinds of bad things?"

"Terrible sexy things with horrible costumes." Klonky shook an admonishing finger at me. "That's not right."

"And what does Bob think about Charlotte Purdy and Donnie Dansicker?"

The puppet seemed to pout. "Oh, they're okay. They don't know as much about working with puppets as they think they do."

"Bob doesn't hate them?"

"Bob doesn't hate anybody! And neither do I!"

"Where was Bob last Thursday night?"

The creature "thought." It stroked its indistinct chin. It scratched its scraggly purple head and rolled its eyes toward the ceiling and murmured, "Hmm, let's see. . . ."

"Say, from ten P.M. on."

"I think I don't know."

"Does Bob know?"

"I . . . no."

"Bob doesn't know where he was last Thursday night?"

"No. He doesn't know *anything*."

"He doesn't know, or you don't know what he knows?"

"I know everything he knows."

So that's how it was. I tilted my hat back in a gesture that even a puppet could read, and I asked, "Is that how it is?"

"Yes," Klonky said. "I know everything Bob Borger knows, and he doesn't know anything."

"So—"

"No, wait. He knows a couple of things."

It was an engraved invitation to inquire. And, of course, I would accept. But first I had a few things to say. "Does he?" I said. "And just what are those things? Do they have anything to do with blackmail? Do they have anything to do with murder? Do they have anything to do with jealousy and betrayal, and the dirty little thrill people all over the world now get, watching fantasy puppet characters simulating human sexual response?"

"N-n-n-nope!" Klonky tilted his head and blinked at me like a flirting chorine. "Bob knows that people should be nice and that learning is fun!"

"Wake up, Klonky. Sure, people should be nice. But a lot of people are not nice."

"That's because they're afraid!"

"Maybe." The talk was getting deep. I wanted to take out a pack of Palmer Impressives and light up, but I didn't, because I didn't have one, and I don't smoke. "But maybe it's because they're weak and corrupt. Or they're greedy and indifferent. Or maybe it's because some people just find it easier in the end to take the path of least resistance, and let others pay the freight."

"But some people are really nice!" Klonky protested. Then his eyes went wide and his mouth opened in delight and he had an inspiration. "Ooh! You know what else is nice?"

"I'll bite. What—a dame? A double with a cool water back? Your long shot winning by a nose?"

"Tropical fish! They're always nice. They're so *pretty*."

"You don't say." It was time to turn on the heat. It was time to tighten the vise. This Klonky joker was fronting for Borger, giving him cover for saying the unsayable and shielding him from having to answer the hard questions. "Let's get back to Marc Cohen, Klonky."

"Awww. Do we have to?"

"Yeah. We do. There are certain issues to straighten out. For example, I wonder if you know that Cohen was murdered last Thursday night."

I delivered it like a slap, but Klonky took it and didn't flinch. Instead, his face went hangdog, and he looked off to the side with deep regret and sighed. "Yeah. I heard about that."

"How'd you hear?"

"Our friend told us. Norman."

"Norman Tibbler?"

The creature nodded in sorrow. "He saw it in the paper and he told us."

"Does Bob have any idea who might have done it?"

"Well . . ."

"Did Bob do it?"

Klonky gaped, and gasped, and looked around in disbelief and indignation—yeah, *that* old gag. "No! Of course not! He could never do something like that!"

"Face facts, Klonky. Borger hated Cohen. Everybody knows that."

"But you don't kill someone just because you hate them!"

I enjoyed a bitter laugh. "Maybe *you* don't, friend."

"Neither do you!"

This gave me pause. For all his nonhuman aspect, for all the fact that he was essentially a manipulable doll made of wire mesh, metal rods, and yarn, he had a point. I didn't kill someone just because I hated them. I didn't kill someone even if I hated them enough so that I *wanted* to kill them. Why might not this hold true for Bob Borger? Was I that much better a man than he? And this thought led to another: Why don't we kill people we hate? We hate them, don't we?

I loosened my tie and said, "Score one for the puppet. You're right, Klonky. I don't think Bob did anything to Marc Cohen."

A tech walked past carrying a pint carton of lemonade and a sub on a paper plate. He stopped and spoke to Klonky. "Hey, Bob. Better eat up. Tea time's almost over; then it's back on our heads." He walked off.

"Uh, I gotta go," Klonky said.

"One more thing." I leaned in to get close to Klonky. "Marc Cohen was running a blackmail scam on DD Productions. He's the one who put the outtake reel from the wrap party up on the Web."

The creature's eyeballs widened to full-size with an audible click. "No!"

"Yeah. My question: Why? Why do you think Cohen ran the blackmail? Did he need the dough suddenly, or was it a long-term yen? Did he have big debts? Was he in hock to the mob? Or did he just want to stop wishing and actually take that dream vacation?"

The puppet looked back at me with that profound, yet frightening expression of animated lifelessness, that unsettling combination of facial mobility and eyeball opacity. Then it spoke. "Marc Cohen was out of ideas," Klonky said. "He hadn't sold even a pilot in five years. That's why he did what he did."

I held out my hand. "Klonky? It's been a pleasure."

The puppet extended its good hand and I grasped it. Then the creature said, "It was nice meeting you. But I gotta go. Bye." As though caught by a vaudeville hook, he contracted backward and fell out of sight.

I tipped my hat forward and started strolling the way I came, toward the entrance. Then I heard my name called, and turned. A tall, broad-shouldered man came hesitantly toward me. He wore a plaid shirt and jeans, had reddish hair on either side of a balding pate and a thick red mustache. "I'm Bob Borger," he said.

I said my name and we shook, and I was surprised at how weak and halfhearted his grip was. "I want to thank you for talking to Klonky," he said in a soft, self-effacing voice. "Not many people bother to do that. I appreciate it."

"I had my reasons," I said. "I'm glad he saw fit to talk to me."

Borger leaned down a bit to speak intimately; he was easily six-two and must have had to do it with most people. "I can see you're a puppet person," he said gravely.

"I won't kick. Let's say I am."

"Well, it was . . . nice." He was ill at ease. "Klonky likes you."

"The feeling is mutual. Oh, one final question."

I asked him why that gal I'd seen watching TV while working was able to get away with it. He looked at me with a boundless pity that knew no bounds. "She's not watching TV," he said. "She's watching herself on a monitor. That's how we see what we look like. Everyone does that. Otherwise how could we know what to do?"

I absorbed this and revised my opinion of the performer. "Thanks, Bob," I said. "I'll keep it in mind."

"Well . . . okay . . . see ya." He turned and did a stoop-shouldered shuffle off toward the buffet in the rear. I shook my head at the varieties of human wackiness that are available for consumption in this world of ours, and headed toward the exits.

I didn't see him at first. But then, at first I could hardly see anything. The sun was a blinding dazzle as I emerged from the gloom of the Astoria Studios and paused on the sidewalk to get my bearings. Then I spotted a faintly familiar figure across the street, leaning too casually against a wall, and it all clicked. It was the lad who had joined me on the train and gotten off at this stop, the gent in the tan suit and the yellow shirt and black tie. I scanned past him, acted busy and unconcerned, and headed off toward the subway.

En route I stopped in a hardware store entrance to eye some late-season air conditioners on sale, and confirmed with a quick glance: He was a block behind me, and stalling.

I was being tailed.

He was a large man, my height but wider, and he carried himself with the physical self-possession of an athlete or a bouncer. I didn't mind the fact that he was shadowing me. I didn't mind the fact that he was almost certainly not a cop and therefore represented a person or persons not necessarily legitimate. What I did mind was that I had no idea who had sent him.

And that rankled. You accept being followed and watched by a known enemy. It's all in the game, and it's part of your job. It's part of what makes you *you*.

But tails of unknown origin suggested hidden enemies with secret agendas, and that was just unfair. Memo to whoever it was who said people should be nice: Nice is nice, but optional. All I ask for is fair.

I walked at a hard stride past the subway entrance and down another block, then went right and ducked into a coffee shop. I headed to the rear, banged through the swinging door into the kitchen, and told the staring cook, "I'm with Steve." I always say that. There's always a Steve. And if there isn't, people think there is.

I found what I was hoping for, a rear entrance, and darted out into the alley. I moved at a brisk trot around the block and lingered in the doorway of an apartment building until I spotted the tail, wandering out of the coffee shop and obviously uncertain as to where I was.

It was time for some turnabout. If I could tail him to his office or apartment, I at least stood a chance of sussing out his name, which would be a first step to learning who he worked for. I shadowed the bird as he stepped quickly down into the subway, pulled out his Metro card, and pushed through the turnstile. When he hustled down the steps to the downtown train, I followed at a discreet distance.

On the platform he checked his watch, tapped his foot, took out a cell phone, then looked at it, saw he had no reception, and angrily shoved it back in his jacket. The train pulled in; during the tumult I bought a copy of the *Post* at a newsstand, boarded his car at the far end, and hid behind the paper during the trip.

The coincidences kept mounting: He got off at the stop for my office. I followed—and with every step felt an increasing sense of amazement, and something I'm not embarrassed to call wonder, as I realized he was heading toward my very street. Was it possible he lived so nearby? Was it possible I actually knew him without knowing it?

We reached my block. He stopped across the street from my office and lingered there. I took cover near a small Dumpster and pretended to read the paper while I kept an eye on him.

For half an hour I scoped him as he loitered. He must have been waiting for something, although it wasn't clear what. A meet? A cab? A drop? The fact that his rendezvous point was so close to my place of business was just one more astounding coincidence in a case that had already seen its share. Finally I decided I could keep tabs on him from inside as easily as outside. I took off my suit jacket and my hat, took off my tie, and rolled up my sleeves. Making sure to avert my face, I skipped rapidly up the steps and into my building.

Stephanie was at her desk, trim and cute in jeans and a white shirt and a little pink zip-up sweatshirt. She practically leaped at me when I came in.

"Pete—"

"Get this," I began, thumbing toward the street outside. "Some joker tailed me from Astoria. I lost him, and then I shadowed him right back here. He's hanging around right across the street."

"Huh?" She looked out the window. "Him?"

"Yeah. He lives there, works there—I don't know. Cute, isn't it, the way he leads me back to my own front door? God knows what he's waiting for."

"He's waiting for you, Pete. He doesn't live here. He figured if he lost you in Queens, he'd just come back here until you got back."

I digested this and appreciated the likelihood of it. "Any idea who he's working for?"

"How should I know? Meanwhile, are you ready?" She looked coy—yeah, the way a bombardier looks just before he pushes the button. "Guess where I went today."

"I don't guess. Stop shuffling and deal, sugar."

"DD Productions. And guess what Charlotte told me when I asked her if Stephen O'Neil had pitched *Henry the Horse at Home* to her and Donnie before he took it anywhere else?" I spread my hands. "Okay, don't guess. *Nothing!* She was totally unresponsive! She said she couldn't remember, and she'd have to check her notes, and all this runaround bullshit."

"Hey—"

"Yeah, I know, the language, sorry. Look: The point is, I got

Ellen to sneak into her office and pull this from her file and make a secret Xerox of it while Charlotte was at lunch. Notice anything interesting about it?"

She handed me a document. It was the proposal for *Henry the Horse at Home* that Jessman Lackluster had given me at Gyro. "Ah, yes," I murmured. "This is what's called a 'leave-behind,' so named because when writers or producers pitch a show, they leave behind th—"

"I know what a leave-behind is. But look at the first page." I scanned the text but drew a blank. Stephanie jabbed her finger in and pointed to the words *Created and developed by Stephen O'Neil.* "See? It's just by Stephen. There's no mention of Marc Cohen."

"Which means what?"

"Which probably means that he created it himself. Charlotte and Donnie said no, so he recruited Marc Cohen for his clout at Gyro or Ronson or whatever. It happens all the time. You share credit in exchange for someone's contacts."

"Tell me why this is something to scream about."

She sighed. "It isn't." Then she brightened. One good thing about having an actress for an assistant: A routine debrief becomes a floor show of starkly contrasting dramatics. "But! Get this! I also talked to Samantha Rosen!" I asked how she had managed to contact Marc Cohen's former head writer, and Stephanie said she'd called the Writers Guild and had Samantha call her back. "We met for coffee. She wasn't exactly heartbroken when I told her he'd been killed. She wasn't exactly surprised, either."

"They weren't true love?"

She laughed. "He threw an ashtray at her. In a fight over casting. God, what a jerk."

I glanced out the window. My shadow was still there, slouched against the building opposite, smoking and gazing around with that unruffled equanimity and deep patience that can be so indistinguishable from stupidity. "Doesn't it tell us what we already know?" I asked Stephanie. "That Cohen was a bad person and people disliked him?"

She looked clever. "Not all people disliked him. The news of the day is that Samantha Rosen told me . . . Marc Cohen has a wife!"

I turned back to look at her. "How can we not know this? How can no one have mentioned it before?"

"Because they're separated, and he never took her anywhere, and she sounds like this cold fish who probably never should have married him in the first place."

"Nice work," I said. "You'll notice, I hope, that it vindicates my theory."

She tore a sheet of memo paper off a pad and thrust it at me. "Here's her name and work address. What theory is that?"

I took the paper. "The theory that I'm the flatfoot and you're the assistant. The theory that I burn up shoe leather going to Queens and running down new contacts, and cope with tail jobs and so forth, while you perform due diligence and chat up the clients, and have fruitful Kaffeeklatsches with nice young ladies. It's called the division of labor and the age of specialization and the separation of church and state."

She snatched the paper back. "Give me a fucking break. I'm doing just as much digging as you. Oh. By the way. My sister called. She and the kids are coming on Thursday. Now, did you talk to Bob Borger?"

"I did more than that, angel." I swiped the sheet back from her and headed toward the door. "I talked to Klonky."

ELEVEN

He was waiting for me.

I headed to the avenue and in my peripheral vision saw he was dogging me from across the street. I hailed a cab, and as one pulled up I noted he had done the same. I climbed in the back and fell into the low, uncomfortable seat. "Looks like rain . . ." I stalled. I turned and peered out the rear window. My tail had gotten into his cab, which was just where I wanted him. "Sorry," I told my driver. "I'm with Steve." It didn't quite apply but it was the best I had. I leaped out and slammed the door.

My cab peeled away with an angry snarl. It took just a second for my tail to spill out of his. As it began to pull away, I held up my hand. His cab saw me and braked with a squeal. I ran up to it and flung a parting shot at my pursuer. "See you next time, pal."

The guy's face, even from ten feet away, looked smeared and out of focus, pale and puffy and slack. He replied with a superior smirk. "Righty-o, fuckwad."

I got in and slammed the door, said, "Fairlane Foundation," and we pulled into traffic.

The Fairlane Foundation had its own building, of course, but it had much more than that. It had a little forest in its lobby. I could appreciate the symbolism: "Our job is *giving money away*," says the structure. "Which is the opposite of every other organization's job. That's why we have a forest inside our building, which is the opposite of every other building, the job of which is to keep the forest out." It was a clever bit of public relations, although you had to wonder just how wild the wildlife in such a forest could really be.

Helen Leeds Corcoran, I discovered, was Assistant Director for Knowledge, Creativity, and Freedom at the Fairlane Foundation. It was a tall order, but maybe she was up to it. Of course, there was no good reason for her to receive me when I first bellied up to the reception desk. But I had the gal convey a message concerning the death of a certain Mr. Cohen, and my involvement in its investigation. I was ushered in.

She had a big office with a lot of sleek modern furniture. Everything—the walnut desk, the teak sofa, the matching armchairs, the glass coffee table—was angled and cantilevered and looked aerodynamic and floating.

So did Helen: She was waiting for me in the center of the room, cool and poised as a runway model, a drop-dead looker in a trim dark blue suit and a white blouse. Her blond hair came to her shoulders and shimmered like a pale honey waterfall. Her perfect legs tapered down to sublime ankles and ended in navy-blue high-heeled shoes, which, when she moved, seemed barely to touch the floor. Her face was flawless, every feature lovingly assembled by the gods of genetics from the most expensive page in the catalog.

"Mr. Ingalls." She extended a slim, cool hand. "I'm Helen Corcoran."

It was like shaking with a fairy princess. She led me, not to the sofa and chairs, as I hoped, but to the visitor's chair opposite her immaculate desk. As I sat I scanned the area and noted an absence of personal mementos. There were no photos of anyone, least of all Marc Cohen.

"I'm sorry to have to discuss this with you," I said. "And I'm sorry for your loss."

"Thank you." Her voice was polite—maybe too polite. "Although Marc and I had been married only two years, and we were separated. Still, it's a shock, and I'm horrified by what's happened."

She spoke as though dictating a letter. I decided to reply in kind. "It is quite horrifying," I said. "Then again, murder is a horrifying thing."

She blinked and offered a slight smile of uncertainty. "Yes, it is."

"One is most horrified when something horrifying happens, because it's . . . it's horrible."

"Mr. Ingalls, if I may, I'd like to ask you: What is your involvement with this matter?"

I crossed one leg over the other and sat back, signaling unflappability. Because I was unflappable. I couldn't remember the last time I'd been flapped, and, frankly, I didn't care to try. "I represent certain parties who shall remain nameless." I smiled and waited for her reply.

"That doesn't really tell me much."

"What do you want to be told?"

"As I said, I'd like to know why you're here. What is your

role in the investigation of my husband's death? Are you with the police?"

I shook my head in a gently negative manner. "I'm a private dick, lady. I work for clients whom your husband was putting the touch on." I didn't like the sound of that. "Sorry. On whom your husband was putting the touch."

She frowned. Her facial features, so fully occupied in maintaining a smooth presentation of beauty, seemed unused to the action. Somewhere inside her head, the little woman in charge of frowning had pushed the button, and while the rest of her mug responded according to the instructions, it lacked some essential spark of authenticity. Not that I believe in that little woman in one's head, not anymore. Call it a metaphor. "I'm sorry; what does that mean, 'put the touch on'?"

"Your husband was blackmailing my clients, Ms. Corcoran. He was threatening to release, to what I call the World Wide Web, some video footage of various puppets engaged in sexual acts."

She blinked again. "I'm sorry—it sounded like you said 'puppets.' Did you mean 'people'?"

"I said 'puppets.' And I meant it. Puppets performing sexual acts. Your husband procured this footage and used it to blackmail my clients. Then—"

"But are you saying your clients *are* puppets? Is that whom you represent? The puppets who were filmed engaged in these activities? Do puppets have legal standing? How is that possible?"

"Let's not kid ourselves, lady. Anything's possible."

"No, it isn't."

"Okay, fine, but we're all puppets of someone. Wouldn't you say?"

She considered it for a moment—to her credit, yeah, but it didn't ring any bells. "I don't know what I'd say at this point."

"Then let me make it easier for you. My clients are the producers the puppets work for. We're talking here about puppets performing lewd acts to and with other puppets they're not married to. Okay, some people don't have a problem with that. Maybe I'm one of them. Maybe you're one of them. That makes two of us—"

"Mr. Ingalls—"

"But put our liberal moral and sexual values aside for the moment. What came next was, your hubby somehow scored these hot-cha clips and put the bite on my clients: Pay up or the pix go wide, with predictable consequences. Then, when my clients acquired the money to pay him off, your husband showed up at my place wearing a harlequin mask, and popped me with an animal tranquilizer dart and stole the dough."

She was as animated as a mask. "I find this hard to believe."

"I imagine you do." I enjoyed a little smirk. "Trust me, Ms. Corcoran, this kind of thing happens every day of the week. You just don't hear much about it up here in the Fairlane Foundation, with your indoor forest and its so-called wildlife."

I was taking a risk. In fact, I didn't know if this sort of thing happened very often. I didn't even know if it had ever happened once. And if it hadn't, did she know as much? I pressed on to distract her from thinking about it. I had some knowledge, creativity, and freedom of my own, and I wasn't afraid to use them. "And then," I said, "even though he'd been paid off, he released the footage anyway, in what I have no hesitation in calling a gigantic act of spite."

"Well, *that* at least sounds like Marc." Helen Corcoran licked her thin, unpainted, pretty little lips and looked away for a moment or two. Then she said, "Mr. Ingalls, why are you here? What do you want?"

"I want to know who killed Marc Cohen. Because whoever did took the ransom money, and that's what I'm after."

"And why ask me?"

"You're his wife. His beautiful, lovely wife . . ."

She didn't blink, let alone say, "Thank you," let alone say, "You're not so bad yourself, flatfoot," let alone say, "What are you doing for dinner tonight?" No, what she said instead was, "I have no idea who killed him, Mr. Ingalls. I did speak to him a week or so ago and he seemed fine. In fact, he was quite optimistic about a certain project."

"Is that a fact, Ms. Corcoran? And why would he share that optimism with his estranged, albeit lovely, wife?"

She shrugged. "The more we fought, the more he tried to impress me. To make me think he was becoming successful again."

"And what was this so-called 'project'?"

"He didn't tell me the title. Or anything about it, really, except that he had pitched it to Ronson Productions along with some performer, and the company was interested."

"And were you impressed?" Somewhere in the back of my mind it occurred to me that I was coming on tough, cynical, and even a little hard-boiled, getting flinty and unsparing with this knockout frail who maybe was exactly as innocent as she professed to be. But that's how it is with beautiful dames. You have to come on strong, and brusque, and indifferent, or they think you're attracted to them. And then where are you?

"I'm past being impressed by Marc." She sighed. "I felt bad for him, and sorry for him, and perhaps a little disgusted by our whole relationship."

"Disgusted?" I leered. "Strong language, wouldn't you say?"

"No, I wouldn't."

I was ready to debate the point when suddenly I became

aware of celestial music from the beyond. It was my cell phone. I pulled out the unit, excused myself, and twisted away from her in my chair, to ensure confidentiality. "Ingalls."

"Pete! It's me! Where are you?"

"In conference at the Fairlane Foundation."

"Oh, shit. Sorry. You should have turned your phone off. Can you talk?"

"No."

"Okay, just listen. I Googled Helen Corcoran, and guess what! I got all these socialite articles in the *Observer* and stuff about how Marc Cohen had to sign a prenup when they got married, and he was contesting it when they got separated!"

"I daresay."

"Why do you sound so weird? Is she there?"

"That's correct."

"Yikes! Okay, look, sorry, one more thing. Her father died a year ago and left her a shitload of money. Cohen thought he was entitled to some if they got divorced, but she said the prenup meant he wasn't. You got that?"

"I do." I glanced at Helen Corcoran. She was reading a document and seemed unaware of the nature of the call. I meant to keep it that way. I said, "Those storm windows sound great. I can't wait until you deliver them to my home."

"Jesus. Okay, get back to her. See you later."

We both hung up and I put the phone away. Helen Corcoran looked up at me, and I said, "Sorry. I get special offers over the phone."

"Mr. Ingalls, I don't know who killed Marc. I know he antagonized certain people, but there's not one person he ever mentioned to me, or whom I met personally, who I think would be capable of killing him."

"But somebody did kill him, Ms. Corcoran. So I guess you don't know everybody who knew him."

"Naturally. But I can only tell you about people who I do know about."

Touché, I thought. Now we were getting somewhere. Or were we? "Very convenient, wouldn't you say?"

"Actually I wouldn't say. I don't know what you mean."

"I'll tell you—"

"But wait, there is someone you can talk to. Do you know Jaxsee Shasta?" I said I didn't. "She does something on MTV. Marc was dating her. I think that's why he left me."

"*He* left *you?* That's interesting, Ms. Corcoran. Because you're a knockout. And a man doesn't leave a knockout. He stays. And why?"

"Mr. Ingalls—"

"Because he can't leave. He can't even get up, the poor bastard. Because he's knocked out. By definition, Ms. Corcoran."

"You know—"

"Are you sure *you* didn't leave *him?*" I was prospecting for leads, throwing out possibilities in the hopes of provoking her into revealing herself. "Maybe he's not the one dating Jaxsee Shasta. Maybe you are."

"I was surprised when Marc moved out. For a while I thought he'd discovered he was gay." She looked away. "Then I heard he'd left me for some rock-and-roll slut. That was quite hurtful."

"So you wanted him to be gay." I spoke cruelly, shooting from the hip and asking questions later, if at all. "You wanted him to leave you for another man—so that *you* could be gay, and leave him for another woman."

She opened her mouth but said nothing.

I pressed on. "But he wasn't gay, was he? He was going out

with Jaxsee himself. It was intolerable—your own husband, non-gayly going out with your own girlfriend. And so you killed him."

Helen Leeds Corcoran stood up. She looked disappointed in me. Well, maybe I was disappointed in her. "Marc wasn't gay," she said. "And neither am I. Lately there had been a lot of hostility between us, but I didn't kill him. And you can ask Jaxsee Shasta if she and I were involved. Now please, I'm quite busy and I'm sure you are, too."

I admired her insight. As a matter of fact, I *was* busy. It was canny of her to know it. I thanked her for her time, advised her not to leave town, and bounced.

By the next morning the clouds had thickened and secreted that slate-gray undercoating that signaled they meant business. Stephanie was scanning *People* and wrestling with a blueberry muffin the size of a fire hydrant when I punched in and made the rounds. I told her what I'd learned from Helen Leeds Corcoran the day before.

She put the mag down and got interested. "So Cohen had a girlfriend."

"Right. So say she comes to the door. You know what you do when your girlfriend comes to the door, don't you, sugar?"

"You let her in."

I looked away and took a six count. I didn't like having my mind read. "Let's call that a lucky guess."

"Pete, Jeez, come on. Or she had her own key. Either way she gets in without a struggle. Still. What's her motive? Why kill him?"

"How about for the dough? A million bucks buys a lot of dirty martinis."

There was nothing she could say to that. There never is. That's the power of the "a million bucks buys a lot of X" statement. You get the other guy busy calculating: What *is* a dirty martini, and how much does one cost? How many *would* a million bucks buy? You tie up the opposing party in mathematical calculations while you skate on home to victory.

Then Stephanie asked if Helen Corcoran had said anything noteworthy about Cohen's work. I told her how Helen had said Cohen was making progress on some project at Ronson.

Stephanie threw up her hands. "Look, we have to see what this Jaxsee Shasta knows. Maybe she has an alibi."

"Let's you call her and I'll go find out."

"Okay, but first we gotta go to Ronson."

"No, 'we' gotta stay here. *I* gotta go to Ronson."

The phone rang. She picked up, gave the spiel, and said, "One moment, please," and handed it to me.

"Ingalls."

"Mr. Ingalls, it's Chris Page. I wonder if we can make arrangements for me to get my necklace back."

It was the last thing I wanted to worry about at that point. "I'll have to get back to you, Ms. Page," I said. "I'm currently involved in pursuing some, ah, current pursuit."

"I see," she said. "Will you call me tomorrow, then? I'm very anxious to get it back."

I said I would and we both bailed out. When I looked up, Stephanie had her finger jabbed into the phone book. "Here it is. Don Ronson Productions. East Seventy-first. Shit, I'd better call."

"Listen, angel—"

"Pete, come on! This case is coming together and we need to talk to somebody up there."

"I talk. You stay. I'm the boss. You're the helper. Haven't we covered this? How many times do we have to have this discussion?"

"Pete—" She slammed her pretty hand down onto the phone book. "This is not about your being the boss. I know you're the boss. This is about getting some very specific information. If I didn't think I had to come along, I wouldn't. Didn't I let you go by yourself to talk to Bob Borger?"

"You 'let' me?"

"Listen." She leveled a look at me that would have singed the eyelashes of a lesser man but which I took in easy stride. "I absolutely must go with you to Ronson, period. Now let's go."

"No sale."

"Let's go."

"Nix it was and nix it is."

"Let's just go."

"Check your listing and dial again."

"Let's go."

The offices and workshop of Don Ronson Productions were on East Seventy-first Street. It was a quick dash from the subway, and a good thing, too. Because it had begun to rain.

It so happens I have strong feelings about rain in New York. I'm against it. Outside the city, where nature exists in all its splendid natural glory, I have no beef with rain. Rain has a place. It rains and you think, *Yes, this is how it should be. This is all part of the cycle of life.*

In town, though, rain seems wrong. It's an anomaly and a violation of some rule. My theory: Because the city is essentially a place of interiors. To be in the city is to be inside. Even when you're outside, skating or playing ball or throwing something at some person or dog in Central Park, you're doing it to improve your health and welfare so you can go back inside. You say to me, "Come on, Pete. Outside is necessary in the city, so you can have somewhere to move through when you get out of a cab." Granted—but why are you getting out of the cab? Nine times out of ten, you're getting out of the cab to go into a building.

A person, in the city, walking through the outdoors into a building, is a person doing what he's supposed to do, wearing his professional clothes and prepared to conduct himself in a professional manner. He's a citizen in good standing in a world predicated on dryness.

And then, suddenly, water is falling on his head—and, worse, onto his professional clothes. You get the feeling that someone isn't doing his job. Your clothes become wet. And it gets worse: You go inside, wearing your now-wet clothes, where everything is predicated on the eternal dryness of the indoors, and yet your clothes are still wet. It's not fair. It's wrong. It stinks.

Small wonder, then, that I was glad to hoof it over to the Ronson HQ quickly. The place looked artistic and swank, as you'd expect. From the street it presented a single ornate facade as wide as two town houses, with one massive oak door of the kind that leads into a castle or a monastery. Not that I've been to either. But I've seen the movies.

I strode in expecting large space and ample elbow room, and maybe, yeah, an echoey hall lit with torches and guys in robes chanting in the background. Instead I got a tiny oval foyer with barely a place to hang my hat.

A receptionist sat at a small desk several feet from spiral stairways leading both upstairs and down. We were actually in a sort of small atrium: A fanciful model dirigible hovered overhead, suspended by wires from the ceiling three floors up. Out of its antique gondola dangled various puppet characters looking jolly and raffish and thrilled about the prospect of plummeting to their death.

Stephanie and I were invited to wait on two small chairs off to the side. Yes, I said Stephanie. The gal was bursting with pertinent questions, obviously percolating up a theory as to who had killed Marc Cohen and where the money was. So it was my professional responsibility to shut her up by allowing her to come along.

There was a niche in the wall above the receptionist's desk. In it sat a puppet like a lifeguard on his perch. Its skinny pink legs were crossed, its cute little pink face was arranged in a perky grin, its fingerless pink hand was held up in a cheery wave. I walked over to the receptionist and asked who he was.

She smiled, as though to a child. "That's Otto!"

The light went on and the bell rang. I thanked her and sat down and kept my hands to myself.

I'd heard of Otto. You've heard of Otto, too. Otto is the little character who plays such a large role on *Abracadabra Avenue*, the kids' show that's been running for decades. Otto is, as you'd expect, adorable. He speaks in a piping high voice and refers to himself in the third person, and has become essentially the icon of the show, and of this company.

Of course, I knew the "Otto" perched above the Ronson reception area wasn't *really* Otto. It was a toy version, just like the millions of Ottos in kiddie bedrooms and kindergarten classrooms all over the world. Although it was possible, I reflected, that the real Otto was in fact somewhere in this building—in wardrobe getting changed, on a workbench being repaired, or just idling in some kind of storage container. You had to wonder

what happened when the real Otto was carried into this lobby
and brought into the presence of toy Otto. You had to ask yourself just what was being represented, and what was a simulation of
who, and to whom, and who was getting rich and who was getting shafted. Cynical? Only when I laugh.

I was primed to begin wondering just these things, because I
knew that my assistant had the theoretical end of the situation
well in hand, when a guy in jeans and a white dress shirt emerged
from the stairway leading up from the floor below. Stephanie
took one look at him and whispered, "Oh, Jesus," and got up and
ran out.

TWELVE

The guy in question never noticed; he just walked through a door behind the receptionist and disappeared toward the rear. But I noticed. I noticed I had set off on a two-man mission and was now flying solo.

Then a woman approached. "Mr. Ingalls?"

She was a slim, sexy dame in a small, stylish black skirt and a deep orange blouse and witty necktie featuring Tweety Bird. She had short, dark hair and a full mouth lipsticked in fire-engine red. "I'm Jane Christoff." She looked around. "Aren't there two of you?"

I explained that my associate had regrettably been compelled to dust. I omitted mention of how she had insisted she be allowed to sit in, how she had systematically busted every one of my chops about it, how she had ignored her vital office duties, and how she had now, suddenly and without compunction, abandoned her post, leaving me without cue cards or talking points.

Instead, I thanked Jane Christoff for agreeing to speak with me. "But then, why not?" I leered. "Everybody's hot to talk about Marc Cohen."

"I know. What a shame."

She led me up the steps, past framed awards and posed puppet memorabilia, to the second floor. It was then that I felt an insistent flutter against my thigh. For a crazy second I thought that some puppet was at my knee, trying to get my attention. Then I realized it was my cell, and fished it out of my pocket. "Ingalls."

"Pete! It's me!" The caller was shouting; I could hear rain hissing down in the background. "Listen, I'm sorry I bailed on you just now. But I couldn't stay there!"

The Christoff woman paused and shot me a sympathetic smile. I nodded and spoke into the phone with my usual self-control. "And why's that?"

"Because of that guy! The one who came upstairs? That's Jason Fielding."

"And what makes him so wonderful?"

"I used to date him. It didn't end so great. Listen, just . . . are you with someone?"

"Yes, I am. Isn't that why I came?"

"Okay, just . . . shit, okay, look . . . um, just be sure to ask what Marc Cohen was doing with them, what project. And who created it. Okay?"

"Yes, and thanks for calling." I flicked off the cell and explained, "It was an individual I happen to know personally." She blinked and walked on. I followed.

Her office was small and stifling. I studied her big brown eyes and expressive eyebrows and struggled against the perception that she was like a puppet herself. Then I thought, *Easy, Ingalls. She might be thinking the same about you. And what if she's right? Then who's pulling the strings?* Then I remembered that these puppets didn't use strings. It helped.

We traded expressions of sadness over the news of Cohen's death. I soft-pedaled my involvement in the case and alluded vaguely to my "concerns." I always do that. You can get by in any conversation on earth if you just keep mentioning "concerns." Then I asked if she had any thoughts as to who might have committed such a terrible crime.

"Well, that's a good question." She sighed. "Marc was difficult. And you got the sense that he knew he was difficult, and didn't care. Which makes it worse."

A thought occurred to me. It wasn't the first time. "Difficult in what way?"

It came out as part grudging admission, part naughty gossip. "He had a temper. And not the kind you respect, either. The whiny, spoiled-brat kind."

I nodded knowingly. "I don't know about you, Ms. Christoff, but that's the kind I don't particularly respect."

She shrugged, as though at the lamentable faults of an otherwise adorable child. "But he was very talented and we were involved in a terrific project with him here called *Henry the Horse at Home*. He was creator and producer. And Disney loved it."

"Interesting," I mused. "Especially in light of the fact that Disney is dead, if memory serves. Still, with the magic of cryogenics—"

"The Disney Channel. We produce the shows and they buy them from us and show them on their channel."

"And Marc Cohen was the creator?" Off her nod I asked, "Ever hear of a lad named Stephen O'Neil?"

She brightened. "Oh, we *love* Stephen! He was in a mob here for a TV special. You know, a crowd of extras. We'll bring in a dozen puppeteers to play, say, the audience at a concert. Everybody wears a puppet on each hand and we do several takes and layer them in, so it's like a crowd of a hundred. Stephen is very quick and has great technique." This, she went on, took place about four months before.

I threw a hard slider and let her react. "I take it, then, that he didn't tell you he had an exclusive contract with DD Productions."

"Oh, he was very up-front about it. This was right after he'd signed for *Playground*. He said Charlotte Purdy had assured him he could do outside projects if they didn't interfere. He came to our set and we did two days and it was fabulous."

"And Cohen didn't mention O'Neil?"

"Maybe as talent. To play Henry. But not for anything else."

"Did he mention Bob Borger?"

"Oh. Bob." She shook her head. "No, not that I can remember."

I caught a flicker of something dark in her tone. "Is Borger not a beloved figure around here? Was Marc Cohen not crazy about the cut of his jib?"

"Well . . ." She stopped, thought better of it, and then got up, moved past me, and shut the door. She sat and, in low tones, explained the history of Don Ronson Productions.

"You have to understand that the universe of puppet performers in New York is fairly small. And the more TV shows and movies that use puppets, the more competition there is for talent. Now, when Don started this place, he was really easygoing. He didn't care who worked for who. The whole idea was to have a good time and invent new ways to do puppets on television. Then he died. And his oldest son took over. Teddy. Who was not even a puppet performer. He has an MBA from Columbia.

"But by then there was this empire. And a lot was at stake and there was a shortage of good people. So Teddy has become very territorial about talent. Someone said he's like Michael Corleone—more ruthless than the father. So Teddy controls these puppet performers as much as he can. If you want to be in the movie next year, you have to sit by the phone and be on call for the special next month. And not take any other jobs."

I opined that that had *raw deal* stamped all over it.

"That's what Bob Borger thought. Marc Cohen set up something here a few years ago, and hired Bob to do the pilot. Then Bob goes out and gets another job while Teddy and Marc shop it around. When Teddy found out he went ballistic, and Marc was in the middle, and Bob got nuts, and everybody hated everybody else."

I put it all together. "So Mr. Puppet is persona non grata at Ronson Productions, and Marc Cohen is the man in the middle. The two of them have a history."

"Everybody has a history."

It sounded interesting. But then, a lot of things sound interesting if you're a student of the human condition. Now, normally that's exactly what I am. You have to be, in my game. But sitting there, in the presence of this insinuatingly hot-cha skirt, and with my assistant AWOL, the only condition I found myself interested in was my own. So I needed distraction.

I found it by looking around the little office. I spied a figure posed on a bookshelf, pink and perky and smiling and waving. "Well, well. Our old friend Otto."

Jane Christoff gave a dry laugh. "Are you kidding? This place is Otto World at this point. Wait until the Christmas toys hit the stores in two months. They're shipping a hundred and thirty million dollars' worth of Otto."

"That's a lot of Otto," I said. For a second I thought I was speaking Esperanto without knowing it. Or maybe something was speaking Esperanto through me, and I was a puppet in the hands of my own brain. I ignored it. "Of course, none of those Ottos are the real Otto, if you take my point."

She laughed. "I suppose. Would you like to see the place? Take a quick tour?"

She led me out into the hallway and up the steps to the third floor. We conducted a series of quick peek-ins at conference rooms and media control rooms, then went back down to level two and made the circuit of executive offices. I went through the motions, greeting people and making noises of admiration, but my mind was elsewhere.

My mind was on Stephanie Constantino. I was having thoughts about her, and about the events of the day. And certain sensations were accompanying those thoughts. You could call those sensations feelings—feelings of annoyance, and irritation, and even of anger.

Naturally, I either shrugged them off or pretended they didn't exist. That's what a private investigator does. Because that's what a *professional* does. Read the literature: When you're a PI you don't get angry. Just like you don't feel self-pity or jealousy or despair. You don't feel these things because you just don't, and if you do, you take steps to remove yourself from their influence, the way you'd remove yourself from the influence of the rain if you were caught outside in a storm. You can do this because the emotion isn't you, any more than the rain is you. Only you are you. Everything else is weather.

We were on the first floor, and Jane Christoff led me through the door behind the receptionist into what looked like an art department. Scattered around, at easels or computers, were young graphic type individuals sketching on big art pads or manipulating images on monitors. I had before me a profusion of Otto pictures: Otto as Robin Hood, as a space cadet, as a doctor, as a basketball player. *Isn't that cute,* I thought. *All those pretend Ottos . . .*

"Now comes the best part," Jane Christoff said.

She led me down the spiral staircase toward the basement, into what began to reveal itself as a huge workroom. I made the final turn in the stairway and received smack in the puss the whole big gestalt of the entire place.

I must have stood there, two steps from the bottom, staring, for some time, because I only dimly began to hear the broad saying, "Mr. Ingalls? Mr. Ingalls?" Then she tentatively took my wrist and shook it, the way you'd try to snap someone out of a hypnotic reverie, or wake them from an involuntary nap time brought on by the application of Mr. Michael Finn's knockout drops.

Before me, all around me, were twenty or thirty Ottos: supine on workbenches, folded up on racks, pinned like butterflies to boards, upright and cheery on stands. The room was vibrant with fuzzy, bright-pink forms—and they weren't toys. Toys, I now realized, were miniature scale-downs for kids' hands and babies' cribs. These were all working puppets, or costume models, or stunt doubles, full-size, two feet tall and able to accommodate an adult-sized mitt. Over here was a disembodied Otto head on a table, smiling. Over there was an eerily headless wire-frame torso, waiting for padding or clothes. Above a workbench hung ten bubblegum-colored Ottos by the scruff of their necks, like an array of identical hats on a line of pegs, ten vaguely smiling heads aimed up, down, at each other, or at me.

"Are you all right, Mr. Ingalls?"

I looked at my guide as though awakening from a dream. "I guess I always thought there was just one Otto," I said. "I guess I always thought that only Otto was Otto." It felt like I was talking to myself. Whatever that now meant.

She laughed. "I know! It's a shock, isn't it? You come down here and you realize that Otto is just a character. Which is really just an idea, actually." She pointed around the room. "Those are for wearing different costumes. Those are for rigging, like if we need him to fly or ride a bike. Those are for if we need him to lie down in a bed. . . ."

The nice lady continued her tourist spiel, but I could have been across town in a sealed room, for all I could hear. It's one thing when you get the answer to a question that you know you're asking. You say, "Oh, I see," and "Fancy that," and "Thank you very much." And the presses keep rolling and everything's okay on the Atchison, Topeka, and the Santa Fe.

Now try obtaining the answer to a question you didn't know you'd been asking. Try learning the question at the same time as the answer. People gas off a lot these days about "information," and everyone and his brother can't wait to tell you something FYI. But when half the payload is the question itself, the answer doesn't arrive FYI. It hits you COD like a sap to the skull.

Of course I had thought there was only one Otto. You think so, too. It's all we ever see: flipping past the show on an early-morning channel scan, a figure glimpsed on a box of kiddie-flavored toothpaste in the pharmacy, in an ad for a movie, on a poster in the video store. You think there's only one Otto like there's only one Pete Ingalls.

But there isn't just one. And there never was. There were thirty in front of me and maybe ten or a million before this. You think there's only one because you only see one at a time. You think there's only one because that's how the very mechanism that delivers Otto to you happens to work. You think there's only one because, out in the world as opposed to here in the workshop, one at a time is all that will work—and all you really need.

That was the answer. It explained how you could really have a multiplicity of something and yet swear that there was one and one only. It opened up a lot of interesting possibilities. Maybe there was more than one God—yeah, maybe there were as many gods as there were Ottos, two or three dozen gods. Or maybe there were six and a half billion, each addressing himself, or herself, or Himself or Herself, whenever somebody prayed.

And maybe there was more than one self in the cranial headquarters of Mr. Pete Ingalls, PI. Maybe Stephanie's theory was right after all. Maybe, no matter how strange and cockeyed it seemed, there were indeed a variety of different selves, each with its own agenda and enthusiasms and fears and hobbies, all clamoring at once in the Macy's of my mind.

The notion got me excited. It got me excited because it came wrapped in the question it now thoroughly and satisfyingly answered, a question I now realized I had been asking for as long as I can remember—me, and every other mug in the gumshoe racket.

It explained how it was possible for me to talk to myself so much.

Because that's what I do. I put on the double-breasted and the fedora and the wing tips, and I go out into the world, and I do what a guy like me does. And that includes describing it, recounting it, chattering on in an endless play-by-play of what I did when, why I said what to who, who punched me how and where, and what it all felt like and who would have to pay what, when, and what for.

You say to me, "Pete—jeez, what's the big deal? Doesn't everyone?" I say: No, I don't think so. Nobody talks to himself like a PI. And sometimes, when he isn't busy chinning away or listening to the result or taking issue with things he's just proposed to himself, he asks himself: Is this normal? Is it physically strong, mentally awake, and morally straight? Or might it not be just a tad unsound?

Because I couldn't square talking to myself with the existence of only one me, a one true Ingalls who had always lived in his head and took it all in and put it all together from that vantage point. How can a single entity address itself? And if it can, how can it listen? And if it can, why bother in the first place?

Then I sauntered down that spiral stairway into the workshop of the Ronson company and took right between the eyes the sight of three dozen bright pink Ottos all at once. That moment obliterated the single, primal Otto, shattering it into a couple dozen versions of itself with nothing left over of the original—no, strike that: There *was* no original. There was no one true Otto. Television creates the impression that there's only one Otto, but it's an illusion. Yeah, I know: You don't like thinking that television can be complicit in perpetrating illusions. Neither do I. But reality doesn't care about what you and I like. Reality is like television: We have to live with what it gives us and soldier on.

And that's when I realized I had to let go of the one true Ingalls, too. The truth was that there were many Petes upstairs, all of them equally Ingalls. The self that talked to myself was me. The self that listened was equally me, equal in stature and savvy and guts. The self that succumbed to Giselle Blanchard's advances was different from but equal to the self that thought deeply about certain things like murder, and blackmail, and puppets.

The world treats you like a single self because it doesn't know any better. But the Ottos set me straight.

Jane Christoff forced a weak smile and said, "Is everything all right?"

"Everything is aces, sugar," I said. "Thanks for the info and thanks for the tour. It's been enlightening."

The rain had stopped by the time I left the Ronson offices. It added to my buoyant mood. That must have been why, when I felt my body hoisted slightly off the ground and moved briskly off the main sidewalk as though on an airport slideway, I took it to be the results of my own uplift. *I'm so happy I'm walking on air,* I more or less thought. After a second or so, however, I realized it was the result of the uplift of a guy having grabbed my arm and lifted me bodily and hustled me into a driveway between the buildings. He threw me against the brick wall and offered a nasty smile.

It was the mug who'd been tailing me. He still had on the tan suit. The yellow shirt had been replaced by a blue one. It didn't go. "You again," I said. "People will say we're in love."

"Can the rebop, fuckwad." His face still had that smeared, indistinct look, with a small mouth, a retreating chin, a narrow nose, and two tiny eyes that teared for no reason. He needed a shave. "We got biz. I'm about to cut you a break big-time, Ingalls."

"Do tell. What makes you so wonderful?"

"Let's talk shakedown."

I began to notice details about his clothes. The tan suit looked slept-in. There was fraying at the seams and street grime on the cuffs. For all I knew this was his only suit. "Meaning . . . ?"

He laughed. "*Meaning,* DD Productions. The puppet perv. *Meaning,* me and you. It's time to play *Let's Make a Deal.*"

I started to shoulder past him. "You've got the wrong contestant, soldier."

"Scope this, slick." He stopped me with a touch. "I've been chasing you from the jump. I've braced your full roster—Marc Cohen's KAs, the ice-queen ex, Donnie and Marie's alumnae—the whole schmear." He plunged his hands into his jacket pockets, and for a heart-thudding second I was afraid he was about to produce a sidearm. But he came up empty and said, "Gotta nail?"

I took my own sweet time in reaching into my jacket for a pack of Preston's Integrals, and slid one out to him. I fired the Zippo. "You might find it interesting to note that I have no idea what you just said, friend."

"Think hard; you'll tumble." He dragged on the cigarette and exhaled. "Feature I know it's you, peeper. Feature I know you tailed Cohen to his pad, clipped him, and glommed the swag. Now tell me I'm wrong."

"Pal," I said, "the way I figure it, you just said one of two things. Either you're accusing me of following Marc Cohen to his office and killing him and taking the blackmail money. Or you somehow think I followed him to his home, gave him a haircut, and did some stylish makeover on the curtains in his windows. I don't know which is more repellent, but I didn't do either."

"Don't shit a shitter, flatfoot."

"Nice talk."

"It gets better. Every wit I spoke to said, 'Crazy Ingalls.' How you sometimes didn't make sense. How you asked screwy questions. 'Is he for real' in full chorus. That don't play SOP."

"I have a distinctive investigative technique."

"My take? It vibes hinky. I give you two options, chum. Either split the kale even-Steven, or I snitch you out and everybody suffers."

"What if I say no?"

He smirked. "You won't."

"What if I say I don't understand the way you talk?"

"Half a million buys a lot of language lessons." He slapped me on the chest. "Think about it. I'll be in touch."

He flicked the cigarette away and strolled back toward the street. I gave myself a minute to digest the experience, then caught the train back to the office.

Ms. Stephanie Constantino was on best behavior when I returned to the place of business. When I mentioned how unorthodox it was to beg and plead to be allowed to attend a meeting, and then to jump ship mere moments before landing, all because some ex-boyfriend happened to be in the vicinity, she actually blushed.

"Yeah. I know. Sorry." She looked away. It struck me how seldom she did that. "I just . . . okay, what happened? I slept with his brother. And so it was like a train wreck, the way it ended. I guess I should have stayed with you, and just said, 'Hi, Jason,' and walked on."

"Let's say," I mused.

"Or what? You're saying maybe I didn't really want to go in the first place? But I did. I was dying to talk to someone at Ronson!"

"Still."

"Yeah, you're right: I bailed out." She shrugged. "It's just that when you tell me no, usually it touches some nerve and I get all insistent."

I soothed the atmosphere by telling her I understood. I didn't, but sometimes you have to say things to make people feel better. Then I asked what she'd been up to, and she told me she'd tried phoning Jaxsee Shasta, Cohen's girlfriend, and learned that the dame was out of town. Coincidence?

I told her about the bird who'd waylaid me and offered a theory as to what he'd said: that he thought I had killed Cohen and taken the dough. Now he wanted half of it to keep mum.

"Fuck!" She looked away, gnawing her lip. "What does he know? Who is he? Maybe he's a friend of Cohen's."

I shook my head. "He talked like a gumshoe. He interviewed all the people I spoke to."

She snapped her fingers. "Let's call 'em back! Sheila and Phyllis and that Helen. And ask how he represented himself."

I shook my head. "It's too messy. We antagonize these people, someone's going to call the cops. Then they come after me, and I can't work. No, I have to deal with that clown myself."

She nodded, then remembered something and lit up. "But wait! What did Jane What's-her-name say about Cohen?"

I recapped the meeting, and told her how Marc Cohen claimed sole credit for *Henry the Horse at Home.*

"And what about Stephen O'Neil?" Stephanie asked.

"Jane referred to him as 'talent.'"

She made a face. "Ooh. That hurts."

I frowned. "Is that bad?"

She never had a chance to answer.

We were both distracted by the sound, at the front door, of several odd, syncopated thuds. Then the door swung open, uncontrolled, revealing a young woman on crutches—the angled aluminum kind, with arm bracelets at the top, the kind that career crutch users use. She was in her early thirties, of medium height, solidly built. She wore dark slacks and a white belted raincoat and incongruous but functional sneakers. Her light brown hair was conservatively styled, and her brown leather shoulder bag looked pricey. She suspended her right foot as she propelled herself in to those syncopated knocks.

I leaped up and shut the door behind her as she lowered herself into the chair. "Thank you," she said in a nicely modulated voice. "I suffer from a chronic condition."

"Who doesn't?" I said politely. I introduced myself and my assistant and asked how we could be of service.

She took her bag off her shoulder and put it on her lap as she said, "My name is Beverly Klosterman, and I think you can do a little job for me that . . . well, it's kind of silly, but I'd rather not do it myself." She opened the bag and peered into it as she said, "Last week I was at a restaurant—the Silver Dove, on Twenty-sixth and Park—and I had a necklace with me. A nice one—not an heirloom, but nice." She produced a photograph and handed it to me.

Or she tried to hand it to me. I seemed to have become paralyzed, with my mouth ajar, because it took Stephanie's prompt of, "Hello? Earth to Pete?" before I came to and received the pic. It showed this gal, in a slightly different hairdo, in front of a theater, the necklace plainly identifiable around her neck. I looked back at her as though I'd been smacked with a stickball bat.

"You, uh . . . this is yours?"

"Yes. It was in a blue Tiffany's box in a shopping bag. And like an idiot I checked the bag at the coat check, and didn't think a thing about it until I got home. Then I realized the necklace was gone."

Stephanie remained deadpan as she said, "Bummer."

Then the phone rang, and Stephanie answered it and said,

"Oh, my God," and handed it to me. I excused myself to the new client and took the phone, said my name, and Giselle Blanchard said, in deep, honeyed tones, "Pete? I was wondering if you've gone to the Silver Dove and gotten back my necklace."

I did some nonspecific stammering, then said I'd call her back. I hung up like a man in a dream who hangs up a phone. "Sorry," I said to Beverly Klosterman.

"Not at all." She looked up at me. "Could I hire you to go to the restaurant and get the necklace? Because if it's there, then no harm done. But if not, I'd want you to do whatever it is you guys do, you know. 'Put the muscle on them,' or whatever. Do you do that?"

I took her name and number and said I'd get back to her.

THIRTEEN

I couldn't sleep that night. The bright-pink Ottos kept me awake. Finally, at around two o'clock, something clicked. I sat up in bed, said aloud, "Well. Okay. Nice," and settled back in. In ten seconds I was out for the count.

Next morning I dragged myself in and lunged for the joe. Then I brought Stephanie up to speed. I told her I had realized who killed Marc Cohen, and that I was about to head out and apprehend the perpetrator. I suppose I had expected a bit of congratulations and a round of admiring applause. But no good deed goes unpunished. What I got instead was a sudden silence and then some cranky skepticism.

"Are you sure?" she said. She spoke to my back as I got more coffee from the pot. When I turned back to face her she was squinting. "Who?"

"That stays under my hat until the perp sings or the johns make the collar," I said. "Then I'll have to deal with that citizen in the tan suit. There's no rest for the weary."

"I don't know, Pete." She was in jeans and a man's pink oxford shirt, and she looked tired; she'd been up late memorizing lines for some class presentation. The short, reddish brown hair lacked its customary luster. She wasn't wearing any makeup. The green eyes looked timid, and the nice wide mouth looked skeptical. "I don't think we know enough to figure it out yet."

"We know more than we think. You of all people should understand that."

I went on to explain my revelation at Ronson and my new-found grasp of the truth. Instead of one guy trying to figure things out, I was many guys, in many centers of the brain, all working on different facts and theories at once. "So I just sat back and waited for one of them to deliver the answer," I said. "Which he did. And I have you and all those Ottos to thank for it."

"Pete—"

"Later, kid. I have an appointment with a killer."

When I got to my suspect's place of business I did what you do when you show up ready to accuse someone of a capital crime: I walked past the receptionist and into the office. The person in question was standing by the desk, on the phone. I strode up and hit my mark.

"It was you, doll. You killed Marc Cohen. You stole the money. And now you have to pay."

Helen Leeds Corcoran said, "I'll call you back," into the phone and gently replaced it on the cradle. She faced me in all her celestial beauty. Today she looked resplendent in a tight maroon skirt and matching jacket over a black blouse tastefully set off by a modest gold brooch. All that loveliness and class, yeah— and all in the service of murder. "I beg your pardon," she said.

"It's not my pardon you have to beg, angel." I did nothing to soften my words. "Try begging the pardon of the deceased's loved ones. Try begging the pardon of the laws of the state of New York. Try begging the pardon of society."

"Are you saying I killed Marc? That's ridiculous."

"Is it? Let's do the math. One: You and hubby were involved in a nasty divorce. Two: He was contesting the prenup. Three: He was seeing another woman. Four: But he still wanted some of your dough, and you found it all disgusting."

"Mr. Ingalls—"

"But here's the punch line, sister. Six: You thought you were the only one for him. Just like you think there's only one Otto. Then you go to where they make them, where all the Ottos come from, and you see twenty, thirty Ottos. And it destroys something inside you. Inside your head. And maybe, just maybe, inside your heart." I paused and thought about it. "Nah. Just your head. Inside, where they keep the brains. That's what Jaxsee Shasta was to you, angel. Your many Ottos. Because if Marc could be seeing her, then he could be seeing other women, too. If there wasn't just one, there could be twenty or thirty. Twenty or thirty women—and all puppets. All puppets of puppet master Marc. Including you. Sure, it rankled. Sure, it got to you. It shattered your universe. It destroyed your conception of him, of your relationship, and of your single, individual self."

"Who is Otto?"

"So you followed him. And on the night of the payoff you saw him pop me and swipe the dough. You followed him back to his loft, waited until the next morning, and paid your estranged hubster an unexpected visit. Of course he let you in. Of course there was no sign of breaking and entering. He knew you. He thought you were there to talk about the divorce. He turned his back, you grabbed the Emmy, and the rest is history—the history of a cold-blooded killing."

"Mr. Ingalls," she said, cool as ice. "What time was Marc killed that morning?"

"Nine, ten o'clock. Why?"

"Because I have an alibi for my whereabouts both the night before and for that morning."

"I'll bet." I leered. "Based on what? On your say-so?"

"Not necessarily. Shall I tell you where I was the night before?"

"Oh, yes. Please do." I normally don't approve of using sarcasm with a woman. But I found her great beauty unnerving, and needed something to bolster my confidence. "For starters, why don't you tell me where you were the night before?"

"I was at a reception at the South African embassy until late, about one o'clock. Then I went home."

"And I suppose there are people to confirm that?"

"Several hundred, yes."

I hesitated. That would be a lot of interviews. "And where might you have been the next morning? When the murder occurred?"

"I was in this office."

I had to laugh. And I did laugh. I laughed the laugh of a man who finds something terribly amusing. "And who can back up that little alibi, Ms. Corcoran? Your secretary? Please. Unless, of course, you were with someone else in here."

"I was with someone else. And he can confirm that alibi."

"Okay, doll, I'll bite. Who were you with? And please tell me the individual in question isn't your father, or your new boyfriend, or someone else who works for you. Please tell me the person in question has at least a modicum of credibility."

"He has great credibility." She pointed past me toward the sofa and chairs. "I was with that gentleman."

I turned. Seated on the sofa was an elderly bird in a dark suit.

I'd walked right past him and not seen him there. He was black, an African-American, with a broad, solid body and graying hair and a handsome, commanding face. He wore big black-framed eyeglasses and looked at me with a combination of curiosity and distaste that, frankly, I wasn't crazy about.

"And who might you be, friend?" I asked.

Helen Corcoran moved in between us and gestured the introductions. "Mr. Ingalls, may I introduce His Excellency Bishop Desmond Tutu. Excellency, this is Mr. Peter Ingalls."

I stepped forward. The guy didn't bother to rise. I stuck my hand out and he gave me a firm but fleeting shake. "How do you do," he said.

" 'His Excellency,' eh? I'll bet." I turned to Helen Corcoran. "You'll pardon my asking, but given the circumstances, I think it's a legit question. Just what is it that's so excellent about this guy?"

"Oh, please, sir," Tutu said. "It is a formal honorific."

"What?"

"Bishop Tutu was the primate of the Anglican Church in South Africa until his retirement," the Corcoran broad said.

"Primate?" My thoughts raced. "I thought primates had something to do with monkeys. Monkeys go to church in Africa? Okay, it's their home turf. If monkeys are going to go to church anywhere, it'd be in Africa. Still, color me skeptical."

Tutu looked at the gal and said helplessly, "Helen—"

"Mr. Ingalls. Bishop Tutu was the head of the Anglican Church in South Africa—"

"Wait a minute." I turned back to the gent. "So you're an African-American actually *from* Africa. Interesting."

"He is visiting the United States on several diplomatic and charitable missions. He is one of the most noble and heroic figures in the world. He will tell you I was in a meeting all morning with him, here, and not killing my ex-husband in his loft. Now please, I must ask you to leave, or I'll call security."

I thumbed toward Tutu. "He'll alibi you?"

"Yes."

"And his word is trustworthy?"

"Most people would think so, yes."

"Oh, really? And who are 'most people'?"

"Most of the intelligent human beings on the planet Earth."

That was a lot of people. The next move was mine. Obviously she wasn't going to crack—at least, not now, not here, not with this Tutu bird available to back her up.

"Okay," I told her. "Let's say I believe you. For now. I'll check his rep and see what pans out. But don't leave town." I turned to the South African. "You might want to stick around too, Your Highness."

I was finished. I bounced.

There was still some late-summer warmth to be savored when I stepped from the Fairlane Foundation building and got my bearings. It was midmorning, and out on the street the air had that hopeful feel that seems to last until after lunch, when everybody gets full and sleepy, and the whole city needs a nap and nobody admits it. I decided to walk a bit before grabbing the train back to the office.

I had barely gone a block when I heard footsteps hurry up behind me and felt myself propelled, via a firm grip on my upper right arm, around the corner into a loading dock and against the rough concrete wall.

"Tick-tock, Ingalls." The tan suit looked worse than ever. The yellow shirt and black tie were back. "Now, why don't you cough up the pelf and we'll mark it closed."

"Careful, pal," I said. "You're talking to a guy who just had a visit with the head of the primate church in South Africa."

"You glommed Cohen dirt to shake down wifey, that's your angle. But I want half the extortion swag."

"Better have your hearing aid checked, friend. I keep telling you, it wasn't me. I took a Mickey Finn to the arteries and was sightseeing through Dreamland when it happened."

"That trank story?" He sneered. You don't see it that often. It was effective. "My nephew could do better than that. He's six. No, see, Ingalls, unlike you, I happen to know all the alibis of the whole cast and crew. You didn't ask them where they were when Cohen was clipped, but I did. Care to hear the rundown?"

"Do I have a choice?"

"The wife was in a meeting with some African priest. Stephen O'Neil? Watching the morning screening of *The Big Sleep* at the local flick, and yes, he had the stub to prove it and was quoting lines up the wazoo. Bob Borger? On the set in Astoria. Donnie and Marie? At the office."

I gave him a tight grin. It wasn't much but he was lucky to get that. "You're forgetting something, genius. I've got an alibi for that morning, too. I was with my assistant the whole time."

He shrugged. "Your gal could be complicit. Wouldn't be the first time."

"You're reaching. But there's nothing there. Now excuse me, I have decent, honest, clean work to do."

I tried to move him aside, but he planted his feet, said, "Clean this, fuckwad," reared back, and slugged me in the stomach. It pushed the air out of me like a collapsing bellows, and all I could do was stagger there, doubled over, waiting for my lungs to refill of their own accord. He wasn't waiting, however. He hauled off and whaled me on the jaw with a cross that threw me back against the concrete wall.

It hurt, yeah. But it was more than a physical pain. This joker had me all wrong but still insisted on administering the rough stuff. It brought pain to my sense of fairness. So when I started punching back, it was with a bit of extra ferocity—ferocity fueled by indignation.

I dealt him a couple of shots across the face, and when he lurched back and lost focus I came in hard to the midriff. But he had stamina. He withstood my body blows, and sledgehammered me with a hands-clasped powerhouse to the gut. I doubled over and again had trouble breathing. That's when he slammed down onto my head.

I lost awareness for just a second, but it was enough. My legs buckled and I fell onto the concrete drive. "Wise up, Ingalls," he said, panting. "The sooner you pony the green, the sooner you never see me again." With that he lurched off, around the corner and gone.

I took a cab back to the office and reeled in, bleeding from several cuts and feeling bruises blooming on my face like malign, terrible flowers. Stephanie took one look at me and went white, then leaped up and ran for the first aid. We'd been through this before.

"Who did this?" she asked, dabbing the cuts with peroxide and wincing more than I did. "And why, for Christ's sake?"

I told her I didn't know his name or what his connection was to the case. All I knew was that he thought I had the dough and he wanted half.

"How does he know about your being shot with that animal

dart?" Stephanie dumped a box of Band-Aids onto the desk and picked out the little ones. "Who did we tell about that?"

I said I didn't remember and didn't care. The important thing was what that guy had told me about the alibis of the suspects and principals surrounding Cohen's murder. If everyone was accounted for, then we were missing something essential and I had to start over. And I knew just how to do it.

"The blackmail was a two-man job," I said as Stephanie taped the final bandage to my face.

"That's what Detective Sandoval thinks, too."

"Who?"

"Detective Clara Sandoval. She's from the Major Case Squad!" My assistant was having more fun than was strictly called for. "The Special Investigations Division! She was here an hour ago. Isn't this cool? It's like TV!"

I didn't think it was cool. I thought the dance floor was filling up with cops. Soon you wouldn't be able to execute a simple allemande left without banging into blue. "How'd she get involved?"

She squinted at my wounds and looked sympathetically anguished. "Thoreau. He finally followed the clues to DD Productions, and of course a minute after he walks in they tell him about the blackmail. So he called her."

"And what did this detective want?"

Stephanie shrugged. "To ask what we know. You were out so she said she'd be back, like, tomorrow. Hey, what *do* we know?"

"I don't know what we know. But I know this: If the blackmail had a cast of two, and Cohen was the star, then the second banana is still in the wings. Let's pry him loose. Take a memo."

"Huh?"

"I'm going to dictate a memo to DD Productions. Write this down."

"Forget it! I can't take dictation! Are you crazy?"

"Okay, fine."

"I mean, seriously. Take it yourself."

"Message received. Just stand by and prepare to disseminate."

"What?"

I went into my office and shut the door and fired up the word processor. An hour later I emerged with a printout. Without preamble, I read aloud: " 'To: All personnel. From: Donnie Dansicker. Re: Recent events. Mr. Peter Ingalls, the first-rate PI we have retained, informs me that he knows the identity of the person who made the illicit copy of the so-called puppet-porno outtake footage. He further informs me that the law will look with greater leniency on that person if he or she comes forward now, voluntarily, rather than having to be ferreted out *and publicly humiliated*. If you volunteer it will be kept confidential. If we have to come after you and find you it will not be pretty. The choice is yours.' " I looked up at her. "Your thoughts?"

Stephanie looked wary. "It's a bluff, right?"

"Let's say."

"Obviously. Because if you really knew who did it, you wouldn't be asking publicly. You'd go to them privately and tell them to confess." She held a hand out. I gave her the sheet. She gnawed her lip and scratched out certain words. I was about to declare a partial victory when she crumpled the whole thing into a ball and tossed it. Then she muttered, "Give me ten minutes."

Nine minutes later she entered my office and handed me a new printout. I read aloud, " 'To: DD Productions staff. From: D. Dansicker. Re: Ongoing investigation. Mr. Peter Ingalls and Ms.

Stephanie Constantino will be circulating throughout the office over the next day or so to affect the apprehension of the individual who made an illicit copy of the *Playground Pals* outtake reel. Please show them every possible courtesy and cooperate fully in their investigation. Anyone with first- or secondhand knowledge of this event should come forward. Legal repercussions will be much less severe for those who voluntarily cooperate, no matter how large or small their role.'" I looked at her. "A few more sentences and we can publish it in hardcover."

"Look, I'm sorry, but there's a lot to say. We want to encourage the person to come forward. But we can't say, 'We don't know who you are,' because they might not bite. But we also can't say, 'We do know who you are,' because they'd wonder why we aren't just grabbing them."

"Sold. Get me Donnie on the phone."

Dansicker sounded like a man in a foxhole—tired, frightened, endlessly apprehensive. I read him the text and said I'd be faxing it to him for general distribution. He didn't jump up and down with joy. "No. Please. I can't have you two roaming around the office. Let the police handle it."

"The police have a homicide to investigate. They have a much larger area to cover."

"Look, Ingalls, I can't keep arguing about this. If you insist on disrupting things here I'll have to terminate our arrangement." He then made some vague excuse about being "busy," and hung up.

I was stymied. My leads had run out on one half of the case, and the client was blocking my progress on the other. Stephanie's reaction, when I told her about Donnie Dansicker's resistance— "I don't get it"—spoke volumes. Or maybe it didn't speak volumes. Maybe it spoke just one sentence, and that sentence was, "I don't get it." But it was enough for me. Because I didn't get it.

As soon as the receptionist buzzed me into DD Productions I started dealing out Stephanie's memo to whomever came within range, like one of those citizens on the street who hands you a flyer for a men's clothing store, and you take three steps and drop it in the wastebasket at the corner, where it settles in with the other ones, and you think, *Can't he just dump the consignment in the trash at the outset, and save all concerned a lot of bother?* I made my way through the office, shoving the sheet into people's hands or slapping it down onto unoccupied desks.

I saved the executive end of the floor for last. Ellen Larraby gave me the covert high sign that the bosses were both in Charlotte's office. I knocked and went in without waiting for an answer.

Donnie was slouched on the sofa in chinos and a white shirt. The wife was prim and upright on one of the chairs, in a light blue silky blouse and a black full skirt. The glass-and-chrome coffee table was covered with folders and documents crawling with numbers, like ants.

Neither of them seemed delighted to see me.

"Mr. Ingalls!" Charlotte turned on the charm. "What brings you here?"

"Oh, Christ, now what?" Donnie sighed.

I handed each of them a sheet. "Hot off the press from the Xerox shop at no additional charge to you."

Charlotte skimmed hers and threw a startled look at her husband. Then she looked at me. "Do you really know who did it?"

"No comment," I said. "Let's leave that for when my assistant and I do another round of questions."

"Forget it, Ingalls," Donnie said. He hauled himself to an upright position and spoke evenly to his wife. "I told him two hours ago that we don't want any more disruptions around here. In fact, I said that if he kept it up he'd be fired."

"You didn't hire me to order me around, Dansicker," I said. "You hired me to do my job my way."

"Maybe. But I don't like your way anymore. You know what? Fuck it. You're fired."

Charlotte, eyes on her hubby, slowly nodded. Then she aimed her demeanor at me and downshifted from sunny to formal. "I agree with my husband. Thank you for your work so far, but we'll take it from here."

"You'll take it? You'll take it where? Over a cliff?" I sat in the other side chair. "You have nothing. The porno's on computers in Timbuktu. The money's gone. You need all the help you can get."

"Insurance will cover the money," Charlotte said.

Donny waved her quiet. "Just . . . forget it; he doesn't have to know anything about that." He looked up at me. "I told you on the phone, Ingalls. We've got police crawling around here now. Some guy named Thoreau. And frankly, we hired you to prevent the blackmail, and you failed. Send me a bill and go with God."

"Our attorney will send you a letter," Charlotte said. "His name is Leonard Finklestein."

Donnie scowled at his wife. "No! We don't have to bother Leonard with this. Everything . . . you want to leave me a note to buy half-and-half, it has to come from the lawyer. It's costing us a fortune."

"He's on retainer."

"Which we burn up on nonsense!"

"It's not nonsense! We're running a business here, Donnie!"

Dansicker made frustrated grasping motions with his hands. "Not every little communication has to come from a guy who charges three hundred an hour!"

"It's not every—"

"Like that letter to Stephen O'Neil! After that Ronson gig? What's wrong with a goddamn verbal message? Why couldn't we just call him in and say, 'You're exclusive to us. No more outside jobs.' I mean, Jesus!"

Charlotte looked haplessly at me, as though inviting my sympathy. "Well, we'll figure it out. In any case, you know you're fired, okay, Mr. Ingalls?"

"I know a lot of things." I stood up. "You're the client. Call me if you change your mind."

I walked through the office toward the entrance and the elevators. Everyone stopped whatever they were doing and watched me as I passed. Maybe it was because I had joined the swelling ranks of functionaries, hired guns, freelancers, and walk-ons who had Donnie and Charlotte stories.

Or maybe it was because a PI commands respect just by crossing a room.

FOURTEEN

It was about ten A.M. the next day when the FedEx gent delivered one of their flat, thin envelopes. Stephanie, fetching in tight black jeans and a raspberry sweatshirt, managed to put her script pages down to take receipt.

It was a letter from a Mr. Leonard Finklestein, of Vartorella, Siegel, Burger, and Knapp, LLP, informing me that my services were no longer required and that my employment by DD Productions was herewith terminated. "Let's frame it," Stephanie said. That remark embodied exactly the kind of playful, robust sense of humor I wasn't in the mood for, and I told her so.

Then I told her about the exchange Donnie and Charlotte had had the day before, in my presence, about the pros and cons of sending a pricey shyster's pink slip when a verbal one would do. "Charlotte had Finklestein send a cease-and-desist to Stephen O'Neil," I said. "Which hubby thought was extravagant, too."

She frowned. "Cease and desist what?"

"After his gig with the Ronson gang."

"The one Jane Christoff told you about? That mob thing?"

"Sounds like it." I looked at her. She was strangely, significantly silent. "Why? What gives?"

"Hmm . . . Nothing. I dunno. Maybe something." Then her eyes went wide and she grew animated. "Hey! It's after ten! Let's call Ellen and see what's shakin'!"

The elves had all had a chance to read my memo. I got Ellen on the horn and asked where Mommy and Daddy were.

"Out," she said. "Donnie's in editing and Charlotte's at a meeting across town."

"Aces. Eyeball the office and give me a rundown. Who's strangely subdued? Who's unusually irritable? Who's acting furtive and then denies it to your face?"

"Uh, let's see. Nobody."

I enjoyed a small chuckle. "Get out the Windex and clean off the contacts, sugar. Who's acting skittish? Who jumps at the slightest noise? Who's uncharacteristically nervous?"

"Nobody. Everybody's completely normal."

"Is that so."

I sensed some sort of motion nearby. It was Stephanie, standing at my desk and gesturing for the phone. I handed it over.

"Hey, El . . ." My associate laughed. "Yeah, really . . . Well, it could happen! Okay, so, how about this: Did anybody call in sick today? . . . Oh, really? . . . Okay, and—" There was a sudden silence and an abrupt plunge in the atmospheric pressure in the room. "*No*. Really? Wow. Okay. Talk to you later."

She hung up and looked at me, and it was with that I-know-something leer she liked to effect when she knew something. "I know something," she said. "Guess who didn't show up for work today and who called in sick and who *never* calls in sick?"

"Say it."

"Norman Tibbler."

We paused to savor the moment. Or, rather, she did. I spread my hands in the manner of an innocent, honest, essentially decent man who doesn't "get" the inference that's making everybody else scream. "So?"

"Pete! It's Norman! That little nerd who runs the postproduction studio. The guy who had more access to the puppet footage than anyone else!"

"Which means what? He made the copy and got in on the blackmail? He colluded with Marc Cohen?"

She lit up. Her aura acquired a kind of celestial golden radiance, if such things existed and I believed in them. *"Yes!"*

"I can't see it."

"I . . ." The lights flickered and went out. She deflated. "Yeah. Neither can I. He wouldn't do anything like that. He's too nervous. He'd be too afraid. And he wouldn't trust Cohen."

"My take? He called in sick because he's ill. People get sick, angel. They get sick and they feel ill and it plays hell with their state of wellness."

"You have to go talk to him, Pete."

Normally I might have challenged this. We'd just eliminated Tibbler as a suspect. But something made me hesitate. Call it something in Stephanie's manner, or in the atmosphere.

Or better yet, call it some still, small voice in one of the departments of my mind, saying, *Heed this, Ingalls. A judicious cultivation of Tibbler might accomplish much by way of securing inside information at DD. Catching him at home, in a debilitated state, might prove the perfect opportunity with which to ingratiate yourself and recruit him to your program.* I don't usually talk to myself in that ornate, fancy way, but sometimes it happens. Fortunately I'm usually able to understand what's being said.

Then, admittedly, another voice might have replied, *You're fired, flatfoot. You don't need inside info. The job is over.* But then a third voice would be "heard" saying, *It's not over. There's a hard boy in a tan suit waiting to feed you a five-finger souvlaki if you so much as step out the door. He's not going to go away until you can prove to him you don't know where the money is by finding it.*

The upshot: Stephanie was right. I had to cultivate the lad. Stephanie got his address from Ellen and I hit the street.

It was a sympathy call, so when I got out of the subway at the other end I did what people do: I stopped at a Korean grocer and bought a pint of Häagen-Dazs, a bouquet of red and white carnations, and a bag of mints. If he really was sick, it would brighten his day.

And if he wasn't, my moral leverage over him would be that much greater. When someone gives you flowers, they're in the ethical driver's seat. Question: Why don't cops, detectives, and private investigators give flowers to everybody all the time? Expense? Not really. You can make the point with a single five-dollar array of daisies or mums. Convenience? You're breaking my heart. The bother is nothing compared to the leg up you get bringing a bouquet to a suspect shakedown, a ransom payoff, a witness questioning, or just any bad-guy confrontation where you seek to influence the behavior of others. Even the toughest muscle boy looking to sap you just for breathing has got to think twice when you hand him a bunch of irises or tulips. "For me?" the hard case stammers, taken aback. "Jeez, Ingalls, I don't know what to say." Then you cash in. You tell him what to say.

Tibbler lived on the Upper East Side over a German coffee shop on Eighty-sixth Street. I didn't call first, but just buzzed the place cold. When he asked, on the intercom, who it was, I said,

"Benjamin Franklin." I always say that. Most people will open the door for Franklin, and those who won't end up not believing I'm him anyway.

I found his apartment and knocked. The guy who answered looked sick, all right. Tibbler appeared diminished in every way, shorter than his customary five-four, even paler than when I'd met him at DD Productions. His boyish, yearning face had gone grim, and his dark eyes looked haunted. He wore baggy white pants and a ballooning white collarless shirt, like a man in pajamas, or an inmate in an asylum. "What do you want?" He sounded panicked. He looked like he hadn't showered or shaved.

"I heard you were sick, Norman." I was dealing with an unwell person. I made sure to speak in a simple, nonthreatening manner. "So I thought I'd stop by with a few things to cheer you up."

"You shouldn't have come here." He stepped back. I took it as an implicit invitation to come in. I crossed the threshold and shut the door behind me. The place was tiny, a single box of a room with a closet-sized bathroom off to one side and a bathroom-sized kitchenette against a wall. A loft bed hovered above it all on wood uprights. The two windows faced an air shaft and gave no light whatsoever.

"What does that mean—cheer me up?" He backed up into the room, hands working anxiously. He looked bloodless and nervous and about ready to scream. I could relate—when I have a cold all I want to do is stay in bed and watch golf on television. That's how I know I'm sick.

We stood in the middle of the small living room, a sofa in nubby, rust-colored fabric to my left, a folding chair beside it, both facing a little TV and a boom box on a bookcase.

"You know. Make you feel better. Look at these." I held out the posy. "Nice, eh?"

He reached forth a trembling hand, then snatched it back. "What . . . what is this . . . ?"

"Carnations." I walked over to the kitchen sink and laid the flowers on the drain board. "Hey, I hope you like Vanilla Swiss Almond." I pulled the ice cream out of the bag. "That means the almonds are covered in chocolate."

"What are you *talking* about?"

"Yeah, I know—what's so damn Swiss about that? Beats me. Let's let it sit a little and get soft."

"What do you want? And what is that supposed to mean?" he said. "What does it mean, 'let it sit and get soft'? What are you saying?"

"Oh, I think you know what I mean." I laughed. "Meanwhile . . ." I rattled the mints at him. "How's this look to you?"

His eyes narrowed. "What are you going to do with that?"

I took a step toward him. "You like mints, don't you, Norman?"

"Stay away from me!"

"Oh, I will. I don't want to end up like you, friend!"

"All right, look . . ." He glanced wildly around the place, gathering his thoughts. Then he practically shouted, "I want immunity!"

I smiled and shrugged. "Pal, I hear you. We all want immunity. But sooner or later everybody gets it."

His mouth worked silently for a couple seconds. Finally he whispered, "Gets it?"

"That's why they call it the common cold. Nobody's immune." I looked around the kitchen, found a drawer, and opened it. A cluster of utensils rattled metallically.

"What are you doing! You don't have to get anything out of there!"

"No trouble at all. You sit down and relax." I gave him a knowing chuckle. "If you can!" I took out a couple of big kitchen knives and gently laid them on the scarred wooden cutting board. I think I heard him whimper. Then I saw a familiar object and it got me to musing. As I reached for it I said, "You know, they're always coming up with elaborate mechanical contraptions and gas-operated gizmos—"

"What?"

"—but in the end, all you ever really need"—I pulled out a corkscrew, the no-frills kind, with a single naked spiral tine emerging from a bell-shaped frame, and a wooden handle. I held it up—"is this."

"Put that down!" He started pacing the little space, rubbing his hands on his shirt. "I didn't know this was going to happen! I swear!"

"Of course not. I wanted to surprise you."

"I did it as a favor! I didn't know what he was going to do with it. It's not fair. It's not my fault!"

"Aha. Here's what I'm looking for." I pulled out an ice-cream scoop—the good kind, with the spring-loaded thumb press that works the ice-cream release.

"Stay away from me with that thing!" He had collapsed onto the sofa, sobbing—a desperate little man in a sad little apartment. "Okay! All right! It was me! I copied the outtake reel! The night before the wrap party! I just did it as a favor!"

I had to shift mental focus, from thoughts about serving ice cream to thoughts about blackmail. No, it's not "easy." No, it's not "fun." But I did it. "Let me get this straight, Tibbler. You're telling me you're the one who copied the porno reel?"

"Yes! All right? Yes! Just put those things down and get out!"

"One question first. Who'd you do it for? Why'd you do it? Okay, two questions. But to me they count as one."

He started to answer, then clamped his mouth shut, ran to the door, flung it open, and fled. I took out my cell phone and hit the speed dial. Stephanie answered right away.

"Pete Ingalls, PI."

"Good news, kid. I found out who made the porno copy."

"Pete? Who? Where are you?"

"Norman Tibbler's place. He did it."

"No shit! How do you know?"

"He just told me."

"Get out!"

"Plus, my little get-well presents seem to have done the trick, because he just made a fantastic recovery and ran out the door on all cylinders."

"He ran out? And you're still there?"

"Roger that."

"Are you nuts? Go follow him! See where he's going!"

I jammed the ice cream in the stuffed, frost-choked freezer and hustled out after Tibbler. When I hit the street I scanned the area and lucked out—he was across Eighty-sixth looking frantically for a westbound cab. I kept a low profile as I subtly hustled west until I was downstream from him. Then I ran across and vamped until I saw him get into a car. I flagged one and we followed.

We snaked through Central Park and emerged on the West Side, where he kept going all the way to West End. Then he turned downtown and pulled over between Seventy-sixth and Seventy-seventh. I had my cabbie stop a block earlier, paid him, and got out. Tibbler dashed into a building I recognized. I legged it to the entrance. The doorman was a tall, smiling Hispanic gent in a pseudo military uniform. I pointed after Norman and said, "I'm with him."

"You seeing Bob? Okay."

"Yeah—that's five-F, right?"

"Ten-E."

"Gotcha."

I approached the elevators warily until I was sure Tibbler had already gone up. I caught the next one and hit ten. When I got out and reached 10-E, its door was shut. I knocked. From within I heard an exchange of whispers and some scuffling. Then footsteps approached and the door opened.

"Oh, hello," Bob Borger said. "Come in."

I entered through a narrow little foyer lined with bookshelves into a nice-sized living room/dining room in which the only other living creature was a fuzzy gray cat, which arched its back at me and hissed and darted off behind an armchair. Borger joined me in the middle of the floor, where we stood like two men waiting at a bus stop. He was tall and stooped in a black sweatshirt with the *Abracadabra Avenue* logo in green, faded jeans, and leather bedroom slippers. Norman Tibbler was nowhere in sight.

"Norman thought that was you," he said mildly.

I looked around the room. It was fanatically neat. The beige puffy sofa, the long glass coffee table, the gleaming upright piano against the rear wall, the shelves of books and puppets and knickknacks: Everything was spotless and aligned and in its place. "Did he tell you what we discussed?" I asked.

"Not really." Borger's pale, open face expressed puzzlement. "He was very upset, though."

"Do tell. He came here to be very upset?" Off the main room was a little kitchen, and beyond it a closed door to what I assumed was the bedroom.

"Yes, he did."

It's my experience that when people talk like that, in complete sentences in which you can hear the commas, they're either hiding something or they're under extreme psychological pressure. I bit for the former. "And where is our boy Norman, Bob?" I said, strolling toward the shut door. "Might he mayhap perhaps be in the bedroom here?"

"Shut up!" Tibbler cried from behind the door. "Go away!"

Borger came after me and steered me back into the living room. "He is in there. But why are you here?"

"Why?" I enjoyed a bitter laugh. Yeah, it was bitter, but I enjoyed it. Sometimes a bitter laugh is the only laugh you can get. "Because of a little thing called blackmail, Bob. A little thing our friend Norman had a hand in recently, as you no doubt know."

Borger looked at me with a perplexed frown on his pale, pasty mug. "What do you mean?"

"Don't tell me you don't know."

"Don't know what?"

"Okay, chief. Let's play Twenty Questions. Truth or Dare the Consequences: Do you or do you not know that our lad Norman is the one who made the copy of the porno outtakes of *Playground Pals,* which Marc Cohen used to blackmail Donnie and Charlotte and company?"

Borger forced a smile. "Oh, I don't believe that," he said.

"Ask him."

When big men have big reactions, it's worth watching. That's what happened now. Bob Borger, for all his mild-mannered, soft-spoken gentility, was a large man, with an open face that displayed emotions with 3-D stereophonic realism. When he grasped what I'd just said he looked away. His green eyes clicked into sharp focus. His thin mouth got tight. His rust-colored brows furrowed. And his whole facial environment began to flush pink.

He pivoted and strode to the bedroom door and twisted its knob, but it was locked, and all he got for his trouble was a friction burn and a sharp noise. He rapped hard. "Norman. Let me in." After two beats the door opened. Tibbler stood in the doorway pale as milk, his hands held limply up before him as though warding off something he knew he was powerless to oppose. Borger loomed over him like a displeased father. "Is that true? Are you the one who copied the outtakes?"

Tibbler looked away and nodded. Then he retreated into the bedroom. Borger pursued him and I followed at a discreet distance. "How could you?" Borger cried. "We talked about that! We agreed you wouldn't do anything! We said you wouldn't take part!"

Tibbler had been sitting on the edge of the immaculately made bed, fretting his hands and fighting tears. Now he leaped up and confronted the bigger man. "*You* decided! *You* said not to do it! I didn't say okay. I said it wasn't a big deal."

"It is a big deal!" Borger looked away and groped for an argument. "How can . . . the whole point of puppets is that they're *not* nasty, and . . . and . . . and obscene—"

"To you! Not to me!"

"And so you didn't tell Rosa to stop it. You did nothing to stop it."

"That's right!"

"And you made a copy of that horrible *shit.*"

"That's right!"

I held up the hand of calm. "Guys—"

"Even after I asked you not to take part."

"Stop ordering me, Bobby! Stop . . . *forbidding* me!"

"Gentlemen—"

Borger's voice plummeted to a frightening hush. "Norman, you're speaking as though I'm trying to control you."

"You are! You try to control everything! All the time!"

"Friends, one question—"

"Please, Norman," Borger begged. "Grow up."

"Fuck you, Bobby. Just fuck you to hell."

"People—"

Norman Tibbler shouldered past Borger and, with a petulant shove, pushed me aside and stormed out of the room. Two seconds later we heard the front door slam shut.

"Just dandy," I said. "But I've got a few more questions."

I turned to follow him, but Borger looked alarmed and used his tall man's stride to get between me and the front door. "Wait!" He put a hand on my arm and said, "Do me a favor. Leave him alone for now. I'll talk to him. He's very upset."

"We're all upset, pal," I said. "DD Productions is upset. Anybody who happened to like Marc Cohen is upset. Puppet fans from six to ninety-six are upset."

"I know. . . ."

I thumbed toward the door. "Does it make sense to you that he'd be in cahoots with somebody like Cohen?"

Borger looked slapped. He glanced away, frowning. "God, no. Absolutely not."

"Then excuse me, but I've got to find your friend and get some answers."

Once again I made for the door and once again he stopped me. "Look, Mr. Ingalls, I know you have a job to do. But I know Norman. He'll catch a train upstate and stay with friends. You'll never find him until he's ready to be found. And it would really make things a lot easier on everyone if you'd let me handle it for now."

I sighed. Or maybe I just breathed heavily. Some days I don't know the difference between the two. "Do your friend a favor, Borger. Find him, tell him he's involved in a couple of big-time crimes, and that one of them is murder. He may not be a material witness, but the buttons are going to come calling for a sit-down and a chin-wag."

"Who?"

"The police. And if they ask me who they should talk to in this case, your chum's name is at the top of my list."

He nodded. "I know. But you should know that Norman and I both have an alibi for where we were last Thursday night. Remember when you asked Klonky about it? We were with each other. Which Norman doesn't want anyone to know."

I smirked. "For reasons known only to him, I'll bet."

"Yes, so I appreciate your holding back for a day or two. I mean, you're a nice person. . . ." He had a sudden thought and said, "Wait here." He disappeared into the walk-in closet in the bedroom and emerged a few seconds later with something in his hands. "I want you to have this."

It was a toy version of Klonky, the puppet character he'd manipulated at the Astoria studio, the little creature with whom I'd had the discussion about who hated whom, and the delights of tropical fish. It was about a foot in length, and wore the character's red vest and yellow pants over its woolly purple hide. I took the doll and said, "For me?"

"You seemed to like Klonky when you met him. And he liked you." He allowed himself a little smile at the toy. "It's nice, isn't it?"

"It is?"

"Are you kidding?" He took the doll from me and examined

it. "It's excellent quality. They used this company in Singapore. Believe me, not every one is made this good. Look . . ." He indicated the creature's red vest. "See how it's a fully independent little garment? You can take it off and put it back on? With the little Velcro strip inside here? His whole outfit is like that. Not like that *Playground Pals* crap."

"Crap?" I chuckled sardonically. "Strong language, friend."

"Crap, shit, dreck . . ." He got agitated. "It's one of the main ways you can tell good dolls from bad dolls. With the good stuff, the clothes are made separately and finished separately and you can take them off. With the junk, the clothes are just sewed or stapled right onto the body. The only way to take the clothes off is to cut them off. It's like you have to surgically remove them. And you destroy the doll. Of course, it's cheaper to make and cheaper to sell, and most kids don't care." He held out the Klonky. "Please."

I took it. But something wasn't quite resolved. "Thanks, Bob. But one question: Why me? Why don't you save this and give it to your girlfriend?"

Shocked? Think about it. Admittedly, it was a personal question. But I'm a PI. It's my job to ask personal questions. It turns out it's Bob Borger's job to laugh at said personal question and to say, "Are you serious?"

"Why not? These dolls are made for kids. And okay, maybe for gals with a taste for the playful and the cute. But I'm a grown man, Borger." It seemed inadequate. I was shortchanging myself. I added, "Of course I have an inner child, yearning to burst free, and maybe he looks at the world with innocence and hope, and maybe he exults with unbridled joy at the glory of existence. But I give him a smack and tell him to sit quietly. And he does, brother, oh, yes, he does."

"Come on, Ingalls!" Borger said. "You're joking, right?" And he laughed.

They always do. You open up your heart, you reveal one of your sensitive, childlike selves, and the world rewards the gesture with a hearty horselaugh to your face. "When I'm joking you'll know it," I said. I hoped it was true.

Borger, though, was unfazed. "Let's just say I don't have girl-friends."

"It's a big world, son. Put down the dolls and find a dame."

"Yeah, uh-huh. Look, just do me a favor, will you? Promise me you won't tell anyone about me and Norman."

"Agreed. Now all you have to do is tell me what not to tell them."

"Okay, fine." He got huffy. Not that I could blame him. In a minute I was going to get huffy, too. You can't avoid it. We live in huffy times. "Don't tell them anything about us. Don't tell any-one we're friends."

I replied that I would honor that request unless I was arrested, in which case I wouldn't volunteer anything but would have to sing the song the bulls had on the lead sheets. Bob Borger said he had no idea what I was talking about and we left it at that.

I returned to the office ready to give Klonky to my assistant, a frail who had shown a penchant for other stuffed creatures from the get-go and who could, therefore, be expected to receive the gift with gratitude and respect. Mark another one for Ingalls un-der the "chump" column.

"Ugh, what's that?" she inquired. Then, before I could answer, she said, "But wait! Did you follow Norman? Where'd he go?"

I recounted the morning's events, including Tibbler's flight to

Bob Borger's, their argument, and Borger's request that I suppress any mention of their being "friends." That brought a curt, "Huh!" and not much more. It was only when I summarized his little lecture to me about the comparative quality of separate versus sewn-on clothes on dolls and puppets that I got a rise out of her.

"No shit!" she said. She grabbed the Klonky doll and suddenly found it fascinating.

"Please?"

"Sorry." She took Klonky's vest off and gazed at it. "Bob Borger sounds like he really hated Marc Cohen."

"Didn't everyone?"

She had gone distracted and remote, but my question brought her snapping back with a quizzical look at me. "Huh? Didn't everyone . . . No, not really . . ." Then she swiveled around until her back was to me, and she studied the Klonky toy.

That was jake. I had an important lunch date.

FIFTEEN

A hundred voices had Roscoe's lunchtime rush buzzing when the first of my guests arrived. It was Chris Page, looking swank and serious in a black skirt and white blouse, clicking in on high heels and made up for business.

"I thought you'd never call, Mr. Ingalls." She sat and smiled at the setup. "A nice big table. Perfect for delivering jewelry and writing checks."

I kept a poker pan and added, "And for other things."

She was about to reply when I spotted my next guest and stood to welcome her—yeah, stood like a DA with an objection. Think I didn't have objections to the recent proceedings? Think something else. Giselle Blanchard approached, a slim, shapely knockout in tight jeans and a clinging light wool top of pale blue. When she saw Chris Page her expression lost the sultry anticipation and became not so happy. "Pete? I thought we would be alone."

"Not this time, doll." I held out a chair. She sat automatically, her frozen smile and unmerry eyes focused on the other woman. I did the introductions. The gals traded polite nods.

"Okay—" I began.

Then Beverly Klosterman made her awkward, attention-grabbing entrance, hobbling in on her angled aluminum crutches. She wore chinos and sneakers and a short-sleeved pink shirt. When the hostess offered to assist, Beverly shook it off and made her way with visible effort toward the remaining empty chair. She scanned our group and seemed undone. Then she nixed my own effort to help, chirped, "I'm fine!" and sat.

My introduction of Chris and Giselle to Beverly provoked stiff smiles and curt nods across the board. You could have chilled a martini in the atmosphere. That was okay by me. I wasn't there to make friends. "All right," I said, eyeing them around the horn and getting a variety of indignant, seductive, and pitiful looks in return. "Let's review how we all got here.

"Chris and Giselle claimed to have had a necklace stolen from the same restaurant on different evenings. You each had a picture of yourself wearing said item or items. And for the longest time I was struck by the coincidence. How could two dames manage to lose apparently identical necklaces in the same joint? It was almost inconceivable. And yet was it? Answer: No. It was damned conceivable. Because I conceived it." I paused. Perhaps someone snickered. Perhaps they didn't. In either case, I'm used to it. When no one snickers, it's business as usual. If they do, it always occurs when I'm about to deal the payoff pitch and proclaim, "Gin."

"The French bird at the Silver Dove said there was only one necklace. We know this because he said it in English. Then Beverly came along with a pic of a third bauble. The inconceivable, however conceivable, became the implausible. There could probably not be three necklaces. Which meant there probably weren't two, either." I allowed myself a knowing sneer. "Maybe if I waited long enough there wouldn't even be one. Yeah, maybe. Well, you can starve to death on maybe. So, quite frankly, nuts."

Chris Page began, "Mr. Ingalls, when I hired you—"

"Not yet, doll." I sat back. "Shall we add it up? Three women asserting three separate claims on a single necklace. How is it possible? It isn't. But I couldn't see that at first. No, I needed something extraordinary to happen to me to make me realize the truth."

Giselle leaned toward me with a devastating smile and purred, "It was extraordinary for me, too, darling."

I kept it deadpan. "No sale, lover. For once I'm not talking about impulsive sex in a swank uptown flat on a big leather sofa, while the maid plays through with the Electrolux and everybody feels sophisticated. I'm talking about a roomful of Ottos."

The bedroom smile evaporated like water off of something hot. "Otto? Otto who?"

For a second, that threw me. It never occurred to me that Otto might have a last name. And if he did, I knew I didn't know it. Solution: Bluff. "There's only one Otto, sugar."

Beverly Klosterman fidgeted and looked sour. "Is this going to last much longer? Because I'm in pain practically all the time."

"Who isn't?" I leered. "It's the human condition, lady. But we're not here to discuss the human condition. We're here to discuss the puppet condition. Case in point: Otto. Beloved puppet star of *Abracadabra Avenue*. Yeah, I know: Aren't there other beloved characters on that show besides him? Don't kid yourself. In my opinion it's practically Otto World at this point."

"We wouldn't know," Chris Page said. "We don't have children."

"Take my word for it," I said. Only later would I realize the implications of her comment, but by then it would be later, and it wouldn't matter. "Now, like you ladies, I always thought there was just one Otto. A single character, a single puppet, a single Otto self. But it's not true about people, so why should it be true about puppets? And take it from me, it's not. I've been there. I've seen the place where they make the Ottos."

"You mean Detroit? Are you saying you've seen where they make *autos*?" Beverly Klosterman looked perturbed. "But that doesn't make sense either—"

"Want the punch line? Take notes: The idea of the single Otto is a *lie*. You say to me, 'Pete,' or 'Mr. Ingalls,' or 'Darling,' 'we only see *one* on TV! It's always the same one. The same beloved Otto.' But it's an illusion—a pretty, lovely illusion. Behind the apparent one Otto there are twenty or thirty." I paused. It seemed called for. Then I continued. "And it's the same with you gals. Except the other way around."

Chris Page turned to the other women. "Does anybody know what he's talking about?"

"Yeah," I said. "Someone does. A guy named Ingalls, who for a long time believed in the apparent coincidence of your three stories, who believed in the multiplicity of you dames and your pics and your ice. Then the shock of seeing a thousand identical puppets made me wise. Behind the one was the many. So flip it with you gals, and the veil falls. Behind the many is the one. Behind your supposed multiple stories is, in fact, a single story. You're not similar strangers. Your cases aren't strangely similar. You know each other. And you're in collusion on some bizarre scheme that smells very, very suspect."

I sat back—or rather, I tried to sit back. But I had already sat back, so I had nowhere to go. That was jake with yours truly. I wasn't going anywhere. Instead, I reached into my jacket and produced the slim, light blue Tiffany's box, and held it out. "All three of you," I said, "are collaborators in a criminal conspiracy. One of you, or all of you, stole the necklace from its rightful owner. One of you, or all of you, lost it at the restaurant. Now you're each trying to con me into giving it to you, so whoever gets it can double-cross the other two and make off with the swag. It was clever, in its calculated way. But the party's over. I'm taking the booty to the buttons and I'm ready to sing."

"No, you're not," Chris Page said. Her handsome, carefully made-up face looked stern. "You're giving it to me. I paid you a retainer. We have a professional relationship."

"Which means nothing," Giselle Blanchard breathed, "compared to the relationship *we* have." She reached out and took my hands. Hers were smooth and warm. "After what we had together . . . ? How can you give it to anyone but me?"

"I would have paid you, but you didn't ask for anything," Beverly Klosterman whined. "And it's not my fault I'm disabled. Can't you see I need it more than these other two?"

Then Chris smirked and said, "Jesus, Bev."

Giselle said, "Really."

"Look." Beverly sulked. "I'm doing what I can."

From a jacket pocket I produced a check I'd written that morning and flipped it across the table to Chris Page. "Your retainer, Ms. Page. Returned in full. Our 'professional relationship' is null and void." I turned toward Giselle Blanchard and spoke with effort. It's hard to turn down a beautiful woman—even if you've already had sex with her. "We're through, angel. Sexual intercourse or no sexual intercourse."

Beverly Klosterman looked sharply at Giselle, eyes narrowed, and said, "What?"

"Nothing," Giselle said. She summoned her resources of dignity and pulled herself up and looked theatrically unperturbed. "He misspoke."

I looked hard at Klosterman and said, "As for you—"

But she wasn't even listening. Still staring at Giselle, she leaped to her feet and forced her chair back. "I don't believe it!" She took two steps away from the table, without the crutches, and turned back to spread her arms wide in protest. "You cheated!"

"So you admit that you three know each other." I felt a quiet satisfaction, the kind no one can hear. "Aces." I was emboldened to speculate: "And just how did this little jewel-thief ring get started?"

Giselle said, "It's not cheating. We said sex."

"We said a blow job!" Beverly said. She shook her head in disgust and flung herself back into her chair. She turned to Chris and said, "She always does this. We follow the rules, and she does whatever she wants. I have to stagger around the city all day, and Gigi *fucks* the guy!"

Chris turned to Giselle and looked mildly chiding. "We did say a blow job, Gigi."

Giselle waved it off. "Fine. I thought we said sex."

"And Daddy always let her get away with it," Klosterman continued. "We get in trouble, and lovely Giselle gets to do whatever she wants."

"Bev, it doesn't matter." Giselle spoke sharply. "The whole thing is off. We'll try it again next week."

"Fine. And you can be the cripple. I hate it and I suck at it. I'm either going to be the client or the fuck."

"Just who are you gals?" I mused. "A trio of high-priced call girls chatting at the water cooler? Three out-of-work actresses frustrated and broke, trying to make it on the Great White Way? A chance encounter in line at the unemployment office?"

"Jesus Christ, isn't it obvious?" Chris Page sighed. "We're sisters."

"I'll say." I savored a knowing world-weariness. "Sisters in crime. Sisters under the skin. Sisters in the exploitation of some poor dame whose necklace got heisted—and of a jerk named Ingalls, who almost fell for it."

"No, you moron," Beverly said. "She means we have the same parents."

I pulled up short. "The same parents as who?"

"As each other! Jesus!"

Chris Page, speaking to me as though I were an addled schoolboy, explained, "The necklace is ours. Our grandmother left it to all three of us, to share. So we play a game every now and then. We hire someone to retrieve it and we see who he gives it to."

"The idea is," Beverly said, "what's the most powerful obligation—money, sex, or pity?"

"Just pick one of us," Giselle said. All the warm honey was gone from her voice. It was business as usual and nothing personal. "Who wins?"

I was still holding the Tiffany's box. Now all four of us looked at it as though it were an award to be bestowed or a dowsing rod for detecting virtue. For a dizzying moment I tried to weigh the merits. Did I give it to the dame who'd hired me in good faith and paid me money? To the one with whom I'd been intimate? Or the one who, through no fault of her own, suffered a deficit every waking hour and who arguably deserved some extra consideration? The conflicting claims tugged at different centers of my being. The professional, the male, and the humanitarian inside me threatened to get at one another's throats. A part of me said, *They're all bogus, peeper,* but I don't know that I was listening.

Then a figure appeared at the entrance, spotted me, and ran up. "Pete! Come on! I have a cab."

Stephanie was distinctly hot and bothered about something, jumpy and agitated in her black jeans, with the sleeves rolled up on her raspberry sweatshirt.

"They're sisters," I said, indicating my three clients. "It's a game. One necklace, three clients. Who wins?"

"Huh? Yeah. Sure. Great." She barely glanced at the others. She was jumped-up and distracted. "But seriously, man, there's no time. We gotta hustle." She stood over me making hurry-up gestures.

I rose slowly. "And why is that?"

"Because I know who killed Marc Cohen. But I have to do a few more things until I'm sure, and I need your help." Then her mind caught up with the rest of her and she stopped, frowned, squinted in bafflement, and looked at the women. "Wait a minute. They're sisters?" She scanned the trio. She looked away. She shook her head, more in sadness than in happiness. Then she snatched the Tiffany's box from me and said, "Like we need this?" and flipped it onto the table. She spied the check in front of Chris Page, grabbed it, and hauled me away.

Our first stop was, for some reason, a Blockbuster on Second Avenue, downtown. "This is it," Stephanie said. "Wait here." She leaped out while I meditated, not for the first time, on the impulsive nature of this thing we call woman.

"How's that strike you, chief?" I asked the cabbie. He was a big, grave black man whose gaze met mine in the rearview mirror and betrayed nothing. "We're on the trail of a killer, and that gal has to stop to rent a movie."

"You live near here?"

"Nah. Neither does she. But she's an actress. They have whims."

"That's not what she told me."

"And what did she tell you?"

"She said we're gonna go pick up her boss, then stop at this Blockbuster, and then go all the way across to the West Side. Wasn't no whim a-tall." He paused and squinted. "You the boss?"

"The same."

He shook his head and laughed and said, "Then I just don't know!"

And I left it at that. Because after what I'd just been through with the three loony sisters, I didn't know either. And we sat there, two men in a cab in the big city, content to not know.

We knew even less when Stephanie came out empty-handed.

The cabbie wasn't kidding when he mentioned far across on the West Side. Our next stop was the Twelfth Avenue offices of DD Productions. Stephanie asked the hack to stand by. I noticed that the meter was running. It always is.

Things looked placid in the loft office, but three steps inside and you could feel the tension. Natalie Steinberg, marching past the entrance, took one look at us and said, "Figures you two would show up." When Stephanie asked her why, she merely said, "Your pal is in the conference room."

We approached it warily, neither of us with any clear idea of who constituted our "pal" at this point. I half wondered if it meant Norman Tibbler, who'd come to earth here, at the scene of the crime, after scramming from Bob Borger's place. Across the space, we could see a cluster of the puppeteers—Susan Bollinger, Stephen O'Neil, Maurice Carnes—gathered around Ellen Larraby's desk, in a confab with Charlotte.

Just then Shirley Takahashi came out of the kitchen and passed by with a steaming mug of tea. I said hello and pointed to the performers. "What's the occasion?"

"Charlotte called us in for a meeting." She rolled her eyes in agony. "We're here all day."

She bounced as we reached the conference room door. I gave a polite knock, and we opened up and peered in.

"Oh, fucking great," a voice said with a snort. "Look who's come to call. Sam Spade and Nancy Drew." We went in, and there he was: Detective Hank Thoreau in a cheap gray suit, his untidy bulk distributed over an upholstered executive chair across the table from a nervous-looking young woman I didn't recognize. "Steph, if you've come to ask for a date, I'll have to check my Palm Pilot." He snickered and looked off into the distance. "There's a joke in there somewhere. Something about a Palm Pilot and a hand job. Ingalls, find it for me, will you?"

Before I could reply Stephanie said to the gal he was interviewing, "Has he beaten you with the rubber hose yet? Because he's not allowed to, and you can press charges."

The young woman turned white as Thoreau leered. "I save all my hose work for you, baby. You know that."

"Is that what you call it?" she said. "That pipe cleaner?"

Thoreau found this hilarious and flopped his loose, heavy arms once or twice on the table as he laughed. "You're a treasure, Miss Stephanie." He sighed. "At least a pipe cleaner's stiff. You could have said inchworm."

"Inch? You wish!"

This set him off for another half minute of chortling and writhing. Finally he pulled himself together and sent a sharp look in my direction. "Ingalls, I can't wait to hear why you've come. So I can get rid of you and get on with my job. I've just been chatting with Miss Leslie Walters here about murder and blackmail and all that good stuff."

"We have a deal for you, Thoreau," Stephanie said.

The big man mugged 'I'm impressed,' which made the acreage of his pale white face seem to grow even more extensive. He turned to Leslie Walters and asked, with surprising delicacy, "Would you mind stepping outside for two minutes? Take a break, have a drink. Thanks." She couldn't scramble out fast enough.

Once the door was shut, paradoxically, things took a less intimate turn. Thoreau sat up straighter and the playfulness evaporated. "I'm not happy, kids, so this had better contribute to the quality of my lifestyle. The worker bees don't know anything, and I suspect Mr. Donnie Dansicker and Miss Charlotte Purdy of willful concealment of shit." He directed his bleary, wet gaze at me. "So what's up?"

Stephanie stepped toward him. "Did you know that Marc Cohen had a cell phone?"

Thoreau went deadpan. "Of course. But we haven't found the instrument. We assume the killer took it."

"Wouldn't you like to get your hands on it?"

Languidly he waved that away. "We have the LUDs. We know who he called and who called him."

"But you don't know who's on his speed dial. His known associates? Is that what you call them?"

For the first time Thoreau looked sincerely amused. "Yeah. That's what we call them."

"What if I could tell you where the phone is?"

"What if I arrested you for obstruction?"

"Fine." She turned to me. "That's it. Let's go, Pete."

Stephanie pivoted and had her hand on the doorknob when Thoreau bellowed, "Wait!" She paused. He sat back in his chair with a squeal and slapped his hands onto his belly. "Miss Stephanie, you and I have our banter, and our badinage, and our roguish flirtation, and it's all jolly good fun . . . but if you've got something pertinent to this investigation, you are required by law to hand it the fuck over, precious."

"In return for one little thing." I watched Stephanie as she paused and tilted her nicely shaped chin up half an inch in defiance. It might have been sincere, or it might have been acting, but it looked real to me, and I bought the whole presentation. Maybe you had to be a gal in your twenties, a showbiz rookie on the make, to behave as though you had nothing to lose. "Give us five minutes in Cohen's loft. We won't take anything and we won't touch anything."

"Then why?"

"We just want to see something."

He nodded. "I've got something you can see right here, right now."

"Yes or no?"

He thought about it like a man considering his bet on a big pot. Finally he said, "And this will result in the phone ending up in my possession?"

"Absolutely."

He turned aside and reached for a phone, punched some buttons, and sighed. Then he said, "Palma. Thoreau. I'm sending two consultants down. Give them five minutes at the scene, and they keep their hands to themselves. Guy named Ingalls and his assistant. Right." Then he hung up and said, "So?"

Stephanie reached into her purse and pulled out the FedEx envelope my notice of dismissal had arrived in. It was unsealed and held a small boxy object. "No charges?"

He scowled. The white face flushed hot pink. "Goddamn it. I should put your pretty little ass in jail."

He reached for the envelope. She pulled it back. He got up and reached out a long right arm and grabbed the package, then peered inside it. He dumped the contents out into his hand: It was a deck of cards.

"No charges," Stephanie said. "Unless you really don't want the phone."

He nodded curtly. "Deal."

She pulled a white business envelope out of her purse and handed it over. It bulged with what was obviously a cell phone. He took it, opened it, peered inside. "Is it too much to hope that you haven't touched this?"

"It is too much. We have."

He shrugged. "Five minutes. And keep in touch." He crossed to the door, opened it, and said, "Miss Walters? We're almost done."

Palma, Thoreau's man at Cohen's loft, was the opposite of happy to see us. He was a lean, edgy Joe in his thirties, in a tired houndstooth sport coat over brown corduroy pants, and it looked as though his job was to house-sit this big, vacant space where someone had been killed.

"You Ingalls?" he muttered. I nodded and he waved us in under the tape. "Ya got five minutes. Don't touch anything."

Forensics had come and gone. The body, the chairs, the Emmy, and all the other paraphernalia associated with the killing had, of course, been carted off to the lab. A path from the door to where the body had been found (by us, I had to remind myself) had been marked off in masking tape on the floor. The room was especially empty and glaring in the afternoon light. On our left was the kitchen area, apparently undisturbed. On our right was the wall of puppets in their S-and-M costumes.

In the cab I had asked Stephanie what it was we were looking for, but she just kept saying, "I'll tell you if I see it," and staring out the window. Naturally I had asked who she thought the killer was, and she had also gone mum about that. I was along for the ride and not especially enjoying it.

Stephanie wasted no time, but walked brazenly over to the puppets along the wall. "How come this stuff is still here?" she asked.

Palma said, "We dusted it. All it had was what's-his-name's prints. Cohen. And a lot of junk. So we left it there."

She nodded, then began a methodical scan of the puppets, eyeballing them one by one. "If you tell me what you're looking for I can help," I said.

"That's okay," she breathed, scrutinizing the dolls. "I'm almost done."

Palma said, "Thoreau said you're consultants?"

"Private talent," I said.

"Oh, yeah?" He looked several watts more alive and interested. "I been thinking about going private. You take the licensing exam?"

"Not yet."

He started and looked confused. "You working without a license? Can you do that?"

"That's it!" Stephanie chirped. Something was making her ecstatic. "We're done!"

I threw at Palma, "I'll get back to you about that," and shifted my attention to my associate. "Did you see what you were looking for?"

"Nope! Which is just what I was looking for. We're outta here!" She turned to the cop, piped, "Thanks!" and led me out.

I had just a half second before getting back into the cab to notice that the lad who'd been tailing me was still on the job.

SIXTEEN

I was in my office, pondering the infinite corruptibility of man, when the visitor arrived. I heard his baritone grunt and Stephanie's practiced, "Mr. Ingalls is expecting you. He has something you two discussed." Hard-shoe footsteps approached; the door opened.

It was the guy who'd been tailing me, the one who worked me over and who was under the tragically mistaken impression that I was sitting on a million clams, of which he hoped to be a partial recipient. "Feature I been chasing you all day, Ingalls," he sneered. He came in and shuffled up to the desk. He jerked his head toward the outer office. "The gash says you got a present for me."

I opened one of my desk drawers. "So I do," I said, searching around for something. "Give me a second."

He pulled a piece from his inner pocket. "Easy, friend. You draw iron, I might get antsy."

I pulled out a big, closed clasp envelope stuffed with take-out menus and let him see the general bulk of it. "I don't like the word *gash,* soldier," I said. "I suggest you choose a different term when referring to women."

He smirked, his eyes on the envelope. "Oh, yeh? Who's gonna make me?"

From behind him a voice said, "The gash," and then Stephanie fungoed him with a Louisville Slugger and the mug collapsed like a circus tent on takedown day.

I took custody of the heater while Stephanie went through his pockets. In the wallet were a driver's license, a couple of credit cards, cash, and the usual personal documents and receipts, but what was of special interest was a little deck of business cards. Stephanie pulled one out and read it. " 'John Panker. Senior Field Investigator. The Basilisk Insurance Company. Insurers and Reinsurers to the Media Industry.' " She looked at me. "Which means what?"

"Which means he's on the trail of the money that Donnie and Charlotte ponied up for the extortion." I peered at his head, wondering if I'd see a bruise or a lump and wondering if I was entitled to hope so. "Their company must carry blackmail insurance. The carrier sent this gent to make sure the claim was kosher."

"Blackmail insurance? Wait a minute." She looked at me. "I thought you told me Donnie said the money in the bag was from their 'Wall Street friends.' "

"He did. It was an advance against the insurance."

"And this guy thinks you stole it?"

I looked somewhat rueful. A private investigator has no business looking entirely rueful. "Kid, I'm as offended by his insinuations as you are."

"I'm just trying to figure this out." She looked away and talked to herself. "So, let's say he's right. You take the million advance from Donnie and keep it. Then this jerk tells Basilisk the claim is legit, and they should pay it to DD Productions. Which they do. What do Donnie and Charlotte do? They know the advance million is gone. So either they pay the Basilisk million to the blackmailer, if it's not too late, or they pay it back to the Wall Street friends. But they can't do both."

"Right," I said. "In which case either the Wall Street friends don't get their advance back, or the blackmailer doesn't get paid off and does bad things with the naughty pictures. Then Mr. Basilisk says, 'What gives? I thought we paid a million clams to prevent that.'"

"Either way somebody gets screwed, Pete."

"There oughta be a law," I observed.

Then we heard a new voice from the outer office, a man's deep-chested basso calling, "Hey, there. You open? Anybody here?"

He was big, one of those behemoths who played football in college and then stayed big even after his gridiron career had ended. His tall, wide body and tree-trunk neck made his head, with its neat, compact black hair, look comically too small. But no one was laughing. He stood at parade rest in a dark blue suit and a white shirt and red tie. He offered a clean-shaven, cheery smile and flashed some excellent teeth. "Hope you don't mind the shouting," he said. "I wasn't sure if they sent me to the right place."

Stephanie became poised and formal. "If who did?"

"The folks at DD Productions. I just got into town and called them to discuss the *Playground Pals* case, and they referred me to you all." He pulled a business card from his breast pocket. He was a pro and knew all the tricks; the card had been pre-placed there for convenient presentation. "Harmon Kirkeby, Greensward Indemnity."

I introduced myself and my associate. Then I took his card and gave him one of mine. And yeah, it felt like Valentine's Day in third grade. Sue me. In my profession you get what little pleasure you can, from wherever you can get it.

Stephanie took his card from me and frowned at it. "Greensward?" She hesitated. "Not, uh, Basilisk?"

"No, no. Different company. Why do you ask?"

She smiled brightly. "No reason." The grin froze on her face and her eyes lost focus. Let's say she was absorbed in thought. Let's further say that that's fine, in its place, but this was not its place, with a potential client standing front and center and the clock, the professionalism clock, ticking. It was up to the boss to bail her out.

"Have a seat, Mr. Kirkeby." I gestured him into the guest chair. "How can we help you?"

The big man perched on the chair as though half expecting it to collapse under him. Maybe many chairs had. Maybe he'd ended up sitting on the floor amid splinters and cushions more times than he could remember. Something like that would change a man. "Well," he said, "we carry a policy on KLAE. The Philadelphia public TV station? They're coproducers of *Playground Pals,* with DD Productions? And . . . well, it seems—"

"Oh, my God," Stephanie said, rejoining us as though from out of a trance. "Are you here about the blackmail of DD Productions?"

The big man nodded. "You got it! And that gal at DD thought that talking to you folks would be a good place to start."

Stephanie squinted. "Really? Who? Charlotte Purdy?"

"Uh, no. I've still got an appointment to talk to Ms. Purdy. No, this was a good-looking young lady, a Natalie something."

"What? Natalie Steinberg?"

"That's her. She said talk to Pete Ingalls, and here I am."

I looked at Stephanie. "Aren't things supposed to be making *more* sense? Are you following this?"

"It does make sense." She looked at Kirkeby. "Then who's Basilisk?"

"Like I said—whole 'nother company, whole different set of policies."

Stephanie's alluring green eyes went wide, and she said, somewhat rudely, "Shit!" She grabbed a pad of yellow Post-its and a marker and started writing. She tore the slip off and handed it to our visitor. "Mr. Kirkeby, the person you should talk to is Detective Clara Sandoval, with the Major Case squad, Special Investigations Division. She's dealing with the blackmail. Here's her number."

"Well, hey, thank you very much—"

"Be that as it may, Ms. Constantino," I said, "I'm sure Mr. Kirkeby has some questions for me, and I might add that I have a few for him."

"Uh, Pete? No can do. We've got that thingie about the thing happening soon."

Kirkeby winked at me. I didn't know men did that anymore, either to women or to other men, but apparently the world was full of things I didn't know. "Sounds important."

"It is," Stephanie said—to me, not to him. "It's very important. Which is why I'm afraid I'll have to ask you to excuse us, Mr. Kirkeby. Mr. Ingalls has a meeting in about ten minutes and we have to prepare."

If Kirkeby wasn't crazy about being handed his hat, you couldn't tell. The big man took the hit and kept on swinging. He stood, said, "Then I'll get out of your way. And many thanks," shook our hands, and left.

The moment he'd gone Stephanie went grim and thoughtful and began marching up and down the office, staring at the floor and pumping a fist and muttering, "Shit . . . that means . . . okay . . . and that means . . . fuck!" I didn't even try to reach her. Instead I went back into my office, stepped deftly over the unconscious man on the floor, and shuffled through the papers on my desk in search of my notes about the upcoming interview.

At first I felt a bolt of panic: There were no notes on any impending meeting of any kind. I returned to the outer office, and was halfway through saying, "All right, doll, put me down as I give up. What meeting, with whom, and why?" when I saw that she was on the phone, agitated and concentrating and waving me away like a lifeguard patrolling a riptide. "Yes, that's right," she said into the phone. "Crucial evidence." I retreated.

I would have to wing it, improvise and take my lead from whomever was about to show up, and try to get by on smarts, moxie, and hustle. I thought: *All right, Ingalls. You've been around the block and you've been to the prom and you've danced with the pretty girls in the moonlight.* Then I had to pause and ask myself just what the hell that meant, because in fact I had never been to the prom, either with pretty girls or anyone else, and I had never danced in the moonlight under any circumstances.

It made me wonder just exactly what was going in my mind, in that special space where the thoughts happened and the different voices all talked to themselves and one another. When you find yourself thinking things you know aren't true, you have to ask, Who's doing what upstairs? Who's in charge and who's just punching a time clock? Who's the thinker and who's just the chump minding the store and maintaining the venue? Who's the master and who's the puppet?

I didn't like wondering these things. I didn't like asking these questions. Mysteries don't belong in your head. There's a place where mysteries belong, a very large place that can accommodate them easily. That place is the rest of the world, anywhere and everywhere except the eighty cubic inches behind your personal, private eyes. But I had one here, right between the ears, and it was getting to me. I was thinking things I knew weren't true, and I didn't know why. Something was wrong.

I glanced at the unconscious man on my office floor. Panker looked somewhere between restful and dead. He was still breathing. But he was closed until further notice and didn't appear to be reopening anytime soon. I let him lie there.

"Okay . . ."

Stephanie had come in, and she looked wound up and jittery. She forced a tight smile and sat in the visitor's chair, but she couldn't sit still. "I just talked to Charlotte at the office. I just . . ." She nodded grimly to herself. "I think I just played a really big card, Pete."

"Is that so?"

"Yeah. I just told Charlotte that we knew who killed Marc Cohen, and who has the money. I told her we have crucial evidence for it." She rubbed her hands together. "Jeez, I'm all freaked out." She looked at me. "I think whoever killed Cohen will be showing up here pretty soon." She glanced at Panker, inert on the floor. "Christ, I forgot all about him."

I sat back, conspicuously at ease. "Care to divulge who it is, doll?"

She hesitated, then made a tight face of frustration and shook her head. "I don't want to say anything until I see if I'm right." Meekly, or fake meekly, she added, "Do you mind?"

I got up. "Not at all. Anything to help." I walked out.

"Hey!" She followed.

In the outer office I made it my business to go to the kitchenette and pour a mug of java without looking as though I was making it my business to do so. She came up fast and gave me a searching look. "Are you okay?"

"I'm happy as a cow in clover, angel. What do we do now?"

"Well . . . I dunno. I guess we wait."

"How long?"

"I don't know!"

"Fine." I walked over to the visitor's chair and sat. Something was digging into my side. I reached into my jacket pocket and pulled out Panker's gun and set it on the desk. Then I sat back and cooled my coffee.

Stephanie made up her mind about something, marched to her desk chair, and sat. Then she turned to me with a sharp look of inquiry. "Okay, Pete. What's going on?"

"We're waiting," I said. "Unless you want to deign to tell me who the killer is and how you happen to know it. Otherwise, get out the cards and the crossword puzzles."

She shook her head. "Not yet. First of all, I want to see if I'm right. And then I'm going to have to tell you, and Thoreau, and Donnie and Charlotte. . . . I just don't want to talk about it yet, okay?"

I shrugged. "You're the boss."

"What? What's that supposed to mean?"

"You're driving the bus. I'll sit here and stay behind the yellow line."

"Get out! I made some suggestions."

"Not this time, kid. You took over the case, and you tied it up with a ribbon. More power to you, I say."

"Pete, come on. We're a team! I didn't do all of this. It's not even over yet."

"No, you didn't do all of it." Somewhere in my head, one part of me saw and listened to another part of me start reciting this litany. Another part of me wasn't crazy about it, but there must have been other parts of me that didn't mind it, or that actually approved. Because at no time did any part of me take any steps to stop the part of me that went on to say, "I did a lot, too. Of course, I did what you told me to do. I went here, I went there. And I reported back with the facts."

She looked confused. "Well . . . isn't that how it works? We both find out stuff and put it together?"

"I find out. You put it together." If I had many selves, then I had one that had a few things to say, things I wouldn't normally give voice to, because it's not what a professional does, and it's not what a man does. Does that mean that in this instance I was behaving like an amateur woman? So be it, I thought. "You want to know the truth, angel, I don't like your giving orders to me. In front of Kirkeby or anybody else."

She laughed, or tried to. "You've got to be kidding! I don't give you orders. We're conducting an investigation!"

"Your investigation. Which you put together. You're the one who says we go to Cohen's loft. You're the one who makes a deal with Thoreau. You're the one who kicks out Kirkeby with some fairy tale about an interview. You're the big expert and I'm the poor chump who runs errands and tries to keep up."

Her look of confusion dissolved into a slack-faced expression of dawning outrage. It gave her color. She looked good. She picked up a white ballpoint pen and started tapping it hard on the desk. "I'm the 'big expert'? What—and that's wrong? Like I'm not allowed to know anything? I'm not allowed to have opinions? I'm not allowed to have ideas? I'm not allowed to figure things out on my own?"

"I—"

"You have no right to say that. You have no right to tell me what I can and can't do."

"I have no right?" It felt like I was piloting a sailboat in a storm. Everything she said hit like a gust or a swell. Everything I said served to channel it or ride through it. "Oh, so now I'm the bad guy? I do everything you want to do, I go along with all your ideas and theories, and I'm the bad guy? Where do you get the crust, angel? Where do you come off saying *I'm* bad? Just because I don't want to be pushed around by you?"

Her eyes flashed. She slammed the pen down on the desk. "Pushed around. Unbelievable. Because I traded something with Thoreau? Because I said, 'Let's check out Cohen's loft'? So if I say anything, it's pushing you around?" She looked away and spoke to the jury. "Great. Just fucking, fucking great."

I loosened my tie. It was supposed to make me feel more comfortable but it didn't. "And with the gutter mouth. Like that helps."

"Oh, fuck you, man!"

"And now I suppose you're going to quit. Like you always do. As soon as I try to stand up for something, for something you don't like"—a part of me couldn't follow exactly what was meant by the part of me that was saying this, but most of the parts of me agreed that we had momentum and should take advantage of it—"as soon as I try to draw a line, and I'm *here* and you're *there* . . . you quit. If you can't control me, you quit."

"What?!"

"But not this time, sugar. Because guess what? You're not leaving me. I'm leaving you!"

"Pete—what are you talking about?"

"I'm talking about breaking away. I'm talking about being my own person. You can have the agency, the office, the whole thing."

"Are you . . . drunk? Am I missing something?"

"I've never been more sober in my life. I'm going to go do something else. I have many selves, right? So I'll listen to one that *isn't* a private eye. You stay and solve the cases. I quit!"

She stood up with a lurch that sent her chair crashing into the rear wall. If my heart was pounding like a pile driver, she looked calm, focused, and in control. But then, she was a performer, and used to making public displays of emotion. "You can't quit! This is your thing. It isn't my thing. I'm not a detective—I'm an actress. Plus, you're out of your fucking mind, and I am totally out of here. Because I quit!"

She grabbed her bag and stomped to the door, flung it open, and slammed it behind her. I sat there and waited for my heart to slow down. I tried to take some kind of internal survey as to how the various parts of me felt about all this, but nothing registered except agitation, the hyped-up arousal of adrenaline, and a vague sense that I had both won and lost.

I don't know how long I sat there, cooling down. It felt like an hour but was probably ten minutes. Was that how time worked? It varied according to your emotional state? Because I had definitely just visited an emotional state, yeah, and I'd taken the deluxe tour, from the capital to the getaway spots. And it was interesting, because I couldn't remember having ever been there before.

I went into my office in the rear. My mind must still have been on my emotions, because I forgot about the special visitor I had back there and stumbled over Panker's body. For a moment I had a vicious impulse to swing a foot at him while he was still un-conscious. But something in me suggested that doing that would come uncomfortably close to kicking a man while he was down. I stifled the urge. Instead I opened the bottom desk drawer and pulled out the office bottle and a paper cup. I poured a couple of fingers of Chivas. Where normally I would sip and savor it, this time I knocked back a greedy gulp and waited for it to burn. It burned.

That was when I heard a sound in the front office. Even in my agitated state I knew it wasn't Stephanie. I had a sudden chilling sense of who it might be just as a voice, shaky and querulous, said, "Hello?" I went out.

It was Stephen O'Neil. He looked bad. He was in a blue checked shirt and jeans—the same clothes I had dimly seen him wearing back at the DD offices in his meeting with Charlotte, what now seemed like weeks ago but was actually maybe three hours before. The shirttail was partially out, the jeans looked somehow defeated and tired. And his face, pitted with acne scars on the best of occasions, looked especially white and ravaged and traumatized. O'Neil was a man haunted by fear and desperate to act on it.

When he saw me he flinched. He forced himself not to turn or leave. But when he said nothing I had to open the bidding. "O'Neil. You look lousy."

"I've been better." He forced a weak smile. "You, uh . . . Are you alone? Here? By yourself?"

"Does it matter?"

"No. No. Nothing matters." His gaze flickered around the office as though looking for my hidden cohorts. It skidded across Stephanie's desk, seemed to stumble over something, and went on. He licked his lips.

"I think we both know why you're here, Steve," I said. And then it hit me. After a lifetime of saying, "I'm with Steve," suddenly I literally was with an actual Steve. Ironic? Not at all. The reason the I'm-with-Steve gag works is because, in fact, the globe is crawling with millions of Steves. Sooner or later you're bound to collide with one.

O'Neil's eyes grew shifty. They kept returning to the desk. "Why am I here?"

"You're here to try to get the evidence I've got that proves you killed Marc Cohen. Am I right?"

He had to think for a few seconds, gazing off into the distance and at anything but me. Finally he came up with his answer. "No. Why would I do that?"

"Why would you come for the evidence?" I laughed. "To get rid of it, slick."

"No, I mean, why would I kill Marc? I don't kill people. So what proof would you have that I did?"

"Oh, there's proof, son. Believe me, there's proof. What I call crucial evidence." I added, "And certain theories."

Now he made eye contact. The nervous drifting was over and he spoke with a sudden sharpness. "Like what?"

I gestured in a general way. "Let's start with a theory . . . let's call this one theory A. Because there may be several."

"What do you mean, 'may be'? Are there several or is there only one?"

"There are several, Stephen. So we'll call this first one theory one." I stopped and looked solicitous. "Will that be all right? Do you prefer theory A?"

"I don't care. Just tell me what it is."

"Fine. Theory A goes something like this. Once upon a time there was a guy. And he knew another guy. And he didn't like this other guy, because the guy was an obnoxious jerk who nobody liked. And so one day the first guy paid a visit to the second guy, and he killed him with the second guy's award from the Academy of Motion Picture Televisual Arts and Crafts. And it was all terribly tragic and illegal. And ironic."

I paused. Actually I stopped. It felt inadequate. And I wasn't the only one who thought so, because O'Neil looked at me as if I were an idiot and said, "That's not a theory. That's just a stupid description of something. Of something that didn't happen, by the way."

"Sure, kid," I said with more confidence than I actually felt. "I'm not crazy about that one myself. So let's move to theory B. In theory B, Marc Cohen won an Emmy for some show about frogs, and you didn't like it."

"Yeah? And?"

"And so you killed him."

He almost laughed. "Are you out of your mind? I would kill someone because they won an Emmy? For a show about frogs?"

"Frogs, horses—what difference does it make?" I started improvising. I hoped that by shuffling the elements of the case, I'd get lucky and they'd all fall into place. "The point is, he won the Emmy. Not you. So let's add it up. The show about frogs wins the big prize. The show about horses can't get arrested. Cohen throws an ashtray at some gal and then marries the cool blonde— and yes, it's the same looker who goes to parties with an African-American from Africa, who just happens to be the most excellent guy in the world. And how does that make our Mark feel? Then Norman Tibbler copies the puppet porno. Bob Borger doesn't like Cohen. Klonky doesn't like Cohen. None of the dames at Gyroscope or anywhere else like Cohen either, but you? You're somehow 'out of town' with Jimmy Farlow. Cohen shoots me with an elephant gun. Somebody steals my chuck roast, and what do I got in return? Some insurance dick tries to shake me down. Meanwhile, Cohen spites the show and puts the porno on the Web. And so it all gets to be too much. You decide a plague on both your houses. You decide a stitch in time saves nine. You decide if you want something done right, do it yourself. And so you do. You visit Cohen, pick up the Emmy, and hand our boy a one-way ticket on the big boat to bye-bye."

He looked pained and somehow resentful. "That's insane. It makes no sense." His expression shifted; his face got a little smoother with relief. "You don't have any theories. You don't have any proof, either. You're just standing here making stuff up."

"It doesn't matter what I have," I said. "What matters is what the cops have."

"Well? What do they have?"

I reached for the phone. "Let's find out, shall we?"

At that he lunged forward and grabbed something off the desk and pointed it at me. "Stop." I had maybe a half second to find that rather amusing, and to ask myself, if only rhetorically, What could possibly be on Stephanie's desk that could enable him to force me to halt? How threatening, in real terms, could a stapler or a computer mouse actually be?

Then I saw he had seized John Panker's gun, and its business end was directed at my chest. I froze.

"Easy, kid," I said. "You were motivated to kill Cohen, and maybe he deserved it, and it must have been satisfying. This will be different."

"Who says I did kill him?"

"You killed him, Stephen."

For a second I thought that one of my selves had resigned from its job in whatever department it worked in and had gone into business for itself. Because I wasn't aware of having spoken that last sentence. Then O'Neil spun and we both looked in surprise at none other than Stephanie Constantino. She stood in the doorway; how long she had hidden there, listening through the cracked door while remaining unnoticeable to those of us in the room, I couldn't say. But I was glad to see her.

O'Neil wasn't. "Oh, yeah? What makes you so sure? Unless your theories are like his—"

"I like his theories," she said. "Even when they're wrong. But I'll tell you, Stephen. First put the gun down."

"Forget it."

"You can't shoot us both," she said. "If you shoot me, Pete'll jump you. If you shoot him, I'll run for the cops."

"Do you want to tell me? Or do you want me to line you both up together?"

That got her. She was silent for a second. "Okay, okay." She turned to me. "Ready, Pete? Here it comes."

I found myself hesitating. How wise was it to prove to a killer holding you at gunpoint that you had the goods on him? But I wanted to hear what she had to say. I wanted to make sure that she was right, so we could solve the case, and wrong, to justify my feelings of abuse. I gestured, *After you.* "You're on the air, kid."

SEVENTEEN

"We know you did it," Stephanie said to Stephen O'Neil, "because you have that naked Jimmy Farlow doll in your apartment."

You could watch the full range of human emotions march past on O'Neil's face, from confusion to mirth to fear. His final response came out as a croak. "So what?"

"Bob Borger told Pete that the *Playground Pals* dolls were the cheap kind, with their clothes sewn on. He said you couldn't take their clothes off without destroying them. And it's true. I bought one and tried it. So how did you happen to have a Jimmy doll with no clothes, that was still intact? You got it from the one guy sick enough to go to the trouble of hiring someone to take Jimmy's clothes off and repair the damage—so he could replace them with S-and-M gear. You killed Marc Cohen, then looked around, and saw the Jimmy doll, and you got so freaked out you grabbed it and took it with you. You threw away the leather and studs and kept the naked doll. It was like you rescued him from an evil captor. Which actually you sort of did."

I couldn't help myself. "Brilliant, sugar," I said. "There's your theory, O'Neil."

The puppeteer got feisty. "That's bullshit. That doll is mine. Not Marc's."

"It's his," my assistant said. "We looked. Pete and I went to his loft. Pete, remember when I said I thought that something was there that shouldn't be? Or something wasn't there that should? All the *Playground Pals* characters were there except for Jimmy. I just didn't quite see it. So that's what I was looking for when we went back. Jimmy was the only one missing."

O'Neil's face betrayed nothing—but that in itself was a betrayal loud and clear. What innocent man remains deadpan when the evidence seems to affirm his guilt?

Finally he calculated the odds and placed his bet. "Okay, I took the doll," he said. "He was a sick fuck and I made him give it to me. But that doesn't mean I killed him. I told that other guy—I was at the movies when Marc was killed."

"Yeah, at *The Big Sleep*," Stephanie said. "The only movie below Fourteenth Street that started before noon."

"Right! At that art house!"

"Except you never went. You rented it. I asked at Blockbuster. It took a lot of flirting. I practically had to agree to date the guy to get him to look up your account. Then he said, 'You know which one, right?' Which totally—"

"Hold the wire." I put up a hand. "What do you mean, which one?"

She rolled her eyes. "Which version of *The Big Sleep*. I didn't know, so he had a lot of fun telling me."

"There's only one. With Bogart as Marlowe. Your video guy has his wires crossed."

"There's two, Pete. The movie downtown is part of a Robert Mitchum festival."

I may have blinked once or twice. Sometimes it helps. "Robert Mitchum's in a version of *The Big Sleep?* What's it called?"

"It's called *The Big Sleep,* asshole," O'Neil sneered.

"Hey, shut up," Stephanie spat. "You rented that movie the day after Cohen was killed."

"I saw it! At the theater! I have a ticket stub!"

"Which you bought after the murder."

"Why would I rent that movie?"

"So you could quote it if anybody asked."

I spread my hands. "She's smarter than both of us, pal. Drop the piece and let's wrap this up."

O'Neil was making a determined effort to maintain his composure. Only his mouth betrayed anxiety. He kept licking and biting his lips. Finally he said, "But why would I kill Marc Cohen?"

"Look," Stephanie said, "you know I know. So why don't you—"

"Tell me!"

She held up both hands, palms out, to placate and assure. "Okay, fine. You killed Marc Cohen because he was going to screw you out of ownership of *Henry the Horse at Home.* You created it. Then you put both your names on it. Then, when they didn't buy it at Gyro, he told you that maybe that was it, and you'd run out of options. Because he didn't know if he was welcome at Ronson. Whereas in fact he had pitched it there under just his name and they wanted it. And at best you might be attached as 'talent.' Right?"

O'Neil muttered, "He was a complete shit."

"I'll say."

"And I knew it! Everybody knew it. But I needed his contacts. And he swore to me we'd be partners, once we wrecked *Playground Pals* and I got out of my contract with the Dansickers."

It was Stephanie's turn to look confused. "After you what?"

O'Neil looked just a bit coy and maybe a little pleased with himself. "The blackmail was never intended to raise money. It was like a blind. It was camouflage, so we could upload the outtakes and destroy the show, without anyone knowing who did it or why. That's—"

"That's why the deadline was so short!" Stephanie was thrilled. She hammered a fist against the door frame. "I'm so stupid!" She turned to me. "Pete? Do me a favor. Don't ever listen to me again. I'm just this dippy *actreese*. It's so fucking *obvious!"*

But with Stephanie's burst of energy, O'Neil went suddenly morose. It must have dawned on him that every smart move he bragged about brought him one step closer to getting nailed. "We figured the deadline would come and go and nothing would happen. We'd upload the footage, the show would collapse, and I'd be free to do *Henry."*

"Mind if I ask why?" I said. "Why destroy the show? You have what all puppeteers dream of, in my opinion. You're a star. You're making money, your character is famous—"

"It's so boring," he said.

I was surprised at the depths of misery that could be conveyed in those three words. But maybe I shouldn't have been. The lad was a puppeteer. He made his living conveying deep feeling in short sentences, for the enlightenment of children. "So unbelievably boring. Doing the same character ten hours a day, answering the same questions, saying the same 'Golly jumpers!' to one interviewer after another. Plus . . ." He shook his head. It occurred to me that he had long since lowered the gun. But we were all frozen in this ritual enactment of the explanation, and nobody moved. "Jimmy is so *dull*. As a character. It's not like doing Victorio, or Ramon—or even Bounce, for God's sake. Jimmy Farlow is just the most boring fucking kid in the world."

"Charlotte told you you could do outside work when you signed the exclusive," Stephanie said. "But then they had their lawyer send you that letter telling you to forget it."

He nodded. "So the show took off. But the merchandise wasn't selling. So CPB and KLAE and everybody decided to make Jimmy the star. And then they sent me on the road, and it never stopped."

"But come on!" Stephanie wasn't buying it. "Isn't this against AFTRA rules or something?"

"It's in my contract. I was fucked."

"Then why didn't you go to Charlotte?" Stephanie fumed. "You say, 'I'm burning out on this. Enough already with the personal appearances.'"

"I did. She said she was sorry, but there was too much riding on it. Then she gave me some speech about the fucked-up politics at CPB, and how our patrons at PBS are either retiring or got fired, and how if we dropped the ball even once they'd cancel the show. Meanwhile, they had an option on me for four more years. I had steady work and was making good money and I wanted to kill myself."

"So instead you killed the show." Stephanie sighed. "Wow."

"Norman Tibbler gave *you* the outtake footage," I said. "Still, color me skeptical. I make our boy Norman for a law-abiding citizen. Why'd he break the law and get into bed with you and Cohen?"

O'Neil shrugged. "As a favor. He didn't know what it was for.

In fact, it wasn't for anything, at first. I asked him for it as a souvenir of the season. And of course he did it to spite his boyfriend—"

"Whoa." I held up a hand. Call it the hand of disinterested accuracy. "You mean his girlfriend."

"Oh, come on."

I looked at Stephanie. "Norman had a boyfriend?"

"Of course!" O'Neil shouted. "Bob Borger. Everybody knows that. I mean, we all pretend we don't, but still. Anyway, every year Bob demanded that Norman not take part in producing the outtake reel. Because he disapproved of it in that lunatic 'pure puppetry' way of his. So when I asked Norman he said, 'Yeah, sure, just don't tell Bob.'"

"Which defeats the purpose of the spite," Stephanie said.

"But that's Norman. He'll rebel as long as it's in private. Anyway, Norman gave it to me, and one day I mentioned it to Marc, and he got all excited and got this evil gleam in his eye, and said, 'This is our secret weapon.' He hatched this wild scheme to use it to blackmail DD and get me free."

"But once Norman heard about the blackmail, he'd know it was his footage." I wanted to sit down, but it seemed rude. "Weren't you afraid he'd spill?"

"Marc was sure he wouldn't. Because he'd get in trouble with everybody—the cops, and Donnie and Charlotte—"

"And Bob Borger," Stephanie said. "Okay, so then you found out that Marc was only going to use you as talent. And not as creator or producer. He probably played you the whole time. He just agreed to partner with you to get his hands on *Henry.*" O'Neil just looked at her. She went on, "But you could have sued him. You could have dragged him in front of the Writers Guild or something. It happens all the time. You must have had proof and documentation—"

"It was worse than that."

The sudden quiet with which he said these last words took us both by surprise. My assistant and I both leaned a little closer to him, as though listening hard to a shy child. I said, "How?"

He hesitated. Then he said, "Marc sent the blackmail message Sunday night in an e-mail. On Monday Donnie and Charlotte sent me to Boston to do Jimmy stuff. I came back on Thursday night, and went to the office of this friend of mine, and asked him to upload the footage. He's good with the Net and he knows how to use false addresses and bogus servers and aliases. So he did. Then I went home and figured it had all gone according to plan."

"But they *had* found the money," I said. "Cohen found that out when Donnie took the phone calls for the payoff on Thursday night. So he tailed us until he saw Donnie leave it with me, then he followed me back to my place and put on the mask and took the cash."

"That's what I think, too," O'Neil said. "The next morning I called the office to ask how things were. And Natalie and everybody said, 'Guess what! Donnie and Charlotte got the money!' So then I went to Marc's loft. And I said, 'So, partner, did they come up with the cash?' And that fucking prick sat there and said, 'Somebody else got it.' "

Stephanie laughed. "I love it. Who? How?"

"Marc said he made Donnie go through the payoff routine. He saw Donnie give the money to Ingalls. He saw Ingalls go home. And then he said, 'I was going to break in and take it, but this guy was tailing Ingalls the same time I was. He put a mask on and went in and shot Ingalls and ran out with it.' "

"Jesus," Stephanie said. "And did little Markie have any theory as to who this mystery guy was?"

"Somebody who knew about the money and the payoff in the first place. Either someone from the office, or from the bank or insurance company or whatever.

"Then he told me he was too scared to go after the guy. He ran into Ingalls's place, saw that he was just unconscious and not dead, and ran off."

"Very thoughtful," I murmured.

Stephanie snorted. "Prick."

O'Neil continued, "And then Marc said, 'I don't think we're going to work together on *Henry*. The partnership—it doesn't work for me anymore.' I said, 'Fine. Then I'll take it and go somewhere else.' He said, 'I don't think so.' I said, 'It's mine, asshole,' and he said, 'Not really. I'm setting it up at Ronson under my name.'"

Stephanie gaped. "And he thought you would buy that?"

"What could I do? Turn him in? I was part of the blackmail. Even if I just tried to keep control of *Henry*, Marc would tell them about Norman and Norman would tell them about me. Was it worth going to jail over who owned a TV proposal?"

"It works both ways," I said. "Would it have been worth it for him?"

"Hey, yeah." Stephanie sounded surprised at my insight. I made a mental note to remind her, later, not to be. "So you had a standoff. He could send you up and you could send him. How did it end?"

O'Neil looked away. "Marc said, 'And by the way, they've got this development money, so we're working on a cool new thing. It's not even going to be with puppets anymore.'"

"Then what would they use? Real horses?" I wanted to laugh.

And I tried to laugh. But I didn't laugh, because it occurred to me that in the past there had been several television shows featuring real horses, and that by now advances in science and technology had probably made such animals even more real and more horselike than ever.

O'Neil looked grim. "No. With digitized puppets. Which aren't really puppets at all."

Stephanie's eyes went wide. "The motion-capture thing. The computer-enhanced puppets he showed us."

"Yeah." O'Neil looked heartsick. "He—"

"That was what he was going to use the money for! Once he got the ransom, the whole picture changed! It wasn't Ronson that was going to put up the money. It was the million dollars he had stolen from Pete."

"So he's sitting there"—Stephen O'Neil's voice took on a sharp, whiny tone of indignation—"in that smug, narcissistic way of his. And he starts talking about how crude and retarded puppets are, and how with this digital idea they'll be able to hold hands and square dance. And I couldn't believe it. You're taking the one thing puppets have over animation, and throwing it away!"

I said, "Which is . . . ?"

"They're actual physical objects! Connected to living people! They're objects in the world! And not in some computer. You turn puppets into digital files and you separate them from everything a person can do. You can program them to play catch and shake hands—but they can't do anything spontaneous. They can't do anything with nuance. They can't be inspired. They can't forget their lines and improvise. They're not real. They're just 'realistic.' Which is bullshit."

Stephanie and I traded a look. It was a look that said both, *This guy is nuts,* and, *This guy must be right.*

"I worked for six months on the character of Henry the Horse. And now this asshole was going to put Henry in the control of programmers and animators and some voice-over person in a booth. The character would have no heart and no soul. He'd be an empty shell. Nothing but graphics and sound effects. He'd have no *self*."

He leaned against the wall in fatigue and misery and despair. The last chapter of this story was implicit, but we all must have felt that he had to describe it. So we waited.

Finally O'Neil seemed to succumb to the logic of all that had come before. He finished the story. "So I went a little crazy," he said quietly. "I'd been under all this stress with Jimmy and the work, and then the blackmail—I mean, I wasn't sleeping, and I knew I didn't trust Cohen . . . so he said, 'Maybe we can use you as talent.' And I said, 'I thought you didn't need a puppet performer anymore,' and he got this . . . this loathsome smirk on his face, and kind of grinned, like I was supposed to appreciate how great this all was, and he said, 'Yeah. You're right. Cool.'"

O'Neil stopped, gathered himself with a big, here-goes-nothing sigh, and said, "And it made me insane. I was just . . . overwhelmed with this *rage*. I looked around, and I saw the Emmy, and I grabbed it, and just started hitting him."

He stared. We waited. Finally he said, "Then something in me took over, and I got very efficient. I wasn't horrified. I felt fulfilled. And relieved. I felt like I'd lifted this huge burden off my back. I saw the Jimmy doll and I went over and grabbed it. That's when I saw the bags of money. So I took them, too. And I went home."

With that we all fell silent, and nobody spoke. A tense pause took hold. Each of us seemed to be lost in his or her own specific reveries about various things concerning the human soul. At least I was. Then I saw Stephanie wordlessly jerking her head from me toward O'Neil. Apparently she was cuing me to take him into custody. I nodded.

"Um, Stephen," she said gently. "That sounds like a lot of extenuating circumstances to me. You have a ton of witnesses who can back you up on his stealing *Henry* from you."

The young man looked up as though emerging from a trance, and gazed at the gal with bafflement. Finally he said, "What are you talking about?"

Now Stephanie's confusion matched his. "When you're . . . you know . . ."

"When I'm what?"

She spread her hands open and groped for the right words. "You can't . . . I mean, the cops . . . You're going to have to be arrested, Stephen—"

"Forget it!" O'Neil's eyes got wide. He looked around wildly and the gun came up again, ready for use. "I can't do that. There's no way. This was *his* fault." He looked pleadingly at Stephanie. "You won't say anything, right?"

I stepped forward. Someone had to. "Let's start with the gat, friend. Hand it here and we'll figure this out."

He gave a high-pitched, near-hysterical laugh. "Forget it! Get back!"

I was about to say, *Listen, O'Neil, violence never solved anything.* But when a man points a gun at you, you don't want to put the word *violence* out on the airwaves for general consumption. I then brainstormed *escaping never solved anything,* but that seemed untrue on its face. I cast about—mentally, of course—until I hit upon an all-purpose warning that would help calm the man down while not committing too specifically to any particular course of action. "Listen, son," I said. "Nothing ever solved anything."

"Huh?"

"Just put the piece down. . . ."

His eyes scanned the room in a frenzy. Then he pointed with the gun to the supply closet. "What's that?"

"What's what?" I played dumb. "Nothing. Certainly not the supply closet."

"Open it!"

"All right, Jesus, take it easy!" Stephanie snapped. "I have to get the keys."

"Get them! Do it!"

She crossed to her desk and opened the shallow, wide drawer. As she fished out a pair of clinking silver keys I probed O'Neil's possible intent with a series of speculations. He wanted to get into the closet to steal our office supplies. He wanted to compose a suicide note and needed pen and paper. He wanted to make sure it wasn't some other room, swarming with people who could apprehend him. Then she opened the closet and he waggled the gun. "Get in. Both of you."

"Stephen—"

"Get in!"

"You can't really believe you're going to get away—"

He grabbed her arm and shoved her inside. Before marching me after her at gunpoint he demanded and got my cell phone. Then he shut the door and locked it with a brisk little clatter and the telltale thunk of the bolt slamming home.

The closet was slightly larger than a phone booth, or than a phone booth used to be, before it stopped being a booth and just became a phone on a post, surrounded by a few small panels offering zero privacy—yes, one more way in which the public realm smiles "Sorry!" and then kicks you in the teeth. Its floor was largely uncluttered. That meant there was plenty of space for us to stand up against each other in the absolute and total darkness, almost touching, like commuters. The door, of course, had no knob for us to twist or rattle. It was a hollow-body, but thick enough to kill most exterior sounds. We were entombed among the boxes of gel pens and steno pads. So we did what people do— we banged on the door and shouted "Help" for about a minute, until our ears rang and we began to feel like a couple of chumps. We clammed up and stood there in the darkness, breathing.

"God *damn* it!" Stephanie banged a fist one final, futile time on the door. "I can't believe we got locked in here by a *puppeteer!*"

"Don't feel so bad." I made an effort to be consoling. I was the boss, the man, the oldest. It was the right thing to do. "He has great manual skills."

"What's that supposed to mean?"

"He went for the gat before I could stop him."

She went suddenly silent. It created a little vacuum of presence in the center of our tiny vertical cave. Then she said, "You *left* it there? Even after he showed up? Pete!"

I iced my tone and came on frosty. "Yes, Miss Constantino?"

"You don't just leave a gun sitting out! When you know a killer is about to drop by!"

"Did I know that?"

"I told you!"

"But you neglected to tell me who said killer was, didn't you? Because you had your little secret."

"No! Yeah. Forget it. It's not your fault."

"Maybe you should have stayed quit." I paused. She said nothing. I pushed it. "So come on, doll. Give. Why did you come back?"

She chewed on this a full ten seconds. Think it doesn't sound like much? Clock yourself next time someone seeks an answer, and hold back for that long. Then try it locked in a dark closet.

It's an eternity. Finally she said, "Because I shouldn't have left in the first place. You pushed one of my buttons and I went into my routine."

"Which button is that?"

"The controlling-man button. The he-can't-tell-me-how-to-live-my-life button."

"Is that what I was doing?"

"No. That's my point. Part of me thought you were."

"Do tell. . . ."

"That's all it ever thinks. That's its job. It's the only thing it listens for. It hears its cue and it takes over and makes me do stuff. Like walk out. I was three blocks down the street before I realized that *it* was in control and not me." She laughed. "Like I'm its puppet."

The explanation rang a bell. Because maybe that's why I whaled into her in the first place. Maybe I had my own buttons that got pushed and pressed, like a button labeled *I'm the Boss, Not Her* or *Just Who Is in Charge Here, Anyway?* Granted, these are awkward labels for buttons. But only literally.

"Or that part of you is just one among many," I said. "And so are 'you.'" I held up quote signs for the last word. She couldn't see them in the darkness, but it seemed important that I make the effort.

I had myself primed for a moment of delighted recognition. Instead I got a beat of silence and a curt, unsatisfying, "Huh?"

"The book," I prompted. "*Consciousness and What Gives.* The many selves. There's no Pete upstairs and no permanent 'I' in control. You were right. It's"—I was going to say, *a revelation that's changed my life forever,* but instead kept it short and sweet— "very interesting."

"Oh." She gave a dismissive little snort. "That. Forget it. I haven't looked at that book in a week. I gave up. It was too dense." She turned away from me. My eyes had grown just acclimated enough to discern that she was exploring the shelves of supplies like a blind person, patting her hands on one thing after another in the darkness. "I think maybe I saw a little lighter here the other day. . . ."

Think it didn't rankle? Think again. It rankled. And that rankling curdled into something sour and smothering. I clammed up. I didn't want to speak. I just stood there in the darkness, waiting for something to change.

"Nah." She stood up from the supply shelves. "I can't find it." She paused as I pointedly, and with great eloquence, remained silent. "What?" I refrained from speaking. "Come on, Pete, what's the matter? So big deal, I can't find the lighter. We'll get out. . . ."

I was struck, at that moment, by the fact that I didn't care. I didn't care if we got out or if we stayed in the closet until . . . well, until some ultimate thing happened. I didn't really know what kind of ultimate thing I was referring to, and I didn't care. I felt robbed and plundered and badly used, and when you feel like that, you don't care what you do, because doing anything feels like a concession to a world that doesn't deserve the courtesy or the effort of your doing something in it.

Stephanie sighed. "Why aren't you saying anything?"

"I have nothing to say."

"Since when?"

"Since nothing."

"Why are you acting all pissy and hurt?"

"I'm not acting."

"Okay, why are you *being* all pissy and hurt?"

"I'm not. Never mind. Nothing." Somewhere in the back of

my mind, in some administrative office that perhaps looks out onto the floors, a voice said, *Ingalls—sulking? That's a first. Is it fun?* I had no reply.

"Wait a minute." In the faint, soft blackness I thought I could see her put her hands on her hips. "You're not hurt because I didn't finish the book, are you?"

"No. I don't know."

"I'm sorry! It's very difficult. I got to the point where I'd read a paragraph three times and have no idea what he was talking about."

"Okay."

" 'Okay'? You sound like my nephew. He's three years old. Pete, look, I'll lend you the book. You can read it and tell *me* what it says."

"Fine."

"Oh, man, fuck this. I can't stay in here if you're going to get all mopey. Let's try to break the door again."

"Fine. Whatever."

"Oh, Jesus. All right, look, on three. One . . . two . . . three—"

We lunged at it with our shoulders and the effect was immediate. There was a short, loud explosion outside, and the door flew open. The notion that the gal and I had somehow beaten down the door and shattered its lock left me stunned and bewildered, so it took a few seconds for the tableau before me to register and leave me stunned and bewildered: Standing five feet away, with his hands behind his back and his mouth bleeding, was Stephen O'Neil. Off to the side and holding a smoking pistol was John Panker, who grinned when Stephanie and I stumbled out, blinking and dazzled in the halogen glare of the office's torchère lamp.

"I tailed him and bagged him when he stopped to hail a hack," Panker said. "Lucky all your 'gotcha' and boo-hoo rebop woke me up. I eavesdropped big-time. Call us even, Ingalls? I spring you; you give me a pass on the shakedown. You don't call Basilisk and we're quits."

I was tempted. But right is right and fraud is fraud, and in my book never the twain shall meet. "Think again, chum. I don't make deals with shakedown sharpers."

Panker smirked. "Yeah, I'm a bent op and you're a gumshoe with a halo. Listen, shamus, this whole grift vibes bunco. Feature Donnie and Marie want me to nix the claim."

For a moment I was paralyzed. Whoever in my head was responsible for understanding what Panker had just said, he was away from his desk. "Come again?"

But Stephanie was electrified. "Really? Meaning what?"

"Meaning, sugar pie, they're paying me five large to tell Basilisk there's nothing to see here and keep moving."

"On their own claim? For the blackmail money?"

"Check." He shrugged. "'Course, you spill to the fuzz, I'll swear on a stack it never happened."

Stephanie opened her mouth, then shut it, then turned to me, started to speak, stopped and looked back at Panker. "It's a deal. Scram." When I started to object, she said, "Something's up, Pete." She thumbed toward Panker and said, "We don't have time for this guy. Let him go."

I agreed, provided Panker gave me O'Neil for delivery to Thoreau. The insurance op, jamming his hands into his pockets in hearty self-satisfaction, said, "Be my guest. He's all yours. Hey, I even got him trussed with twine."

Then out of nowhere came a little burst of pixie music, and all four of us jerked in response. Stephanie looked toward her handbag; I reached into my pocket. But the cell in question was Panker's. He pulled it out and touched a key. "Yeah? Okay. Great." He touched another key and jammed it into his pocket and said, "Gotta run, gang. Ingalls, see ya around campus. Miss Constantino, a pleasure. Stevie, boy, crime doesn't pay." He left in a gust of sleaziness that left me feeling just a little besmirched.

"He's going to my place," O'Neil said quietly. "That call was probably fake. He called himself just now."

I looked at him. "How do you know?"

"He beat me up until he could look at my driver's license with my address. He thinks the money's there." Then a thought occurred to him, the same thought that occurs to all of us, sooner or later, the thought that you can save yourself from the consequences of your own corruption by offering corruption to others. You could tell, because he started squirming and twitching. "If I tell you where the money is, will you let me go?"

My assistant and I looked at each other for two solid seconds before she said, "No."

"Why not?"

"Because they'll catch you and you'll turn us in," Stephanie said coolly. "And who wants to live the rest of their lives running from the law? For what? A Ferrari? Who cares?"

"Plus," I was careful to point out, "it's immoral, Ms. Constantino."

"Is it? I guess. But like insurance companies never do anything immoral? Please." She went to her desk, consulted a number on a slip of paper, and punched it in. "Detective Sandoval? Stephanie Constantino. At Pete Ingalls's office? Yeah, well, then, guess what? A guy named John Panker is on his way to break into Stephen O'Neil's apartment. That's probably where the extortion money is." She gave the cop the address and bailed out.

During this time I had remained immersed in that strange, glum, but somehow beguiling, magical mood of what I dimly realized was self-pity. It was a new experience. My usual self normally gave self-pity the bum's rush whenever it showed up at the back door, looking for handouts. I did that because it was what I was supposed to do. Or so I had thought. Now I had grounds to ask, *Who's "I"?* And, *Maybe this self, the source of this so-called "self-pity," is someone I should meet and chat with, to debate the issues with and learn to appreciate for his particular qualities, and learn to feel pity for. Because it feels good, in a bad kind of way.*

All of which means I was swimming in the warm, slightly rancid bathwaters of feeling sorry for myself when I heard a fuzzy snapping sound, and looked over toward O'Neil.

The wisps and threads of torn twine floated from him as he wrenched his hands free. So, yeah, his writhing around and squirmy twitching were those of a guy wrestling with what tied up his hands, not with his conscience. He clawed the twine off and lurched toward the door. And then he was out and gone.

"Shit . . ." Stephanie said.

I looked at her. I looked at the door. A summons had been issued, and I felt poised between answering it and defiantly refusing. And then . . .

Who was it who said, *You are what you is?* Maybe nobody knows, at this point, because it could be from the Bible or some other ancient text of anonymous authorship. But he said it, and it's true. You really are what you is—meaning, no matter what you're made of, one self or a thousand, you do things. Things get done. You act, or fail to act, and it's all done by you in collusion with whatever other parts of you there are, if there are any. And as long as you've got a hand in electing what to do, and then doing it, you might as well do the right thing.

I pounded out the door and down the steps, and then raked my searching gaze left to right, up and down the street. And I made O'Neil—a turbulent, bobbing figure unwisely running, conspicuous amid the late-afternoon walkers. I ran.

We both faced the obstacles of pedestrians and dogs and cars. But he couldn't very well hide or stop for a cab. I kept pace with him north on the avenue for a block or so. Then he ducked east on a street, but that was a mistake: There was less foot traffic and I was able to close the distance. I caught up with him halfway down the block, reached out to grab his flying shirt, and pulled him harshly to the sidewalk.

He scrambled to his feet and flew at me, flailing and swatting me with wild, desperate blows. I had to endure them like a swarm of bees until I found an opening, but I was glad for it—it hurts the hand less if you punch out of anger and not just tradecraft. I subdued him with a good right cross and barely felt it. He collapsed onto the sidewalk. "I'm not evil," he said, panting. In his fear and exhaustion he sounded high-pitched and plaintive. He sounded like Jimmy Farlow. "I'm not a bad person like he was."

"You weren't at first, but you became one," I said. "You listened to the wrong voice."

I hauled O'Neil back to the office, where Stephanie was at her desk, on the phone. She held up a wait-a-second finger and, into the mouthpiece, said, "Good. We'll see you there." Then she hung up and handed me a roll of duct tape.

I was taping our lad's wrists together, for convenient transport, when Stephanie reached over with a folded sheet of paper and said, "Wait! Pete! Take this. We might need it."

I glanced at it, then put it in my jacket pocket. As I dragged the sullen O'Neil outside for a cab, I saw her squinting at a business card and punching numbers on the phone.

The offices at DD Productions felt like a funeral home just prior to a service. A lot of people milled around acting sensitive or brave, while the guest of honor was offstage and beyond helping. Make that plural, in this case; the guests of honor were elsewhere. A brief confab with our inside gal, Ellen Larraby, revealed that Detective Hank Thoreau was still on the premises, and was in fact at that moment questioning Donnie Dansicker and Charlotte Purdy in Charlotte's office.

"El, see if you can hang out," Stephanie said. "It's going to be fabulous." She knocked once and opened the door and led us inside. I did the honors of dragging Stephen O'Neil, the killer puppeteer. Ellen Larraby followed. She shut the door, then crept in discreetly and drifted to the periphery.

Donnie and Charlotte were on the couch, acting morose and besieged. Thoreau, whose light gray suit looked like several people had slept in it at the same time, sprawled across one of the facing chairs. He glanced up as Stephanie breezed in. He started to leer. But his expression curdled from lascivious to calculating as he saw O'Neil and tried to add up what it meant. Stephanie gave him a helpful hint. "Guess what, Detective. Case solved."

He gazed at her in lewd and horrible admiration. "Is that a fact? Tell me about it, sweets. And be sure to include the part about why this guy's hands are taped together."

"Detective Thoreau, Stephen O'Neil."

"We've met," the cop said.

"Maybe," she replied. "But you only know him as the voice of Jimmy Farlow. You may be surprised to learn that he's also the guy who killed Marc Cohen."

The room went silent. Thoreau actually hauled himself to his feet, enduring what was surely a massive inconvenience, and looked from O'Neil to Stephanie to me. He stayed on me when he asked, "Is this for real?"

I nodded. "He admitted it an hour ago."

He turned to O'Neil. "So? True?"

"No comment."

Thoreau nodded. "And I am suddenly not bored." He turned to me and said, "You know, Ingalls, I don't want to come on like a big buzz kill or anything, but you and the gal Friday here technically aren't really cops."

"We never said we were."

"Of course not. But it's illegal to hold someone against his will."

"Oh, for Christ's sake," Stephanie muttered, and tore open her handbag and dug around in it. She came up with a little pocketknife, opened the blade, and went up to O'Neil. "Gimme your hands." He held them out, and with a grimace and a sawing motion and a concentrated slash she cut the tape. O'Neil wrenched his hands apart and massaged his wrists. Stephanie said curtly, "Fuck it. Go. Leave."

Thoreau put a restraining touch on the young man's upper arm. "Stay put. I have a few probing questions." He stepped out into the main office and, a second later, returned with a uniformed cop I hadn't seen. The cop led O'Neil away. Out in the office, whispers and gasps erupted like little geysers.

I sat in the other chair opposite Donnie and Charlotte as Thoreau turned to the rest of us. "Ingalls? My darling Stephanie? If this pans out, you have the thanks of a grateful city. If not, we have a date to discuss certain malfeasances on your part." He lowered himself back into his chair gratefully. "Is there any other new business?"

Stephanie looked vexed. "Yeah. Wait." She edged past Thoreau's slouching bulk and the seated, tense forms of Donnie and Charlotte until she reached the door, then opened it and darted out. In a second she dashed back in with a look of sly triumph and said, "Okay!" It piqued my attention. Some subtle windup toy of a stratagem had been cranked into readiness and was about to go ticking across the carpet.

Behind her came our old crony John Panker, scowling and seething and all dressed up—for a night on the town or a quiet evening with that special someone—in shiny silver handcuffs. He was escorted by a short, handsome Latina in a navy blue skirt and jacket and a white blouse. She and Thoreau exchanged nods.

"Lieutenant."

"Detective."

"Pete," Stephanie said, enjoying herself perhaps a bit too much. "This is Lieutenant Clara Sandoval of the Major Case Squad, Special Investigations."

I nodded genially. "You're the blackmail lady?"

She wasn't amused. "That's one way to put it. Detective, thanks to Ms. Stephanie Constantino I was able to apprehend this man tossing the apartment of Stephen O'Neil."

Thoreau chuckled. "Miss Stephanie, you're as smart as you are intelligent." He looked at Panker. "And you are—?"

"John Panker," Stephanie said. "Field agent for Basilisk. They sell blackmail insurance. Like anybody knows there is such a thing. Which I completely didn't."

"And what was he looking for?" Thoreau stared at Panker, all amusement gone from his manner. "A lost contact lens?"

"He was looking for this." Sandoval leaned out into the main room and gestured. A uniform plodded in like a bored extra in a nonspeaking role. He was carrying two familiar dark red nylon sports bags, and they were bulging. Sandoval unzipped one and revealed the gray-and-green paper contents. "It's about a million dollars. Hidden in the sofa cushions."

I looked at O'Neil, who had gone even whiter and clamped his pale lips shut. He didn't say anything. I didn't say anything. But maybe we were both thinking the same thing, which was that we lived in a world in which you could sit on an old sofa for two hours, and drink tea and gas off about PBS and puppets and the issues of the day, and not know you were riding a million clams.

Then our festive group was treated to the arrival of yet another guest. A cheerful voice called, "Hey, is this a private shindig or can anyone crash?"

In the doorway stood solid, beefy Harmon Kirkeby, a trim linebacker in a brown sport jacket, blue shirt, maroon tie, and tan slacks, and looking both pleased as punch and confused as all get-out at the spectacle before him. Stephanie invited him to come on in. He entered with a big man's delicacy and found a space for himself on the edge of Charlotte's desk.

Meanwhile, at Sandoval's gesture, the cop retired with the bags. Or he started to. But I had a question of my own. "Officer," I said. "One more thing. Is there any raw beef in those bags? What one might call chuck steaks?"

The cop started to reply, then got wary and turned to Sandoval. "That mean something?" he asked.

She rolled her eyes. "Not that I know." She looked at me and said, "No, no chuck steaks. Just a million dollars in stolen money."

I nodded my thanks. "Just thought I'd ask."

"A million dollars?" Kirkeby looked baffled. "Say, that's kind of funny."

"Where can I buy a program?" Thoreau murmured. "I don't think I know this individual."

"Lieutenant Thoreau, meet Harmon Kirkeby," Stephanie said. "Field op for Greensward Indemnity. They, uh, also issue blackmail insurance."

"What?!" Thoreau said sharply, then lapsed into thoughtful silence. We were like a class of graduate students waiting for the professor to snap out of a *petit mal* epileptic trance. Suddenly his eyes resumed their squinty calculations and his little beaklike mouth curled into an amused, horrible smile. "You don't fucking say."

"You know what, you guys?" Charlotte Purdy beamed with forced cheeriness. "You know what would be really great? If we called our lawyer."

"You can call your lawyer," Thoreau said carefully, "or you can call out for pizza. We're just talking here. Just having a friendly chat with our friends and associates about two insurance companies and two million-dollar payoffs when everybody thought there was only one."

"I'll say!" Kirkeby slid off the desk and stood poised, ready to shift with the audibles. "Namely, ours! Frankly."

"And how is it you happen to be here, Mr. Kirkeby?" Thoreau asked.

"I got a call from Ms. Constantino."

"Did you, now?"

"Yeah," Stephanie said. "He did." She was standing by the windows and had a commanding view of everybody else. She pointed to Kirkeby. "He's from Greensward. They represent KLAE, which is DD Productions' partner in Philadelphia and co-producer of *Playground Pals*. Why is he here? Because KLAE filed a claim and his company sent him to check it out. What did they file a claim *for?*"

"The million they gave to DD to pay the blackmail," Thoreau said. "Which we just all admired in those bags."

"Not quite—" I began.

"Ingalls. Not another word." Donnie Dansicker had come to life. He glared at me from the couch. "You work for us."

"Dial 'N' for 'Nix,' Dansicker," I said. "You fired me, remember?"

This brought Charlotte sitting up primly at her husband's side. "We most certainly did not."

"Um, actually?" Stephanie said. "You most certainly did so. Pete?"

My assistant was behind me. I had to turn around to make eye contact and saw her gesturing. "Yes, Ms. Constantino?"

"The thingie?"

For a second I balked. "Thingie," in my game, could mean many things, not all of them nice. Then the fog lifted. I reached into my jacket and produced the folded letter Stephanie had slipped me at the office. I let it fall open and displayed the contents to the staring throng. "From attorney Leonard Finklestein, thanking me for my services and giving me the large kiss-off. Whatever confidentiality deal we had ended when the FedEx man delivered this." I turned to Thoreau. "The money—"

"I told you!" Donnie snapped at his wife. She sighed and with a wave advised he shut up.

"The money," I repeated. "The bucks in the bags aren't from KLAE or Greensleeves. The dough is from the so-called Wall Street friends of Donnie and Charlotte. But let's not jump up and down and clap just yet." I had the floor, and I used it. I ruminated aloud. "These so-called Wall Street friends. Who are they?

What's their angle? That's one thing we don't know. And, in my view, unless Donnie or the missus here decides to sing, it may be that we'll never find out who they are. I don't know about the rest of you, but I can live with that. Some things remain a secret to the end of time. And, hell—maybe they should."

I stopped and let it sink in. And it would have sunk in, if Ellen Larraby, over in the corner by the potted ficus, hadn't said immediately, "What are you talking about? Everybody knows who they are. It's Gromyko Securities."

I nodded encouragingly. "Nice effort, El, but you're half a quart low on motivation. Why would Gromyko do it? What's in it for them?"

"The stock! Charlotte kept saying all week, 'Tell me if the media call.' They were terrified word would get out, and people would think the company's finished and dump the stock. Gromyko is a market maker in the stock and they'd be screwed, too, if it went down."

Thoreau stretched and sighed. "The stock. The stock. *Cherchez* the fucking stock."

"So Donnie and Charlotte borrow a million from Gromyko," Stephanie continued. "How do they plan to pay it back? From *their* insurance. From Basilisk. So they file a claim and the company sends John Dickhead here."

Panker roused himself from his sulk enough to snarl, "Watch it, sweet chips. I bounce on this beef and then you and I got business."

"Stephanie? Ms. Constantino?" I threw her a chiding look. "Let's keep it professional."

She gave me a killer smile. "Sorry, Pete. The company sends Mr. John Dickhead here. Who snoops around and follows my boss and decides that Pete has the missing million. He tries to force Pete into splitting it with him. Which of course goes nowhere, since Pete doesn't have it. Marc Cohen stole it from Pete's apartment, then Stephen O'Neil killed Cohen and took it."

Thoreau, not looking at her, his eyes aimed at the floor and doing the mental math, nodded. "Good. Keep going."

"Of course, KLAE doesn't know any of this. So they send their million, thinking it's the only million and it'll be used to save the show." Something occurred to her. She turned sharply toward Donnie and Charlotte on the sofa. "Which means KLAE sent it *before* the outtake footage hit the Web Thursday night. Because once that happened, they wouldn't have sent it. There would be no point."

Donnie shrugged. "They sent it Thursday afternoon. Just after you guys left the office."

"Donnie!" Charlotte glared at her husband in that special, intimate way only married people have of glaring at each other. "Will you shut up!"

Dansicker swiveled his head and just looked at her for a beat. Then he said, "They know everything."

"I don't care!" You could hear the gears turning in her head. She had to make an adjustment. "I mean they *don't* know everything. I mean there's nothing to know!"

He started to reply, but the heat of his embarrassment and, possibly, shame, got the better of him. His face colored with that ominous purple that seems to afflict bald men, and he sank deeper into the couch and tried to fold himself into invisibility. It didn't work.

"Miss Stephanie?" Thoreau directed toward her the wet, deferential gaze of a chivalrous dolphin. "May I?" He looked dead ahead at Donnie and Charlotte. "So you have an extra million bucks sitting here in a box. You decide to keep it for a rainy day.

Then you hear that Cohen is dead and the other million is gone. It's perfect. If you can get each insurance company to think that theirs is the only million, you can keep the second one. But how?" He looked at the rest of us. "Anyone?"

"Just don't tell the companies about each other," I said. "And don't tell KLAE and Gromyko about each other, either. But there's another problem. If the bulls get wise."

Clara Sandoval said, "What? Who?"

"The johns," I explained. "They compare notes, they see the books are cooked, and they come calling with an engraved invitation to the hoosegow."

Stephanie intervened. "What Pete means is, how does your department find out about cases?"

"Oh. Really? He said that?" Sandoval shrugged. "We're informed by the insurance companies. It's mandatory." She bit her lower lip. "But I never heard of Basilisk."

Thoreau turned and said to Panker, "John. My man. You didn't call it in."

"They paid him!" Stephanie yelled. "Donnie and Charlotte bribed him not to okay the claim." She turned to Sandoval and said, "You're only here because of Greensward, right? So you never knew there were two separate claims."

"That's right."

"And," she said with excitement, "there was one other thing that had to happen for them to keep the money. The killer had to get away. Because if he got caught, then we'd probably find the million he stole. And you'd have two groups waiting for the same million. Gromyko and KLAE. You could pay one back, but not both." From behind me, Stephanie slapped me on the shoulder. "Get it, Pete?"

"Got it, doll," I said. "That's—"

"That's how I knew I could get O'Neil to show up at the office. I called Charlotte and told her we had crucial evidence that could prove that O'Neil had killed Marc Cohen. And I knew they'd want to help him! Because the only way these two could possibly get to keep the second million was if the killer was never found."

I said to Charlotte, "So you told O'Neil we were looking for him. Either so he'd get away or so he'd come to my office for the evidence."

Donnie started to speak. "That's why I didn't want to circulate your memo. And why I couldn't wait to fire you."

"Don't say anything," Charlotte said. It was without her usual spark and pep. She was collapsing.

That fact didn't cause Donnie to handle her gently. He screamed, "Shut up! Shut up! This was your idea and now look!" His face again flushed deep crimson. "We had this extra million dollars delivered to us. And we thought, what the hell. Let's just keep it."

I shook my head, more in sorrow than in moral disapproval, and said, "Why?"

"Because it's all over anyway!" Charlotte Purdy said. Her eyes had gone puffy and now welled with tears. She didn't sob, but just let them silently drip down her face as she went on. "It was all over as soon as we read the first e-mail. We knew that. We could have paid Marc Cohen *ten* million dollars, and he could have destroyed his copy, and sooner or later it would have ended up on the Web. It's digital. You can't control it. Maybe he made ten copies for friends. Or one copy, and the friend made a hundred. The point was, we worked so hard, and now this shit creep asshole is destroying it. We *deserve* this money. So we took it."

Ellen silently floated to Charlotte's desk and returned with a box of tissues, which she handed her boss. Charlotte sniffled, said, "Thanks, honey," fluffed out two, and honked a big one.

Everyone seemed exhausted and we all took a breath. Charlotte's tears signaled the collapse of all secrets, the relenting of the tension we all had, for one reason or another, been enduring for a week and a half.

Then some kid knocked and opened the door and stuck his head in. "Um, Stephanie Constantino? You have visitors."

Stephanie's eyes went wide. "Gail! And the kids! Fuck!"

"Oh, yeah," the intern added. "Tim was just here. He dropped off the puppets."

EIGHTEEN

Stephanie dashed out into the main area while I followed more slowly, with a boss's calm. Thoreau, plodding behind me, joined O'Neil and the cop who held him in custody in an unoccupied carrel. He picked up a house phone and started making quiet calls. Kirkeby wandered out and drifted around, looking both fascinated and lost. Clara Sandoval, Panker, and the Dansickers were still in Charlotte's office as Ellen shuffled to her desk, sat down, and started to sob.

By now normal business had stopped. No one typed at their computers or chatted brightly on the phone. People milled around in little clusters, and everyone whispered or sniffled or sighed—everyone except Stephanie and a perky gal in her thirties, who conferred in muffled, happy tones way across the room, at the reception area.

Stephanie led the visitor toward me. That's when it hit me that she looked vaguely familiar. It took me a second to place the resemblance, but I got it. She looked like Stephanie.

"Pete?" My assistant spoke softly, damping down her pleasure to suit the somber mood of the room. "This is my sister, Gail. Honey, this is my boss I told you about."

The sister and I traded greetings, and then Stephanie introduced two kids, who stayed close to their mother's legs and stared in childlike wonder at the whimsy and disaster all around them. There was a girl around six and a little boy, call him three, three and a half. But don't quote me. What I know about the age of children could fill a book full of nothing.

"Aunt Steffie?" asked young, wide-eyed Brianna. "Why is everybody crying?"

Stephanie bent down to the little girl's level and began, "Oh, sweetie, something sad happened here today." Then it must have struck her that the job of explaining murder, blackmail, and insurance fraud to a first grader might be better left to experts. She stood up. "I'll tell your mom and she can explain it to you guys later." She drew Gail aside and started murmuring.

If you're keeping score at home, you've noticed that the subtraction of the two broads left Ingalls with the kids. That was jake with yours truly. Not to toot my own horn for more than a bar or two, but let's just say I can handle myself with the juice box crowd. I happen to believe that an adult who is ill at ease among children isn't quite the grown-up he thinks he is. Yeah, I know: Neither is anybody else. But children—and dogs, for that matter—instinctively trust me. Why? Maybe because I treat them all like human beings.

That's why, when young Dominic pointed and shouted, "It's Jimmy!" and ran over to a line of boxes along the foot of a wall of partitions, I followed in a responsible, attentive manner.

The lad stood staring down at eight black fiberboard cases, all lying flat on the floor. They were open, their lids stacked nearby. Inside, like grinning corpses in coffins at an open viewing, were the *Playground Pals* characters, the six kids and Bounce and Pounce. Their vividly colored costumes were pressed and perfect, their hollow bodies inert, their hands, with the rods attached, brought together in front of them, one atop the other, in demure patience. The oversize faces were frozen in cheery smiles, the bulbous eyes staring but lifeless.

"I want to talk to Jimmy!" the kid yelled.

Then I heard noises from Charlotte's office. It struck me that it might be advisable to get the kids away before the sad, tawdry parade of perps in bracelets began. So I picked up the case holding Jimmy Farlow and said, "Then let's talk to him!" and herded the kids into Donnie's office—deserted, now and maybe forever—and shut the door.

"Can you make him talk?" Brianna asked.

"Are you kidding? Jimmy and I are old friends."

I hoisted the puppet up from its case and experienced that immediate sense of disorientation and ineptitude you get when you pick up any unfamiliar mechanical device. Never mind wondering how to operate it effectively. You're back at the square one of childhood, asking the primal question, "How do I *hold* this?" With electronics, it always comes down to the central issue of the digital age: "What button do I push?" But with mechanical implements, there are moving parts, and hinged armatures, and weight to distribute properly, and controls requiring manual skill.

I put my right hand into the puppet's body and found my way toward the head and its cold metal devices. There were triggerlike studs to pull against, to make the eyeballs shift, and odd springloaded fingerloops to make the mouth work. My left hand found the rod attached to Jimmy's left hand; by moving and twisting it I could make him gesture and gesticulate. The whole creature must have weighed close to ten pounds. I hoisted it up over my head, the way I'd seen the puppeteer do at the Astoria Klonky shoot, and got a feel for how taxing the work must be.

I turned Jimmy's face to myself and observed the bright blue eyes, the corn yellow crew-cut hair, the gap-toothed mouth that opened, revealing a small mound of felt that read as his tongue. It was eerie. It was unsettling. By the time the craftspeople and the costume folks had built and dressed this item, most of the work toward making it seem like a living being had been done. A small swivel of the head, a slow blink of the eyes, and this inert bundle of metal and cloth seemed at least half alive. I didn't know whether to laugh or scream.

Then I lowered the creature and aimed it at the little boy.

The effect was instantaneous.

I could have been Superman himself, in cape and boots and blue body suit. It wouldn't have mattered. Little Dominic had eyes only for Jimmy. Even older, worldly Brianna was transfixed.

I moved the head, I gestured with the arm, I blinked the eyes. "Hi, Dominic!" I had Jimmy say. "How are you today!?" I used a kiddie voice, like the ones employed by the skilled professionals. Sure, it meant ransacking my vocal cords for some kind of chirpy, zesty falsetto. But I did it. I found the sweet spot and stayed there. But how would I know what to make Jimmy say?

The kid looked hesitant. "Okay . . ."

"Is this your sister?"

"Yeah . . ."

I froze. I vamped. It's like anything else. It looks easy from the outside, but when the puppet's on your hand and it's time to make it talk, the mind goes blank and you have to scramble.

I addressed the girl. "What's your name?"

"You know my name," she said.

"It's a courtesy question, doll." It came out with more back-spin and edge than I intended, less out of the "Jimmy Farlow" character and more along the lines of the "Pete Ingalls" character.

"My name is Brianna," the girl said. "You talk funny."

"It's my job."

"You're weird."

I could feel myself starting to sweat. "Sez you, missy." I moved the head and blinked the eyes. But I was holding the puppet out at arm's length, to isolate it and keep myself as much in the ob-scure background as possible. So I couldn't see the effects of my manipulations. Too late I thought of the Klonky show gal's little monitor, and silently vowed that I would never disparage a pup-peteer watching a small TV ever again. "So, uh, what should we talk about?" I looked at the boy. "Dom? Your thoughts?"

"Huh?"

"Any issues on your young mind?"

He shrugged. "I don't know." Then he said, "I want to go home."

"Who doesn't, kid?" I—or, rather, Farlow and I—indulged in a bitter laugh. "It's been a long day for everybody. I'm a puppet and even *I* need a drink!"

"I want to go home!"

Somewhere upstairs, in my head, a voice said, *Easy, Ingalls. You, a grown man, in a closed room, with two little tykes, "having a talk with Jimmy Farlow"—sure, you know it for what it is, a cute and wholesome activity for children and adults alike. But some people might not under-stand. Better quell this lad's outburst.*

I was about to argue, in another voice, with that voice. I was about to reply, internally, that "some people" could go soak their head. To which another voice was ready to say, *Why don't you two pipe down and give Jimmy some gab for the kids?*

I didn't care for that voice's attitude, frankly. But what was I going to do? Send it to bed without its supper? It didn't have a bed and it didn't eat supper. Demand its respect? Respect has to be earned, not coerced. Besides, it was right. I was paralyzed by my own internal debate. I couldn't make Jimmy speak because I was stuck in my head, in the dark, narrow supply closet of my mind, refereeing disputes between the selves that constituted me.

It made me wonder: How does anybody ever manage to say anything? Ordinary citizens, men and women and boys and girls: How are they able to fight through the clamor of all the contending voices inside, and pick one to actually give voice *to?* And yet we know they do. Because let's face it: People say things. It happens all the time. How?

The kids were staring at Jimmy, who'd grown inert and lifeless at the end of my arm. So to keep up appearances I had him turn his head toward me. I looked into his bright blue eyes and made them blink.

The puppeteers who improvised the porno scenes, reeling off dialogue and jokes and comments without a script or notes or practice: How did they do it? Maybe it all came down to: You wing it. You pick something to say, and you say it. If it plays, you're a hero. If it's wrong, you're a chump. It's trial and error, the scientific method that goes all the way back to our original caveman Founding Fathers. You pick a self, and be it, and see what it gets you.

"Hi, kids!" Jimmy said. "Say, listen. Pretty soon your mom's gonna come back here, and your aunt Stephanie, and you'll have to go. But before they do, can I just give you one word of advice?

Will ya let your old pal Jimmy teach you one special lesson, so you'll never forget our visit here today?"

The kids stared. Maybe they nodded slightly.

"Ya will? Great! Then have a seat." The kids sat on the sofa. I stood above them, brandishing Jimmy. "Now, I've been thinking about this for a whole week, and I think I figured it out. It's real important, though, so pay attention, okay?"

The kids nodded, spellbound. It gave me a second to flex my right hand inside the puppet's head, to regrip the loops and studs, which were growing slick with sweat. I considered taking my jacket off but rejected the idea. I didn't want to break the spell.

"You say to me, 'Jeez, Jimmy, I'm a young, growing, innocent young person. I'm standing at the kickoff of my whole moral education. So how do I know what's right? I mean, in the world, and with my life, and everything. Why *shouldn't* I bash a guy's head in with an Emmy? Or steal a million bucks when nobody's looking?' We've all had thoughts like that, right? And, as everybody knows, we're supposed to be ourselves. Right?"

I paused. Dominic stared. Brianna frowned.

"The answer, kids, is: Be yourself, yeah, but be your best self. Forget all those other selves, blabbing away in your head, telling you to do naughty things, or bad things, or criminal things, or homicidal things. Or just those dirty, wrong things that people do. Remember: Just because they talk to you doesn't mean they're right. Those voices. Those many selves. Maybe they exist, and maybe they don't. Let's all read the book and see if we can follow it. And if they do exist, and you talk to them, don't worry. It doesn't mean you're crazy. I talk to myself all the time, and look at me! So, to summarize: Listen to yourselves, don't be afraid to talk back to them, find your best one, and stick with it. Okay? Ya got me?"

Dominic leaped to his feet, his face creased in a ferocious frown, and pointed an accusing finger at me. "You're not Jimmy Farlow!"

It threw me. I had to regroup. "Sez who?"

"That's not Jimmy's voice!"

Then the door opened and in breezed Gail, the mom, and Aunt Stephanie, the dick's assistant, buoyant and refreshed from their tête-à-tête while Pete Ingalls, PI, thoughtfully provided child care and character development with puppets and amusing voices. "Here we are!" Gail laughed. "Everything okay?"

Dominic's face began to melt as the tears began. "He said he's Jimmy Farlow but he's not!"

"Oh, honey . . ." Gail, to her credit, gave me a quick eye roll—*kids*—*good luck trying to please them*—and mouthed, *Thanks,* and took him in her arms. I lowered the puppet and gave Constantino a look that suggested she reconsider laughing.

Then Gail told Brianna they had to go, and told both kids to give Aunt Steffie a good-bye hug. While they did, Gail took me aside and whispered, "She told me what's been going on. My goodness. She's my little sister, Pete. Should I worry about her in this job?"

I looked at her, at an older, slightly less refined version of my associate, with her sensible clothes and bulging tote bag, her workaday haircut and delicate crow's-feet, saw her radiating that combination of fatigue and watchful competence that mothers acquire, and said, "Don't kid a kidder, lady. Her job is nothing compared to yours—and she's good at it."

Then I had other things to think about, so I walked off and gave them my full attention. Because that's what I do.